She knew that when she took over as head of the family, she would learn some dark secrets, but she hadn't expected this...

Oh, no, what else? Lydia thought. Her aunt's eyes filled with the age-old suffering of time as she prepared to disclose a secret too painful to speak out loud. She pulled a small tape recorder from her robe pocket, set it on the table, hit play, then left the room. Lydia heard a familiar voice along with that of an unidentified man.

"Mr. James sent me. Your husband's the mark, right?" the unidentified voice asked in a cold, emotionless voice.

"Yes."

"Are you sure about this, Mrs. Mayers?" he asked again in the same frosty less animated voice.

"Yes, I'm sure."

The vengefulness in those words moved Lydia to tears. She heard the clicking of high heels against the pavement as the woman hurried away. With a loud pop, the recorder shut off. Shocked and gasping for air, Lydia shook her head from side to side. She felt her body falling deeper and deeper into a damp, dark place like the confines of an old abandoned well. The more she clawed and struggled the farther she sank.

Finally, Lydia knew what Regina had meant. "Oh God," Lydia cried out.

Those monstrous words kept ringing in her ears over and over again. As her throat tightened, she stumbled over to the sink, coughing and choking on the madness of her aunt's deed.

Dr. Lydia Giddens has taken an oath to do no harm. But now she stands in the shadows of her success, wondering if honoring her profession is even possible. Surely, her family doesn't expect her to jeopardize everything she's worked so hard for all of her life. No matter. Age, death, and declining health have forced her predecessors to appoint her to this new role. She isn't given a choice. As her powerful family's new matriarch, she understands how their world works. She's seen it up close, but she isn't sure if she has the strength or the prowess to take on such a complex responsibility. There are certain obligations, and certain risks, associated with this hierarchy. What were they thinking? she wonders. After all, she has her own challenges, battling an incurable disease that could take her life at any moment…

ACKNOWLEDGMENTS

Much love to my husband, John; my daughter, Jay; son-in-law, Eric; grandchildren Zachary, Ericka, and Stormy; and much love to our dear friends, Sam and Valerie Golden.

For your honest critiques of this book, I want to thank Dr. Celeste Clark, Pam Mitchell, Helen Lewis, Ron Williams, Linda Walker, Julia Lawrence, and Sandra Holloway. Your comments made a tremendous difference.

Thank you, thank you, Sophia Lecky, for helping me to navigate the world of Southeast Asia and Dr. Cecily Ganheart for sharing her knowledge. A special thanks to my nieces, Andrea Turner and Latasha Abraham, for bringing our family together.

Also, thank you, Carolyn Barksdale, Jeannette Macha, Diane "Duchess" Thompson, Pourchia Cockrell, Malinda Fowler, Linda Allen, and Joyce Carey for listening and encouraging me along this amazing journey.

WOVEN

BERTHA CONNALLY ABRAHAM

A Black Opal Books Publication

GENRE: WOMEN'S FICTION/FAMILY LIFE

WOVEN
Copyright © 2017 by Bertha Connally Abraham
Cover Design by Jackson Cover Designs
All cover art copyright © 2017
All Rights Reserved
Print ISBN: 978-1-626948-35-8

First Publication: DECEMBER 2017

Published by Black Opal Books **http://www.blackopalbooks.com**

DEDICATION

In loving memory of Michael Derrick Abraham
4-10-2017
Big smile, Big Heart

CHAPTER 1

Why her? Lydia had sworn to uphold the Hippocratic Oath. What made them believe she had the strength to lead a family shrouded in controversy? That unthinkable idea had her head reeling and her thoughts breaking off into tiny pieces. Taking on such a powerful role deeply rooted in an unconventional tradition scared her.

The magnitude of their expectation forced an old nemesis up from the abyss. Suddenly, the bold untimely attack of sickle cell anemia had her questioning her life expectancy and their decision. Beneath her unrelenting pain, she saw bits and pieces of her life flicker then leap like scenes in a movie.

She juggled a challenging career, a health crisis, and her new appointment. Lydia's multifaceted lifestyle broached her from every conceivable direction. She thought no one noticed those half-eaten dinners.

Her husband gleaned every tangible clue. He knew he'd put it off long enough. "Babe, I'm worried. I think you need to see a doctor," Jake said.

"I am a doctor, and I'm doing just fine."

Her apparent arrogance shocked him. He snapped,

"Babe, you're not fine." His agitation mimicked a spirited stallion prancing anxiously with a burr trapped beneath his saddle. "Lydia, unlike you, I'm obviously no Bible scholar, but I believe Dr. Luke can offer you some practical advice."

As he watched, a tiny frown etched a wrinkle in her forehead until a smile appeared. It redefined the scowl.

The words "physicians heal thyself" popped into her head. She laughed out loud, amused that Jake, of all people, could recall any scriptures. Like a restless two-year-old, church service lasting longer than an hour usually drove him insane.

"Jake, I know you love me. I love you, too. What about all those people who depend on me?"

"Who will care for them when you're not here? What about me?"

His selfless questions had merit, although investing in his worries had to wait. Her aging predecessors had chosen her. Their unanimous vote placed a monumental task upon shoulders they believed strong, courageous, and capable. What made them so sure of her? she wondered.

The role tugged at her rapidly beating heart with persistence like a deadly merciless force of nature. Scared? You bet. Could she willfully trample her oath if necessary for duty, for family?

Doubt crept in. Besides the rumors, Lydia knew her predecessors operated outside of the law.

Long after Jake kissed her good-bye and walked out, his concern shook her concentration, stripping away the enjoyment of her morning ritual. Suddenly, her usual second cup of coffee lost its appeal.

When she arrived at work, the clinic's waiting room was already bursting at the seams with hopeful patients.

She checked in. Then she grabbed her lab coat on the

way to an unscheduled appointment.

The technician looked up when she entered the lab and smiled. "Good morning, Dr. G."

"Good morning." Her voice quaked as the air surrounding them filled with an immediate urgency. "I'll need this test ASAP," she said then passed him the handwritten request. Please let me know as soon as the results come back."

"Yes, Dr. G." *Huh, no polite chatter*, he thought.

Dr. G., the name a patient adoringly bestowed upon her quickly took on a life of its own then spread like germs in a classroom filled with sneezing, coughing kindergarteners. No one bothered calling her Dr. Giddens anymore. Well, almost no one.

All day long, an exhausting number of restless patients paraded through the exam rooms. In-between patient visits, she daydreamed about cuddling with Jake after a pleasurable and intimate candlelight dinner. When the last patient left, she hung up her lab coat flung her stethoscope on her desk, and walked out. Except for a few stiff joints and that nagging headache, their romantic evening turned out almost perfect. Around eleven o'clock he asked, "Babe, you coming to bed?"

"In a little while."

Overseeing her dysfunctional family terrified her. Gatekeeper, wow! Her temples throbbed as sweat oozed from her pores. Even if she could muster enough courage to question their choice, she couldn't rescind their decision. An already paved road stretched out before her. It wasn't as if she could say no thank you. In the prime of her life, she discovered secrets destroy even ordinary lives. The things she knew seemed more threatening than the effects of her illness. One evening after tossing a little black book onto a burning fire, she watched the flames destroy its pages, but the memories remained forever

seared in her membrane. Family secrets selectively
haunted her daydreams. More often they caused her to
wrestle with the small amount of sanity in her nightmares. Her aunts B J and Regina, those kindred spirits,
shared an amazing sisterhood. But her Aunt Regina, the
catalyst, secretly guided, always carefully grooming Lydia to accept the full weight of her destiny.

As Lydia and Jake lay next to each other, a sliver of
light penetrated a small crack underneath the bathroom
door then moved into their inner sanctuary. Her head
sank into the softness of her pillow as each rhythmic
breath played its own beautiful unrehearsed melody. He
sighed then closed his eyes and tried not to imagine his
life without her.

The next morning when Lydia woke, he had gone.
Early or late, it didn't matter what time she got to work,
the overcrowding filled her day with predictably long
hours. Finally, around mid-afternoon, she caught a much-
needed break then sat down and massaged her aching,
calloused feet. While she rested her weary eyes, the tech
walked in. He found her slumped over a pile of patient
files. "Dr. G., are you all right?"

She nodded. He handed her a battery of tests then
quickly walked away. His abrupt departure came as a bla-
tant reminder that not everyone had the strength to face
her truth. She understood that all too well. The unsurpris-
ing results revealed an aggressive downward spiral of the
disease. Sharing her concerns with someone who understood her disease like her friend Tommy—Dr. Tommy
Calvin—proved hard enough. Certainly, she knew, it was
almost impossible for a stranger to grasp. Tommy and his
team had developed a new exciting drug that offered
hope for thousands of others like her. Now, they awaited
the FDA's approval. She and Tommy chatted weekly
about his mother's progress after her stroke. From time to

time, he voiced concern about the red tape encumbering the release of the drug. She listened attentively. He told her an anonymous donor funded his research for years. He had no idea who to thank for such a generous contribution.

Like today, every day brought something new. While those annoying aches and pains kept her up some nights, her patient load presented her with yet another challenge.

Lydia sighed. "Oh well!"

Her last patient sat waiting in a cold, isolated exam room. She got up and slowly pushed back her chair. Her legs folded like an accordion and then her body hit the floor with such force the loud thump echoed around the room.

"H-e-l-p! H-e-l-p!"

She heard someone repeatedly hurl those anxious words. Then the shadowy outline of her nurse, Rebecca, came into focus. Curious onlookers watched the staff lift her onto a gurney and then wheel her down a long narrow corridor into a waiting elevator. Before she could catalog that frightening moment, a man's familiar voice snapped orders as the nurse gingerly wiped tiny beads of sweat forming on his brow.

He grabbed her hand. A faint smile crossed his lips. "You're out of danger, Lydia."

The underlying sincerity in his voice gave her reassurance. She closed her eyes. Obviously, the medication had stolen some consciousness. Every attempt to speak or swallow tickled the back of her irritated throat. She licked her parched lips. Nothing else worked. She kept repeating *stay focused* over and over in her head. Even that seemed an impossible task.

By her standards and those of her colleagues, Dr. Justin Rodgers tipped the scale. Her friend Justin's boyish physique demanded more than a quick glance.

"Don't try to speak, Lydia. You've had a rough time. Slow it down, girl. I'll call in, Jessie." Justin figured she needed no explanation. He smiled, rubbed her hands gently, then walked out.

Justin, Jessie, and Lydia—the trio met in medical school. The smart, beautiful Jessie had naturally tanned skin that appeared more luminous against the backdrop of her thick, coal-black woolly hair that, like hers, it had a mind of its own. Her suspenseful dark-brown eyes, with russet colored specks like rings of fire circling their circumference, lay hidden deep beneath layers of thick black lashes.

The door swung open. Jessie walked in. Lydia shivered then reached down and pulled the sheet up over her aching shoulders. Her jumbled thoughts bounced like a Ping-Pong ball from one corner of her mind to the next. Momentarily, all clarity fled.

Then she remembered her deceased friend, Jackson, saying, "Always trust your instincts, Lydia."

Lydia savored Jackson's wisdom. She hoped to one day scatter his knowledge like desirable springtime rains upon desolate crops. "Well, hello, Jessie! It's wonderful to see you." Then jokingly she asked, "What does my friend, the good doctor, think about all this?"

Lydia appeared calm. But, underneath, her nerves began disintegrating like splinters in a wind storm. Her eyes darted from one corner of the dismal room to the next. Empathy spilled out from every pore like sweat on a hot summer day. Finally, she understood how overwhelmed the families of her patients felt, squeezed into small cramped rooms bulging with intimidating monitors. Until this untimely episode, she'd successfully concealed her illness. Now in the wake of such a brutal assault, a tinge of regret made its debut. Life wasn't fair. Sadly, she had experience in both arenas. She needed no reminder.

The door opened slowly. Jake walked over to Lydia's bedside. Jessie pulled up a chair. Under her pensive stare, Jake's lower lip quivered. *Man up!* he thought. No way would he fall apart in front of the stone goddess. Lydia would've seen shades of red if she had any inkling her knight in shining armor dubbed her friend cold and unfeeling. He liked Jessie. How odd that her lifestyle choices bothered him. Suddenly, as if she felt his distress, Lydia gripped his arm reassuringly.

Jessie took Lydia's hand. "You really had me worried, girlfriend. I'm relieved you're doing so much better. I'll stop in again after rounds."

The compassion in Jessie's voice soothed the uneasiness building up inside of Lydia.

"Thanks, Jessie."

"Lydia, I'll be right back," Jake said, and then he followed Jessie out of the room.

It seemed like he stayed gone a long time. Lydia felt disoriented. Every once in a while, a lucid memory traded places with voids in time. Briefly, she glanced backward at an evening when the dimly lit doctor's lounge played host to a private moment. She'd forgotten some papers. In her haste to retrieve them, she stumbled upon a clandestine rendezvous. Low pleasurable moans floated through the air. Her lips curled upward into a fanciful smile. Everyone knew the lounge had a notorious reputation. She tiptoed in the direction of her locker. As she turned the corner, she glimpsed Jessie pinned against the wall in the devouring grip of Dr. Anthony St. Johns. Their eyes locked for a split second. Jessie looked away. The papers slipped from Lydia's shaky hands and scattered all over the floor. Quickly, she scooped up the disheveled pile then backed out of the room.

Where had everyone gone? She sat alone, holding the same pile of crumpled papers when Jessie walked into the cafeteria. "Lydia, I hope you didn't get the wrong idea. The situation's more complicated than it looked."

"Complicated! Carnal lust looks the same from any distance."

The color drained from Jessie's cheeks. She snapped. "How dare you judge me, Lydia?"

Lydia felt betrayed. No matter what, she expected that her friend would confide in her. Ironically, Jessie's denial offended Lydia's jaded sense of decency. She knew once fully vested in her family's affairs, her duties would require unpleasant and sometimes distasteful tactical maneuvering. All of a sudden, she felt like a hypocrite.

After that breach of trust, Lydia and Jessie vigorously pursued their careers as an escape from the strained memory that evening left behind. Their friendship suffered, time passed, and despite the brief lull, the wound healed. Eventually, their friendship recovered. Destiny's stake in their lives slowly began unfolding. Still, Jessie's rapidly tumbling life resembled a powerful avalanche accelerating with reckless disregard down her own manmade mountain.

Lydia's hospital room grew more daunting. She felt like a hostage trapped and completely alone. The drugs numbed her body, but her mind drifted through corridors, bridging the past with the present. She vividly recalled the anger and shame she felt after tossing a plate of soggy overcooked pasta into the trash. The statistics loomed. Sadly, every single day people somewhere went to bed hungry. Because of Jackson's legacy, his endowment to her, Jake, and their friend Margie, his restaurant continuously met the needs of the community he loved.

The past kept hijacking her thoughts until the sound of their voices nudged her gently back into the present. Jake and Jessie walked back into the room. Lydia sat upright, relying on the pillows positioned directly behind her head. Year after year, the search for a cure taxed her spirit. Finally, she understood the crushing reality—this hospital visit gravely affected not only her but the future of her family. Her sisters and Jake needed the whole truth and not another layer of her lies. Maybe, that's why their Aunt Regina created and strictly enforced an unwritten in case of emergency rule. She didn't want any of them to ever feel alone or suffocated during a crisis. Her oral decree mandated that only one family member at a time travel into the eye of the storm out of a city to the south, east, or west. Fortunately, her aunt considered their husbands a bonus.

Lydia understood her family's bedrock ideology. After a drunk driver killed their parents, she and her four sisters became wards of the court until their Uncle Roy and Aunt Regina assumed legal guardianship. They drilled the same unorthodox family principles into Lydia and her sisters with such force they smashed every idea that stood contrary to their beliefs. Their new guardian's philosophy of dependence on God uncovered a fallacy that in their own power, they found it hard to accept His. By now, Lydia's heart beat so loudly she thought they heard it pounding in her chest. She looked directly into Jessie's eyes. Her voice shook. "Jessie, I need to tell Jake something." Jessie stood up. "No, please stay."

Jake raised his hand and pressed his fingers gently to her lips, "Everything will work out, Lydia, I promise. I've been waiting for you."

How long? she wondered. She paused then turned her attention back to Jessie. "So, what's the verdict?"

Confident she had another powerful advocate on her side, she grinned.

Jessie was shocked. She couldn't believe Jake and Lydia kept something so life-changing from each other.

Then suddenly, her pager buzzed.

"I need to take care of this," she said and stepped out.

Jake picked up a magazine. He pretended to read. Again, Lydia's mind stumbled backward then forward through the archives of her past. From the moment they met and, even during their grueling residency, Jessie kept disrupting the order of things, like the time she presented an alternative slant on a technique their instructor spent a lifetime perfecting. Very quickly, their worlds collided. Dr. Martin's angry words soared like hot lava forced up from an active volcano. Jessie sprang to her feet. Finally, she'd had it up to her beautiful eyeballs with his pompous attitude. As she hammered home her point, her high-pitched attack grew more threatening. The veins in his neck bulged, his cheeks turned beet red, and his eyes popped like kernels of corn exposed to extreme heat. Her colleagues gaped.

Jessie bravely challenged a man powerful enough to crush her dreams. As a flicker of recognition flashed between them, Lydia proudly added courage to the evolving list of qualities she admired about her friend. However, it seemed strange that, with their distinctly different backgrounds, a solid friendship sprang up so quickly. But, over time, common threads of wisdom stitched their lives together like tiny squares in a quilt. Each stitch united their professions and, ultimately, their friendship until a workable and beautiful piece of art emerged.

Jessie stepped back into the room. Worry lines creased her forehead and arched her eyebrows upward. Lydia felt partially to blame for Jessie's solemn disposition. Jake appeared more anxious than before. He tossed the magazine aside. It missed the chair. Then it hit the floor. The pages fluttered noisily. Jessie looked directly at him and then at Lydia. "Guys, I just received word that the preliminary tests show sickle cell anemia, but I won't make an official ruling until the final test comes back."

"I understand. Thanks, Jessie."

"You're welcome. Try to relax. I'll see you in the morning. Jake, keep an eye on her," she said, staring at him. He flinched. Then she looked at Lydia. "Absolutely no calls to the clinic, Doctor's orders."

Lydia smiled and raised her hand as if taking an oath. "I promise."

Jessie walked out. Again, Jake followed. Lydia sat up, straining to hear as their mingled soft whispers floated through the slightly ajar door.

Minutes later, Jake returned to her bedside. He whispered the same reassuring words. "Everything will work out, Lydia, I promise." Briefly, his smile hid the fear masquerading as hope.

Without asking, Lydia would never know exactly how long he'd known. Certainly, she had a pretty good idea how he'd found out. While watching him frantically fade in and out of consciousness, she wanted to say don't worry. On second thought, what good would come from interrupting the little bit of sleep he'd stolen? Her mouth opened wide into a yawn and then closed almost immediately. The beautiful soft glow of the moon cascaded through her window. She watched as it played peek-a-boo with a host of twinkling stars. Their breathtaking performances lifted her spirit then sat it high upon a cloud. While he slept, she prayed for sustainable faith to endure the long, painful journey ahead.

Disappointments spanned decades, but she never gave up hope. She believed that one day modern medicine working alongside an infinite God would produce a plethora of possibilities. New medical breakthroughs happened every day in labs all across the country. Tommy's miracle drug became her new beacon.

Jake stirred as she gently stroked his head. "Good morning, sleepy head."

"Good morning, Lydia."

A lack of rest left his muscular form less brawny. Jake looked ragged. His puffy red eyes, which once signaled a night of binge drinking with his boys, now sank deeper into their sockets.

"Go, get out of here. Grab some coffee. Jessie normally starts her rounds much later. Grab some breakfast, too. I'm still a little groggy."

Jake kissed her. Reluctantly, he walked toward the door. "I won't be long."

That little white lie seemed like the right thing to do. It was painfully obvious that he couldn't handle much more. Lydia watched him shuffle out the door. Then she leaned her head back, adjusted her pillow, and shut her eyes tightly.

"Good morning."

Lydia recognized the voice. She opened her eyes. "Good morning, Jessie! Timely, as usual. I knew you wouldn't disappoint me."

"It's all in what you get used to."

They laughed.

"How did you sleep?" Jessie asked.

"Last night or a few minutes ago?"

"Both."

"Last night fair. Much better a few minutes ago."

"Where's Jake?"

"Getting breakfast, he had a rough night."

"And you haven't?" Jessie asked.

Lydia's silence froze time. When she spoke her shaky voice sounded like ice cycles crashing onto the pavement. Watching her wrench in pain, Jessie purposely steered the conversation away from her illness. "Anthony walked right pass me the other day like what we once shared meant nothing. The word's out that he's got a new woman in his life."

"Do you miss him?"

"I suppose I miss a skill that extended beyond the operating room." Then she laughed while fanning her hand in front of her face. Lydia laughed too. Seconds later, Jessie recoiled as a glint of sadness filled her eyes. She then walked over to the window and stared out across the hospital parking lot. "Poor Anthony, I'm sure you heard his wife left him shortly after our breakup."

"I heard a rumor," Lydia said, and that's all it took.

Jessie didn't need any coaxing. Her sharing produced a therapeutic high void of any vindictiveness.

"Lydia, sometimes I wish he'd understood the meaning of faithful. I realize now he enjoyed too much privilege to care. A few short months after our breakup, his wife caught him in their bed with the help."

Much too late, Jessie had learned his wife overlooked his sexual improprieties with women of reputation too many times to count during their ten-year marriage. Usually, he received a slap on the wrist as punishment. That weak gesture didn't deter his bad boy behavior. As it turned out, he continued to cheat. Finally, he went too far. When he cast his net in waters filled with shoals of what she deemed a socially unacceptable catch, she kicked him out on his butt. Rumors took flight.

While Lydia faced one of her greatest challenges, she felt grateful for Jessie's presence, not just in her hospital room, but in her heart. Jake's low threshold for the suffering of those he loved rendered him mentally distraught and sometimes physically ill. If possible, she wanted to spare him what she couldn't escape. The air stilled. In the quietness, her mother's spirit spoke comforting words to her heart. *It's out of your hands now, Lydia. Trust God to do what he does better than anyone. Who do you think kept you all these years?* The words resonated so clearly, Lydia felt her presence.

No amount of stalling would change the facts. Since last night, Jessie had rehearsed this scene a dozen times. Briefly revisiting the past had simply postponed the inevitable. Her uncompromising words, like clumps of frozen water flying through the air, pelted Lydia with such force her body ached at each point of impact. Jessie leaned forward.

Gently, she repositioned a lock of hair dangling over Lydia's glassy stare. Far removed from shock or fear, she knew. Now, Jessie knew, too.

"If you need me please ask the nurse to page me. I'm around here until midnight. I took over Dr. Clay's shift since her daughter and sitter has the flu." Then Jessie walked out.

Their colleague, Dr. Clay had flirted a few too many times. In the same year, she toiled through a nasty divorce and custody battle. Her husband's inadequate defense couldn't prove allegations of adultery. As a result, the promiscuous doctor had walked away unscathed.

Jake appeared in the doorway. "Looks like I missed Jessie."

"Uh-huh. Babe, please sit down." This time Lydia didn't let him stop her. He took a deep breath and moved slowly over to her bedside. "Jake, I'm sorry. You deserved the truth. I've always had this need to take care of everyone else. I didn't want to burden you. Yes, it's true. I've lived with sickle cell anemia my entire life. I know it intimately, and it knows me. Normal red blood cells resemble round, soft doughnuts without holes. My sickle shaped hemoglobin makes traveling through the bloodstream much harder and painful. Until recently, my old medication worked. Of course, like everything else even old medicine needs improving."

As Lydia detailed this worst-case scenario, his heart braced against every sharp prick. The secret he had kept seemed more real now. Suddenly, he felt an urge to shield her with his body as if from falling debris. Additionally, he wept. With her fingers, she traced the stream of water trickling down his cheeks. Silently, he uttered a prayer. Surely, his tiny semblance of faith counted for something, he thought.

His muscles grew tense. "Jake, honey, relax."

"Why didn't you tell me?"

"You wanted children. I knew the limitations."

"Lydia, we can adopt."

Then Jake wrapped her in the warmth of his body and smothered her with affection. Now looking ahead, she wondered how the news would affect her sisters. Mostly, she feared Jake would grow weary in a climate hosting more bad days than good.

She looked over at him and smiled. "Jake, don't worry. God has a plan for my life. We've talked. He heard me."

"I sure hope you're right, Lydia. Anyway, I prayed, too."

His bold confession shocked her. No way! Surely, this wasn't the same man who eyed the clock impatiently the moment he took his seat on Sunday mornings? Then she looked at him. "Jake, He hears and answers every prayer. A few days ago, I danced a melancholy waltz with death. Look at me now. Although I certainly can't boogie yet, I don't doubt it will happen. Hopefully, Jessie will release me in a day or two."

"That's good news, Lydia. Get some rest. I'm going home to shower, if that's okay. I'll be back soon."

"Of course."

Lydia couldn't shut the flood gates fast enough. Memories rushed in like rising flood waters. This attack thrust her entire medical history out into the open like books on display in a public library. She knew Jake dreamed of a home filled with children. In many ways, he reminded her of her father. Her sisters fantasized that Jake like their father and Uncle Roy had a hand in hanging the moon. With all that praise pumping him up, he confused her goals with those of her sisters. Unlike them, she never expressed a desire to become a mother. Adoption scared her. Why? After all, she and her sisters turned out fairly well. Maybe, her fear had nothing to do with adoption. Perhaps, the hurtful knowledge that their parents unknowingly passed on a debilitating disease delivered one final powerful blow which left her grappling with the unshakeable truth of her destiny.

She hoped Jessie would release her soon. Minute by minute her hospital room grew increasingly more confining. Her restless body contorted in sweeping discontentment while her mind searched for escape in the shadows of all those old memories. Jessie's intriguing lifestyle dominated Lydia's thoughts. At the point of suffocation, it was as if the walls took a deep breath and then exhaled. She relaxed, but the memories continued. In such a short time frame, she and Jessie shared a lifetime of memories. Dr. Anthony St. Johns, the man in Jessie's life, inherited his sculptured good looks from his French and African-American ancestors. Proudly, the renowned doctor skillfully molded Jessie's career. He believed his protégé could never surpass him. That lie fed his narcissism. Gradually, his possessiveness eroded their romance. As a result, their inseparable teacher-student relationship crumbled, too. Jessie never considered those teachable moments under his tutelage a total debacle, and rightly so. After all, the world revered this gifted doctor. Sometimes though, he scared her. The evil in his eyes matched the evil in his heart. He took pleasure in destroying careers. She feared someday, he'd snatch away her life's work, too. Therefore, she sank alongside him in the gutter like a grungy sewer rat.

CHAPTER 2

Nearing the end of the day, an attractive couple sat waiting. When Jessie entered the room, the woman jumped up. "Hello, Dr. Cooper, I'm Keisha Foster, Lydia's sister and this is Frank, my husband. May we speak with you please?"

"Of course, come on in. It's a pleasure to meet both of you." They shook hands and then with a slight hand gesture, Jessie ushered them toward her office. "Please hold all my calls," she said as they strolled pass her receptionist. Inside diplomas and awards lined the walls like priceless paintings hanging in a museum. Her desk held the basics: pad, pencils, papers, and computer.

It struck Keisha odd that her desk held no mementos or family pictures. "How's my sister?" Keisha asked then took a seat.

"She's improving and getting the best care possible."

Keisha wanted more, but expecting the doctor to divulge privileged information wasn't going to happen. Leave it to Frank to fast forward to the obvious question.

"May we see her now?"

"Of course, I'll take you to her room." On the way out, Dr. Cooper stopped at the receptionist desk.

"Mrs. Johnson's running late again. Please page me when she arrives."

"Yes, doctor."

They took the elevator up to the third floor, criss-crossed between two long purple color-coded corridors, and through a set of automatic doors before reaching her room. Keisha forced a smile then pushed open the door. Her hand went up then casually brushed away a single teardrop teetering at the corner of her eye. Keisha held her sister close as her aunt's stern advice "only let them see what you want them to see," played once again in her head. Apparently, all of them paid close attention since an onslaught of heartaches gave them a whole lot of practice time.

"It's good to see you, Lydia. How do you feel?" Frank asked.

"Better today, thanks."

He kissed Lydia gently on the cheek then asked, "Jake, you okay man?"

"Not bad," Jake said as they exchanged that manly handshake.

Jake hugged Keisha then moved over to the window.

Lydia grinned. "Frank, please tell me my sister's behaving herself."

"You're kidding right?"

Their explosive laughter momentarily relieved the tension hovering overhead.

Jessie stepped forward. "Give us a minute, please."

They walked out. Moments later, the door reopened. As she turned to leave, Jessie looked directly at Lydia. "Today, you're the patient. You know what to do."

Then she left them alone to make sense of an illness stripping them naked before a cruel and insensitive world. Keisha sat on one side of the bed. Frank sat on the other. Jake remained at the window absent-mindedly looking out across the parking lot. Lydia imagined him counting the cars neatly lined up in their proper spaces. Even this simple task demanded total concentration, much like detailing her illness over and over again. During those early years, she dealt with petty nuisances disguised as childhood illnesses.

Eventually, they progressed into a few bruising attacks. But, with her aunt and uncle's help, she successfully kept her illness a secret.

Today, for the very first time, Keisha learned her sister had sickle cell anemia and what it meant in full disclosure. She blinked fast several times then shut her eyes tightly. That ritual didn't halt the effortless flow of salty water running down her face.

The tears came anyway along with her volatile outburst. "Lydia, why didn't you tell me?"

"Why unload that burden on everyone?"

"You had no right to shut us out. We're family," Keisha shouted in a shrill, angry voice.

"I had every right," Lydia snapped back. Seeing the fear in her sister's eyes, she immediately regretted her sharpness. "I'm sorry, Keisha."

The minute the battle of wills started, the guys backed out of the room, using a cafeteria break as their cowardly excuse. Keisha frowned at them and then turned back around. Their conversation got nowhere. An onslaught of incoming calls kept interrupting them. Calmly, Keisha took charge. In a polite, yet firm tone, she began screening the callers. Of course, Rebecca's call made the cut.

"I'm glad you're feeling better. Everyone sends their love and well wishes, especially your patients."

"Thanks, Rebecca. Please tell everyone I'm doing much better."

"Please follow Dr. Cooper's orders, okay."

"I promise." Lydia's body grew tired as mere minutes seemed like hours.

Off in the distance, a phone rang. Immediately, the new caller's authority superseded Keisha's brief power play.

"Lydia, we're all here."

"Aunt Regina, I'm really very tired, please explain everything to Patsy and Pauline for me."

"Of course, sweetheart."

"Thank you."

"We're sorry we're not there," her sister's said.

Her voice barely audible, Lydia offered them a gentle reminder. "You know the rule ladies."

Their heartfelt goodbyes trailed softly behind their aunt's hacking cough. No doubt, she'd held her breath. Shortly before visiting hours ended, everyone left. Two days later, Jessie released her. A week later, Lydia returned to work on restricted duty. The clinic's doors swung back and forth continuously with patients exchanging places like players at a roulette table. Some of them limped away while others seemed to glide.

Jessie had a smile on her face and joy in her heart after she received the good news. Finally, Tommy's medical research had gotten the necessary approval. She couldn't wait to make that one important call. Before she got the chance, her phone rang. She answered hurriedly.

"Hello, Dr. Cooper, it's Regina Mayers."

"Oh, hello, Mrs. Mayers, how are you?"

"Very well, thank you." Regina's strong, distinctive voice shook slightly despite an attempt to mask the distress lurking behind an obviously forced cheerfulness. Without delay, she got straight to the point of her call. "Dr. Cooper, Lydia commands a special place within our family structure. I'm entrusting her to your care. Please do your very best to ensure she gets well."

"Of course, Mrs. Mayers, you have my word."

"I'm sure I do, honey. Thank you. Good-bye."

The authority in Mrs. Mayers's sweet, yet menacing, tone delivered the same urgency that Jessie felt. If only she could've given her the good news, but her obligation to Lydia came first.

Lydia's private line rang once and then in a soft self-assured voice came, "Dr. Giddens."

"Lydia, he has the approval," Jessie shouted excitedly into the receiver, all the while suspecting Lydia had already heard.

"Thank you, Jessie. I'm overwhelmed. It's hard to explain how I feel right now," she said in a voice packed with an unusual calmness. "We'll talk later. Thanks again."

Lydia's tear stained cheeks still held the remnants of an earlier long-awaited call. Tommy Calvin's research had given her and thousands of others a fighting chance. When a bone marrow search didn't yield a single match, her life hung in limbo. Now years later, due to extensive and careful research, his lab produced a miracle drug. It claimed less frequent attacks in most patients and possibly extending the life expectancy of others. Lydia laughed out loud when she thought about her two best friends. Like Jessie, Tommy's private life kept drenching the appetite of those speculating about his single status. Interestingly, Lydia never worried about any aspect of her life fueling the flames of the gossip mill. Perhaps, people understood the danger in spreading rumors about her. Regina owned everybody's secrets, and her influence had a far-reaching effect.

❧❧❧

A few weeks before Jake and Lydia got married, he

received a strange call. "Jake, it's Aunt Regina. Lydia's stubbornness has left me no choice. I'm in Philadelphia on business. Meet me tomorrow morning in the coffee shop at the Charleston Hotel. I'd appreciate it if you keep this between us."

Jake took an early lunch. What on earth? he wondered. Surely, she knew he loved Lydia. Minutes later, he stood in the hotel lobby, clasping sweaty palms, while ignoring the sound of his knees as they knocked frantically together. Before walking into the coffee shop, he pulled in a long deep breath.

She looked up and smiled. "Hello, Jake."

"Hello, Mrs. Mayers."

"Please call me Aunt Regina, we're almost family now," she said as she stood and embraced him.

She seemed uncharacteristically different from the other times he'd spent in her company. Lydia and her sisters needed their aunt's approval as much as they needed each breath that ushered in the next heartbeat. He found her mysterious, her control intimidating, but he didn't dare speak ill of her. A queasy feeling like butterflies fluttering about rose up from the pit of his empty stomach. He coughed uncontrollably. Then he gripped the back of the chair hoping the floor beneath him would stop spinning. Slowly, he lowered his limp wobbly body into the seat across from her and felt his masculinity begin to wane.

"Jake, Jake, are you all right?"

"I'm okay, Aunt Regina."

Right away, he figured she had bad news. She didn't waste any time before she let Lydia's health challenge roll painfully from her lips. It took strength to expose such a heartbreaking secret. Lydia's story pierced his heart and sent a rush of tears running down his cheeks. He no longer cared about his manly image. That day, the vow he made etched an indelible imprint into his memory.

"Jake, she's afraid that she can't handle this. Watch her for me. In addition to her love, when she's ready, she'll share her burdens, too."

Hum, burdens, as in more than one, he thought.

Aunt Regina stood up slowly and, ignoring the dampness, patted his moist hands affectionately. "Great to see you again, Jake. My flight leaves in an hour, I've got to hurry. I'm looking forward to the wedding." Then she turned and walked out.

Jake remained seated long after she had gone. Sunbeams danced across the window pane. They hit him squarely in the face. He squinted. He hadn't thought of that day in years. *Why now?* he wondered. Lydia's last attack happened over six months ago. She looked and felt better than she had in a long time. The improvements in her and the other patients had even the skeptics singing a new tune.

🙐🙐🙐

A cool snap rushed in, announcing a seasonal change as the last weekend of fall made its exit. Jake pulled out of the parking lot heading home when his cell phone rang.

"Hello, Jake. I'm sorry for spoiling your weekend, but one of my forensic team's results took a troubling dive. I just got wind of an unscheduled review. I need you and your team back today."

His boss didn't think twice about rearranging his weekend plans. He knew Jake had lofty goals and thrived on challenges.

"Yes, sir, on my way. I'll contact the team as soon as I get back." Then hesitantly, he dialed, "Hey, babe!"

"Hey, Jake, what time are you getting home? I'm already here. I'm hoping we can get an early start on our weekend."

"Sorry, babe, the boss called. I'm needed back at work."

"Again, so soon?"

"Yep, I'm afraid so. I'll miss you."

"I'll miss you more."

"What will you do?"

"I'll think of something," Lydia said and hung up.

Four times already this year, his call outs interfered with their plans. Just like before, Jennifer, their restaurant manager personally handled the preparation and delivery of all meals for his crew. Knowing Lydia absolutely hated dining alone, he figured her finger had already hit the speed dial button.

Lydia did the expected. "Hello, Jessie."

"Lydia, how are you?"

"Disappointed, Jake's working this weekend. Are you free?"

"Yep. My date had an emergency. I took a rain check. I'll see you around six, if that's okay."

"Terrific." Lydia sat in that special booth and watched as a hostess escorted Jessie to where she sat waiting. "Hey, girl, you look great."

Jessie smiled. "Thanks, and so do you. How's that handsome, hardworking husband?"

Lydia smiled. "Hardworking!"

As soon as Jessie sat down, the waitress took their drink orders.

Several merlots later, Jessie mellowed. Tonight, for whatever reason, she allowed a small glimpse into her troubled past. Lydia knew Jessie grew up on Martha's Vineyard. She didn't know her family still lived there. In fact, she never knew Jessie spent her early childhood in

California. Jessie's unrehearsed, but rare disclosure stunned her. Lydia wondered if her choice of wine or perhaps the ambience created the perfect platform for Jessie's new revelation. None of her colleagues really understood her. Lydia knew more than most. Of course, everyone knew she had a peculiar aversion to going home.

Despite her aloofness, Lydia felt deeply connected to her. Jessie drew people like a magnet then abruptly pulled away when such proximity left her feeling vulnerable. These friends, Lydia and Jessie, had different starting points, but secrets like the insidious flames from a welder's torch fused their lives.

As each holiday approached, Jessie voiced the same unrealistic reasons for not spending time with her family until finally, she believed her own lies. Then it happened. Ginny, the sister no one knew about, came. Her visit fueled the rapidly burning flames of the hospital's gossip mill.

CHAPTER 3

From all angles, Jessie's life looked a mess. Lydia praised her best and held her accountable for her worse.

Dr. St. Johns's power over Jessie's life worried Lydia. Repeatedly, she begged her, "Jessie, report the abuse."

"I will, I will," Jessie said. Nothing happened.

Her nonchalant attitude bothered Lydia. Finally, she backed off. "Jessie, I'm here whenever you need me." She'd wasted enough energy telling Jessie what she already knew.

"Lydia, stop worrying about me, I'm done." A few days later, Jessie collapsed on the well-worn sofa in the doctor's lounge.

"Jessie, what's wrong? Are you okay?"

Lydia's empathy broke through a barrier of pent-up emotions with such conviction it gave Jessie the strength she needed. Tears ran down her face. Mascara streaked her cheeks. She licked away tiny drops of water near the corners of her mouth. Jessie appeared visibly shaken. While listening impartially to details of her friend's torrid affair, Lydia stripped away her imaginary robe. Finally, she had validation for her dislike of the conceited doctor.

As Jessie's teacher, he knew better. The turning point came in their relationship when she found out he had a wife. Among the things she and Jessie had in common, they had somewhat misguided views on morality.

"Lydia, please don't misunderstand. The affair didn't start out one-sided. In the beginning, we both got what we needed until his possessiveness took over. I'm no fool. From the beginning, I knew his reputation. Playboys don't usually grow up, they merely grow old. However, I regret he knowingly railed against the sanctity of his marriage. Stakes that high leave permanent scars."

"I'm sorry too, Jessie. I thought you knew."

Embarrassed, Jessie looked away.

Wait a minute. Permanent scars! Now what? Lydia thought.

Jessie's earlier candor seemed refreshing. After Lydia witnessed her attack on Dr. Martin, Lydia wondered why she tolerated such a sleazy relationship. Was the sex that intoxicating? According to hospital gossip, her relationships usually fizzled out very quickly until Dr. St. Johns came along.

Then late one night, an explosion at a local plant pushed the understaffed hospital almost beyond its breaking point. The emergency room filled with casualties as worried families piled into the already-crowded waiting room. Jessie had spent thirty-six straight hours on her feet, providing care for the injured and comfort for the grieving when she saw the posting. A dozen down trodden interns gathered around to check their schedules. Quickly, she scanned the sheet. Suddenly, she felt flushed. The great Dr. St. Johns stood at the nurse's station, looking smug. Jessie pushed her way through the crowd until she stood looking up at him. "You possessive little worm," she shouted hysterically. Her hand flew up into the air and landed hard on his face. "I hate you."

"Get over it, Jessie," he snapped then rubbed his jaw and walked away.

Their on-again, off-again affair kept the rumor mill buzzing like a hive of angry honey bees. When they were off, he acted like she had a contagious disease with quarantining the only solution. By assigning less senior interns preferred shifts, he flaunted his control over her life. Until she confronted him publicly, she naïvely believed no one knew the real answer behind that mystery. But they knew. Nothing happened in that den of sin without getting broadcast over human airwaves. Lots of affairs happened and a few divorces as a result, but mostly just hot and sweaty sex. Deep down, surely, Jessie knew her life looked like a used book with its dingy, crumpled dog-eared pages attesting to its worth.

Her crime—she believed his lies until that shameful discovery banished his power over her. Everyone knew. No matter what others might think, only the abused knew how far from grace they were willing to fall. No matter what Lydia or anyone else said, no one could make that decision for her. Then one cold, blustery afternoon, Jessie sat waiting. The door opened wide. Daylight, a gust of wind and haze competed for the open space. He stood for a moment before his cold, deep-set eyes saw her. As he leaned in, she turned too late. His lips brushed across her cheek.

"What's wrong, sweet thing?" He loved the way she flipped between hot then cold in the same span of time. He leaned in, again. He couldn't resist the fragrance of her charm. "What's this?"

A tattered piece of ordinary notebook paper ripped from the confines of its binder lay face down on the table in front of him. His grin widened when he remembered how much he enjoyed her surprises.

Suddenly, the twinkle in his eyes faded, his jaw

tightened. The scribbled words began registering. Then she saw it. His eyes held the same terror seen in the eyes of those who feared him. Through clenched teeth, he hurled obscenities into a cloud of smoke as he walked away. She watched the crumpled piece of paper fall aimlessly onto the floor. Not so long ago, he thought of her as a worthy conquest. Even after their hot-blooded affair ended, she remained his greatest challenge. In the time suspended between blinks, she regained her freedom.

Now, she and Lydia sat facing each other. Jessie had her undivided attention. When a noticeable frown formed wrinkles in Lydia's forehead, Jessie laughed. "Relax, girlfriend. I gave Anthony too many liberties. Guess what—he took advantage of them and me. I had the solution. I wasn't sure I had the courage. I guess I had that, too."

They talked a while longer. Jessie walked out of the lounge carrying a much lighter load and a renewed confidence. A few days later, she checked in.

"Lydia, thanks for listening the other night."

"No problem, I'm glad we finally talked."

"See you around, girl."

Finally, with the affair behind her, an amazing metamorphosis gave birth to a new emancipation. Her hiatus stunned the gossipers. Except for the times she joined Lydia at the restaurant, she stayed off everybody's radar.

Lydia, Jake, and Margie owned the restaurant called Jacksons. On those days when Margie didn't feel like dining in, Lydia ate dinner upstairs with Margie in her apartment. Their popular eatery kept evolving into this wonderful place Jackson dreamed into existence. Had he seen it today, Lydia envisioned his chest extended and his eyes gleaming with satisfaction.

Most evenings, she and Jake ate dinner while enjoying lively conversation, but tonight Jake sat unusually quiet at their mid-week dinner. Finally, she asked, "Are you okay, Jake?"

"Lydia, my boss asked me to attend a three-day seminar next week in California. Can you manage alone?"

"Of course, I'm not an invalid Jake," she snapped and rolled her eyes at him.

"Lydia, I didn't mean it that way."

Her tone softened. "I know, Jake." She had a laundry list of character flaws. Never had she considered selfish one of them. Before she joined the clinic, her on-duty calls surpassed his out-of-town seminars and occasional weekends with his buddies. "When do you need to leave?"

"The meeting starts Monday afternoon. I'd like to get there early."

That earlier sharp outburst fueled her guilt prompting preparation for a fun-filled weekend. Friday night, they went to the movies. Later, they dined on pizza and beer. Early Saturday morning Jennifer's energetic voice set the tone for her dinner plans. "Oh, hello, Dr. Giddens, how are you?"

"I'm terrific. Jake and I will see you tonight around seven o'clock for dinner."

"Great, I'll see you later."

They had two days together before Jake's boring business trip. The image in the mirror stared admiringly back at her. Black stilettos accentuated her toned legs and seemingly, every curve of her petite body melted into a sensual bright-red dress. Her choice of a gold filigree clamp held every strand of her upswept hair in place. Large gold hoop earrings shimmered as they hung from her delicate ear lobes.

Every seductive sway of her body held him captive along with the soft jingle of a dozen gold bracelets dangling freely from her tiny wrist.

"You look delicious." As his emotions churned, they fed his insatiable appetite. He pulled her close and kissed her lips passionately.

She pushed him away. "You know I hate arriving anywhere late."

He winked and pulled her playfully back into his arms. "Who cares? You act like we need reservations."

"I care," she snapped.

He released her abruptly and walked off. "Lighten up, Lydia, it's just dinner for goodness sake," he yelled and tossed his damp towel onto the bathroom floor.

The sudden spike in his blood pressure caused a thudding in his head. Sometimes, her mood swings drove him nuts. He dressed quickly while she sat waiting in the car. The silence exacerbated their mood like a thick fog. It lingered long after they took their seats at the restaurant. The relaxing atmosphere at Jacksons never changed, but tonight gloominess surrounded them and wouldn't go away. They left early.

Why had she reacted so poorly?

Sunday morning, she sat, spellbound, as their pastor delivered another stimulatingly intellectual sermon. Reverend Kettle had an amazing memory. He could effectively articulate a message like the Apostle Paul. But today, Jake's leaving ambushed her thoughts.

Monday morning, she drove him to the airport. "I'll miss you, Jake Giddens." Then she gave him a long passionate kiss.

"And I'll miss you even more, Liddie."

Shock replaced the loneliness already choking her. All at once, her legs felt heavy, as if cement blocks held them firmly in place. Early on in their marriage, at the mere whisper of her pet name, their lovemaking soared. Later, she'd lay blissfully extinguished in his arms.

She smiled approvingly and watched as he smiled

knowingly back at her. "I'll call," he yelled as he rounded
the corner and vanished.

Still relishing the moment, she got back in her car
and drove to work.

"Good morning, Dr. G."

"Good morning." Lydia looked around at a room
filled with sitting, crouching, and standing patients. Already her morning was in full swing. The affection in
Rebecca's greeting reminded Lydia of their very first
meeting. She traded her hospital scrubs for the clinic's
the same month Rebecca came. The patients readily recognized in Rebecca a genuine gift. With Lydia's encouragement, and a rather significant financial contribution,
Rebecca enrolled in nursing school. Lydia wagered the
money she and Jake spent on Rebecca's education would
yield its own rewards in time. Surprisingly, their return
came sooner than either of them expected.

"Looks like another long day," Lydia said as she recalled the waiting room brimming with patients.

Rebecca grinned sheepishly. Then she passed Lydia
a chart and stepped aside. Wow! Her patient looked
amazing. Evidence of iron pumping exposed arms as
strong as steel with a rippling six pack bugling from beneath a tightly fitting spandex shirt. Working outdoors,
balanced high above the Earth, enhanced his now darker
sunbaked complexion and boosted his confidence.

"Good morning, Rob, please sit down."

The light in Rebecca's eyes shone even brighter in
Rob's presence. Shortly after his wife lost her battle with
a slow agonizing cancer, he started showing up at the
clinic with countless imagined illnesses manifested from
his sense of helplessness.

He had a sweet loving demeanor that presented no
danger to himself or anyone. Lydia had suggested many
times that he seek help from the on-site mental health de-

partment, but her soft prompts never got any serious attention.

Whenever she ventured off in that direction, he'd laugh and say, "Nice try, Dr. G."

What brought him here today? she wondered. Thus far in her career, she'd only treated one other hypochondriac. What a way to start her morning. She waited for his long list of ailments.

He surprised her. "I'm feeling great. What about you, Dr. G.?"

"I'm great too, thanks for asking."

"I've just returned from a weekend of hiking."

More like hiding out from the world, she thought, until she noticed the poison ivy. It had spread quickly. Almost every inch of his red blistery body had deep gashes and skin torn away from continuous scratching.

During a couple of visits, she found herself daydreaming amid his habitual rambling, but after that humbling experience, she never lost sight of any of his complaints.

"Dr. G., thank you. You knew I had head problems, yet you let me barge in here every few months with one fake illness after another. You never gave up on me. Thank you, again. Now, I'm ready."

Her voice shook. She could hardly contain her excitement. "That's wonderful, Rob." Immediately, she dialed a colleague, and they spoke briefly. "Tomorrow at three, Rob, okay?"

"Sure thing, thanks, Dr. G." Then he stood up.

"Take care of yourself, Rob. I'll miss you." She walked from behind her desk and gave him a hug. His touch warmed her all over. He walked out, stopped in an open doorway, and smiled at Rebecca.

"Thank you, God, for the miracle of new beginnings," Lydia whispered.

CHAPTER 4

Lydia hadn't eaten a single morsel all morning. After Rob left, she closed the door and sat lost in her thoughts until a voice called out, "Dr. G., it's' Dr. Cooper on line three."

"Hey, Jessie, what's up?"

"Work and more work. How are you feeling?"

Lydia welcomed the interruption. "Great, Jake's out of town on business, I'm meeting Margie for a business update and a late lunch. Can you join me for dinner say around six?"

"Sure, dinner sounds wonderful. Your favorite place?"

"Is there any other?"

They laughed.

"See you at six."

Frequently, Jessie stopped in at the iconic eatery for food or late night drinks either alone or with Lydia or a companion. After Margie's stroke, Tommy made frequent unannounced trips home. He relaxed only after Lydia promised she would keep an eye on his mother. As a single mom, Margie made many sacrifices for him, although she never considered them as such. "We do whatever it takes for the people we love. It's a lesson from Calvary," Margie said.

Lydia couldn't wait. Lunch sounded like a nice treat. Today, Margie felt well. She looked forward to their meeting. Whenever Margie felt inclined, she shared some of her customer's delightful stories with Lydia, always careful that she never disclosed their secrets. No doubt she knew many personal things, but only talked about their already public escapades. They talked for hours, first about business, life, and then everyday things. Margie looked toward the entrance and waved. "I like your friend Dr. Cooper." Then she got up and headed out the back entrance. Her apartment sat a few yards away.

Lydia grinned. "Hey, Jessie, glad you made it."

"Ladies, what can I get you to drink?" Jennifer asked as she stepped forward.

Jessie ordered a chardonnay. Lydia ordered her usual.

"Where've you been hiding, Dr. Giddens?" Jennifer asked. "I've missed you."

"Under a pile of work, I'm afraid."

"I'm glad you're back. I'll get your drinks right out."

Jessie looked over at Lydia. "I know doctors make the worst patients, so tell me what's it like following my orders?"

"Better than I thought. Maybe it has a lot to do with our friendship."

"Maybe."

They laughed.

Jennifer placed Lydia's drink down first. The other drink slipped from her hand and spilled out running like tributaries in all directions. She scooped up the mess quickly then summoned a waitress. "I'm so sorry, Dr. Cooper."

"Don't worry about it, Jennifer."

"Bring another chardonnay please," Jennifer said addressing the waitress.

"Enjoy the rest of your evening ladies." Embarrassed, Jennifer walked off. Her cheeks glowed like red hot coals.

Four years of outrageously funny stories had them strolling joyfully down memory lane. "Well, from all accounts, I can seriously say doctors love their nurses," Lydia said.

Jessie winked. "And doctors love their doctors."

Lydia fondly embraced the memories of the naughty boys of medicine with a gentle toss of her head and a hearty laugh. She saw so many affairs come and go, she considered writing a steamy novel. Her book, *Swinging Doors*, would tell all.

Jessie never forgot their last outing. She successfully steered Lydia away from any talk of her family. Lydia got the hint. Not tonight. Those waters would remain murky a little while longer.

"May I get you ladies another drink before dinner?"

"Another chardonnay, please."

"Water, please." Lydia's illness put a cap on her alcohol consumption.

The evening started out perfect until their jovial chatter briefly stalled. Then Jessie blurred out, "Lydia, I desperately want to forgive my parents. I thought I knew them. What liars! The sum of my existence equals one big fat lie." The sour-tasting words left her lips in such a flurry, she couldn't retract them in time.

Lydia felt the bitterness embedded in her words and the awkwardness of not knowing how, or even if, she should respond. Then, as if she'd arrived at a party in her honor, Jessie's anger quickly changed into gaiety. Lydia missed an important opportunity. Jessie's pain slipped through her fingers with the grace and speed of an eagle.

Perhaps, Lydia should've said she once faced the same
reality. Why didn't she say she discovered that her parents in their humanness had flaws, too? But before the
little voice inside could guide her, Jessie asked a profound question.

"Lydia, do you believe God forgives our transgressions?"

"I absolutely and unequivocally believe in God's
forgiveness."

"Perhaps, one day I will too."

Lydia felt a tinge of guilt. She had seen the troubled
look in Jessie's eyes many times. She did nothing. They
spent a lot of productive time working and too many su-
perficial evenings pretending they lived unencumbered
lives. Lydia's tightly woven circle shunned outsiders, but
somewhere along the way, the ebb and flow of their
shared times changed the dynamics of their friendship.
The evening ended with Lydia promising she would
check in at least once every month with her doctor and
more often with her friend. After they said goodnight,
Lydia remained seated. How many times had she sat either alone or with a member of her inner circle preparing
to grab hold of her destiny?

While sitting there undisturbed, some good and not
so good memories inundated her thoughts. After a fire
partially destroyed the restaurant, it underwent a few
structurally necessary along with aesthetically noticeable
changes. Jennifer added a few of her own concoctions to
an outdated menu. She brought in some great music on
the weekends. At first glance, watching Jennifer in Margie's role seemed too surreal. Lydia once thought no one
could ever fill Margie's shoes until fate showed her another possibility. Loyal customers rewarded Jennifer's
adeptness with the same well-deserved accolades bestowed upon Margie. Lydia watched these same custom-

ers dip in and out of relationships like seagulls searching for food along a white crusted sea shore.

Margie's not so uncommon story had a happy ending. One poor decision rewired the destiny of a pregnant, scared teenage girl with no idea what life had in store for her. Then one day she met a man who literally saved her life. From far and near, customers came. The restaurant provided relief for their burdened and broken spirits. They needed an escape. In this most unusual place, they found hope. Everyone found their answer. Margie found a refuge. Lydia discovered genuine love transcends a simple friendship. Jennifer found peace.

Of all Jennifer's regrettable choices, her difficult marriage left her threadbare. At times, she felt mentally wounded. Young, foolish, and in love made for a devastatingly insane combination, but, against all odds, Jennifer still believed good triumphed evil. Somewhere in all those memories, Lydia lost track of time, as if it no longer mattered. The rest of the evening, she watched Jennifer hop from one table and then the next before plopping wearily down across from her.

Beneath those droopy eyes, an unmistakable smile radiated its usual warmth. "What a long night. Would you like anything else, Lydia?"

"No, I'm good, thank you."

"Enjoy the rest of your evening."

Before stepping into the night air, Lydia blew Jennifer a kiss. Jennifer smiled then closed her eyes as she listened carefully to the words of "At Last" playing softly in the background. No one could electrify an audience with her soul stirring lyrics and incredible vocals like the accomplished Etta James.

The next morning, Lydia arrived early to get ahead of the paperwork. The clinic always seemed chaotic, but she loved everything about it. Every day, her patients, family, and friends got better than one-hundred percent, while she sometimes neglected the most important people in the equation. What about her needs? What about Jake's?

"Dr. G, you've got a call."

Excitedly, she picked up, expecting Jake's voice.

"Hello, Lydia, how's your day?"

"Hey, Jessie, it's going very well. I'm finishing up a routine exam, thanks for asking." The glee in her greeting hid her disappointment. She hoped he would call later.

"Any problems you need help with?" Jessie asked.

"Not unless my patient requested your services, too. If not, your patient feels pretty terrific, and as for my patient, she's well, too."

Jessie laughed. "Well, take care of your patient. As for my patient, I believe she knows where to reach me."

"Thanks, Jessie."

Still, Lydia's day ended on a high note. As she pulled out of the garage, the smell and image of scented bubbles caressing her body took control of her senses. Only minutes later, she heard him calling out. "Hey, babe!"

Where had the time gone as she lay covered from head to toe in a fragrant liquid grave of tranquility?

"Hey, Jake, did you pick up dinner?"

"Yep. Spaghetti with meatballs."

"Great."

Jackson's spaghetti recipe traveled comfortably and intact down the proverbial pipeline. Lydia enjoyed having some of life's chores handled. She changed and then sat down on the sofa to wait.

Jake sneaked up behind her and kissed her neck. "Let's eat."

"I've got a better idea," she whispered softly as she led him into the bedroom.

He kissed her gingerly and then passionately on her lips. All cares fell away as she surrendered her mind and body over to him.

"I've missed you, Liddie. Welcome back."

She giggled then jabbed him hard on his arm. He laughed so loudly his shoulders shook. The sight made her laugh out loud, too.

They enjoyed dinner and each other as their toes touched playfully beneath the table.

"Jake, I think Jessie would enjoy Aunt Regina's birthday party next month. I'll invite her." Already, she anticipated what he would say.

"Really, you think that's wise?"

"And why not?"

"Just because she's a great doctor and your friend doesn't make her any less weird."

"Jake, I agree she's different, although eccentric sounds like a stretch of the imagination." Lydia couldn't deny that Jessie kept things lively around the hospital and the clinic.

He shot her an obviously annoyed look. "Anyway, I didn't say eccentric. I think I used the word weird."

"Same difference." Then she tossed her napkin across the table at him.

"Lydia, once she encounters our loud, opinionated family, she might feel out of her element and freak out."

"And do what, Jake?" She snapped. Definitely more put out with him, she threw up her hands.

He surprised her, talking as if Jessie had some mass murderer tendencies and, at the right moment, would slaughter Lydia and her entire family in their sleep.

"Okay, you win. I can't wait. This should prove interesting," he murmured.

She'd heard enough of his nonsense for one night. So what if Jessie followed a different set of rules? Lydia's family had rules too. Even if the love of her life perceived problems, she couldn't let him cloud her view. Just like the ever-shifting wind, she deliberately changed directions and speed so quickly, he barely noticed. After dinner, she fell asleep in his arms half way through a romantic comedy.

Gently, he nudged her. "Lydia, Lydia, let's go to bed."

Her eyes sprang open capturing the brilliance of a big golden light as it spilled through the partially open blinds. "Okay, I'll be there shortly." She remembered her very last words.

Every morning, a second cup of coffee always kick-started her day, but before walking out the door this morning, she called Jessie.

"Dr. Cooper's office."

"Good morning, this is Dr. Giddens. Is Dr. Cooper in?"

"Yes, Dr. Giddens, one moment please." They had private lines, but they rarely spent enough time in their offices to answer them.

Jessie's voice was cheerful. "Hello, Lydia. How's your morning?"

"Wonderful. My aunt has a birthday in a few weeks. Please come."

"Really!" An octave higher, her surprised voice came through loud and clear.

Lydia pretended she hadn't noticed. Of course, she had.

"Please, please come. It's always a blast."

Jessie concluded from their too much sharing over late night dinners that Lydia's aunts came from a long line of spoiled little girls who grew up into society's pampered women. Jessie hesitated. *Why not?* she thought.

She'd heard so much about this birthday tradition, she couldn't resist.

"Okay, I'll come."

"You won't regret it." Lydia gave her a few highlights and left her puzzled about the rest. Out of love for his wife, a husband created a party that blossomed into an elaborate celebration. Her aunt loved crowds, "the more the merrier," she always said. Lydia thought she'd let her aunt know that she'd invited a friend to her celebration, but before she dialed her aunt's number, an overwhelming urge took over. Instead, she called someone else.

"Keisha Foster." Her voice exuded confidence, despite the colossal demands of her job. Keisha knew what she wanted. She let nothing stand in her way. Immediately after graduation, she hired on with a prestigious law firm, made partner and snagged a husband in unprecedented time.

"Hey, girl, what's going on?"

"Hey, Lydia, I'm glad you called."

"Why, anything wrong?"

"Everything's fine, Lydia. You're always so uptight. Relax. I've got some great news." Keisha paused.

"Well, do you plan to keep me waiting all day?"

"I'm preg—nant," she yelled excitedly.

"Congratulations, honey! Give my best to Frank." Lydia's voice cracked slightly.

"Lydia, you okay? You sound strange."

"I'm fine. I'm so happy for you guys."

Lydia felt conflicted, knowing she and Danielle would never experience the miracle of childbirth. Danielle had the trait and, unfortunately, she inherited the disease. Ironically, providence granted safe passage for her sisters Keisha and the twins, Patsy and Pauline.

"Does everyone know?"

"Only Aunt Regina."

"When's the baby due?"

"Early spring."

Keisha's excitement soared. When she came down from her inflated high, she proudly enlisted her sister's opinion of their choice in baby names. "How does Matthew Roy or Stormy Regina sound?"

"Good choices."

Long after they hung up, Lydia stood fixed in the same spot. Keisha's news stunned her. Sure, some of them wanted children. Lydia chose a career. The family chose her. No one gave her a choice. Pauline's engagement, the other big news had the family anxiously waiting for the other big announcement—a wedding date.

While honeymooning in Cabo San Luca, Jake almost drowned. A stranger named Rick Parker rescued him from the warm waters off the southern tip of the Baja Peninsula. Jake literally owed Rick his life. Later, they introduced him to Pauline and magic happened. Had a brush with death not paid Lydia and Jake a visit, Pauline and Rick might not have met.

Aunt Regina's birthday celebration drew near. Danielle and Pauline worked really hard. They wanted their aunt's big day memorable. When Lydia and her sisters spoke earlier in the week, Danielle assured them she'd checked every box. Lydia didn't care about party details. Her aunt hadn't called any of them. The phone rang a little longer than Lydia expected. Her aunt's winded hello gave the illusion she'd just returned from a brisk run.

"Aunt Regina, are you okay?"

"Oh, I'm fine, Lydia. How are you?"

"I'm doing great."

"That's wonderful. I'm glad. I got preoccupied with all that stuff I've accumulated over the years. I forgot to check in with my girls. I'm a little breathless from carrying all those boxes from room to room. Barton promised me he would stop over later and help. Tell the girls I'm sorry."

"Of course. Now, why don't you wait so he can help you?" The new man in her aunt's life had everyone taking notice.

"Maybe I will." Then like a skilled magician, she cast aside any talk of her tiredness. Lots of exciting things started happening in their family. They had an upcoming birthday party, the anticipation of a wedding, and now the birth of a child to celebrate.

"A grandmother again, how exciting," Aunt Regina said, sounding elated.

For more than a decade, Danielle's adopted son Joey had dibs on the title of grandchild, and their hearts.

Somewhere beneath all the excitement of a new arrival, a fallacy lived that this announcement should've come from the oldest sibling. *That's silly and pure nonsense*, Lydia thought. They talked non-stop about family business as well as her aunt's hopes and dreams for her family. Lydia actually invented an excuse so her aunt would move the conversation along, but today time actually got away from them. "Aunt Regina, I'm late. Oh, I almost forgot. Jake and I invited a friend to your party."

"I hope it's another nice guy like Rick. Patsy could use a change of scenery."

"Not this time, I'm afraid. It's a girlfriend. I think you'll like her. Goodbye Aunt Regina."

"Goodbye, sweetheart."

CHAPTER 5

Row after row of big red Xs systematically counted down the rapidly approaching days. Why had she agreed to go? How weird that people carried out grandiose birthday parties beyond what she considered their prime. Secretly, Jessie wondered why Lydia and her sisters made such a big deal out of these parties. Except for this bunch, sixteen and perhaps twenty-one marked the most significant years in the lives of most people. Anyway, she hoped those etiquette classes paid off and, if all else failed, she'd pretend. Regardless, like every doctor in her workplace, she needed a respite.

At seven o'clock in the morning, the terminals boasted of bustling crowds. It looked like some of them had slept there all night. Perhaps, they had. An unstable weather pattern crouched over the city, bringing with it high winds, blinding rain and hundreds of delays. From everywhere heading somewhere an influx of people sat and waited.

Lydia started laughing.

Jake looked at her. "Don't tell me."

Of course, she couldn't resist. The congestion conjured up a laughable reminder that, no matter where she went, she couldn't escape the crowds. "Look around you. Does this remind you of anything?"

He chuckled. "Your clinic."

Boarding had begun. The aftermath of bad weather, combined with an unexpected last-minute patient consult, created a long, treacherous trip. Jessie arrived at the airport, panting, but safe. "Hey, everybody."

Lydia hugged her. "Hello, Jessie. Glad you made it."

Jake stepped forward. "Hello, Jessie."

They boarded quickly. Lydia flanked Jake on one side and her friend on the other. *How funny?* she thought. Countless times Lydia sat trapped like a middle child between Jake and a stranger. No wonder she harbored a deep resentment for that seat. Fortunately, a tail wind pushed the flight a little ahead of schedule. They grabbed a cab and endured a shaky twenty minute ride. Lydia felt like ducking every time the driver bobbed and weaved in and out of traffic. When he finally pulled into the driveway, she jumped out, happy she could feel an unwavering earth beneath her feet.

"Welcome home, Lydia!" Aunt Regina pulled Lydia into her outstretched arms. Then her mouth fell open at the sight of the beautiful woman strolling alongside Jake. "Hello, Dr. Cooper. Welcome to our home. I'm so glad you finally came."

"Thank you, Mrs. Mayers. Please call me Jessie."

They smiled politely at each other.

"Thank you. Come on in, Jessie."

Lydia thought she glimpsed some semblance of familiarity during their exchange of pleasantries. Her aunt's comment sounded as if she expected Jessie would drop in one day. Had she mentioned that Jessie would join them? A month earlier, she discussed the idea with her sisters and perhaps, one of them mentioned Jessie would be their guest for the weekend. Sometimes, Lydia got so busy

with work and other issues her siblings filled the gaps in
time for her. Those belated birthday and anniversary
cards became her signature trademark. While Jessie
freshened up, she joined her aunt in the kitchen.

"Your sisters called. They'll join us later. We can
catch up. Tell me what's going on in your life? How's
your health these days?"

They talked weekly. Still, Aunt Regina had lots of
questions.

Lydia turned around as Jessie walked in. "Perhaps
you should ask my doctor."

"Well, Doctor, do I have anything to worry about?"

"Not a thing. Lydia's actually a pretty good patient.
The improvement in her and other patients has the medical community hoping that, one day, an off-shoot from
this drug will produce a definitive cure."

Aunt Regina threw her head back. She laughed. "Jessie, I've known Lydia all of her life. Quite frankly, my
dear, your assessment surprises me." Everyone laughed.
Then she got up from the table and walked over to the
stove. "However, I owe you and Tommy a debt of gratitude. May I get anyone some tea?"

Lydia nodded.

"Yes, please," Jessie said. "Tommy and his team de-
serve all the credit. Because of their doggedness, I can
offer help to hundreds of patients."

"That's wonderful. Is chamomile okay, ladies?"

"Of course," they said.

"Nothing warms the soul like a piping hot cup of
tea."

Jake blew Lydia a kiss as he headed outside. A half
hour later, Danielle and her family arrived. "Hey everybody!" she yelled out. "You look great, big sister."

"Thanks."

"I'm happy you're looking well, Lydia."

"Thanks, Mark."

Joey ran into her arms screaming, "Auntie Lydia, Auntie Lydia," and wrapped his arms around her neck before she could introduce Jessie.

It seemed he grew an inch every time she saw him. Danielle looked on affectionately, reliving the memory of their father as Lydia swung him around. Finally, Lydia caught her breath and made the introductions.

"What about the food?" Lydia asked.

"It's covered. By the way, Lydia, the theme's western."

"I'm miles away from home, and now you tell me. Little sister, it looks like you kept too many secrets."

Their laughter filled the air.

Danielle had their mother's flair for the theatrics and, in a deeply Southern drawl, she said, "Sweetwater got rid of the horse and buggies decades ago. There's a mall in town now, sugar."

Jessie laughed so hard tears rolled down her cheeks.

"All kidding aside, Lydia, I doubt you left home without a pair of jeans."

Lydia didn't respond. Instead, she cast a questioning look in Jessie's direction.

"I brought a pair, too."

The key made a clicking sound. The door swung open. "Hey, everybody," Pauline shouted and intentionally ignored the disapproval on Lydia's face.

Her aunt's eyes pleaded. "Lydia, let it go."

Pauline sometimes misunderstood her boundaries. The sisters greeted like long lost strangers. Had they forgotten they talked at least twice a week if not more?

"Anybody heard from Keisha, today?" Lydia asked.

"Keisha will be here in the morning. Frank's traveling on business. He sends his love," Pauline said.

"There's plenty to eat. Is anyone hungry?" Aunt Regina asked.

"I'm starving. Those peanuts only teased my appetite," Lydia said.

"You mean you didn't enjoy those yummy calorie busting peanuts?" Jessie asked sarcastically.

"Nope, and I'm famished."

They raided the refrigerator like old times. Lydia stuck her head out of the door and yelled, "Jake, you want a sandwich?"

"Uh-huh. Thanks."

"Mark, you and Joey want one?"

"No," came once and then twice. "Late breakfast," Mark yelled back.

Jake grabbed his sandwich and then went back outside. Over lunch, their overlapping chatter transported them back in time. At one point, Patsy's eyes held so much sadness they looked lifeless.

"Patsy, what's wrong?"

Immediately, a hush settled over the room. Patsy broke down and shared her pain openly.

Her nightmare began with an invitation from her friend Marvin. Going to a club in the middle of the week never appealed to this workaholic. She hesitated, seeing the work piled three tiers high on her desk, but relented. He drove to a characterless building on the out skirts of town where a brightly painted rainbow made of stained glass hung over its door and underneath it a sign with the words, *Welcome to all Shades of Amsterdam.*

"It's really okay, Patsy," he'd said, laughing as she nervously fumbled with the door handle.

They stepped into a very stylishly decorated room. Once inside, it appeared larger than she envisioned from the outside. The beautifully stained concrete floors and massive dark mahogany counter created a sophisticated vibe. Customers completed the spectrum of age, race, and gender. Deducing from their attire, most had left a professional job in the city for an evening of fun. The waiter immediately found a table and took their orders. They talked about the usual work stuff then threw in a few tidbits about their personal dramas for good measure. Out of the corner of her eye, she noticed that Marvin kept staring toward the entrance.

"Marvin, do you have plans for later?"

"No, I'm just having trouble unwinding from a maddening work day."

"For you, my friend, I left a ton of work on my desk."

"Gee, I knew you loved me." His deep raspy laughter and dry wit made her laugh even on her worse day. Time passed quickly as the band played a hodgepodge of music.

"Eleven-thirty, goodness, tomorrow's a workday," she said.

Suddenly, he looked impatient, almost uncomfortable, in a setting well suited to his sexual preference.

"Anything wrong, Marvin?"

"No, no, everything's fine."

He hadn't mastered the art of lying. Another awkward few minutes passed before she suggested they call it a night. He pleaded then confessed he'd requested the band play one of his favorite songs.

"Okay, just one more song."

"Another drink?"

"No thanks, I'll quit while I can still walk out of here knowing my name and my address."

He laughed and ordered another. His face lit up as the band started playing, "Midnight Train to Georgia."

She tossed her head from side to side in a sing-along. Instinctively, she turned toward the entrance as the door opened. Her boyfriend, Elliott walked in holding the hand of a lanky, well-dressed man.

Marvin winced. "I'm sorry, Patsy. I didn't know how or what to say."

A gray shadow drifted across her mind. She gasped. Marvin squeezed her hand tightly.

With familiarity, the hostess greeted the couple warmly as she escorted them to a table near the dance floor. Patsy's legs wobbled slightly as she stood. Then she moved briskly toward them. She wanted to heave, but fought the urge. *Not a bad idea*, she thought later. Elliot saw her. Quickly, he jumped to his feet. Patsy moved in so close, she heard his erratic breathing.

"Stay the hell away from me," her eerie voice squeaked. The hatred filling her heart matched her scorn.

He reached for her as she pulled away. "I'm sorry, Patsy."

"Don't worry, he's all yours." Her eyes dared his companion to move as her trembling fingers frantically wrestled with the zipper on her handbag. "If you come near me again, Elliott, I promise I'll kill you."

Like a dagger, her cruel words sliced through all the lies he ever told her. Fear paralyzed him. He couldn't move. Marvin felt the hair rise upon the back of his neck. Heads jerked around. The room fell silent. In her haste, she almost tripped over her friend. Patsy never made idle threats. Right about now, Marvin worried he'd made a terrible mistake. At the time, his decision to bring her here seemed like the right thing to do for a friend.

The half-hour drive to her house seemed like hours. "A penny for your thoughts," Marvin said, encouraged as a brief smile appeared and then saddened as it quickly vanished.

"Thanks, Marvin." Then she gave him a peck on the cheek. "Goodnight."

Unfortunately, Elliott's secret left her bitter. Why didn't she see through his lies? As if the thought that he found a man more desirable wasn't tormenting enough, his preference made her question her own sexuality. Patsy stared across the room as if she could see clear through the plastered wall. "I'll always love Marvin for saving me."

Her revelation sent a shock wave rumbling throughout the room. Then, one by one, they gathered around her. Jessie sat quietly. She'd never seen such an outpouring of love.

Poor Elliott! Lydia pictured his grim future in the beautiful vengeful eyes of the very capable woman sitting across from her. Poor thing! He had no idea he'd stepped into the lioness's den. Much to his dismay, his troubles had only just begun. Nothing serious came out of Patsy's dates after his unveiling rocked her world. She waited on Mr. Right. He never came.

Lydia couldn't believe how smoothly Jessie fit in. Lydia's polished aunt cautiously sized their guest up. Of course, Jessie pretended not to notice. *How strange,* she thought. Her aunt's behavior reminded Lydia of a funny anecdote. Whenever something made no sense, her aunt's friend would always say, "Somewhere, there's a dead cat on the line." Although still humorous, she suppressed her laughter.

"Aunt Regina, where's the sergeant tonight?"

"Barton's out of town. Why do you ask, Pauline?"

"Just curious, I haven't seen him around lately."

Another man had fallen under Regina's bewitching spell. She never discussed her personal affairs with her children. But, strangely out of character, she didn't leave Pauline hanging. "Barton's visiting his brother in Detroit." Her slightly edgy pitch gave Pauline pause.

"Oh," Pauline said. She remembered the hostility

Danielle encountered when pointing out the obvious.

"It wasn't a date, young lady," Regina had snapped.

The burning sting of those words felt like a hard slap across Danielle's face. If their aunt hadn't figured out that the sergeant had stolen her heart, they had. Selfishly, all of them held out hope their Uncle Roy would remain the only man she ever loved.

At the pre-party celebration, Lydia and a few others sat around shamefully overindulging until the lateness of the hour spoke to them through yawns, stretches and the exhaustion blurring their senses. A watery glaze covered her aunt's beautiful eyes. Clearly, she missed all the noise that once filled their home. The twins left first, everyone else followed. Their home had grown rather old and subdued without those sibling squabbles. It no longer embodied the loving playfulness of their beloved protector. Had her sisters felt it, too?

All evening Jake's skepticism slowly wiggled its way into her sub-conscious. On the way to her room, Lydia stopped and knocked softly. "Come in."

Jessie sat child-like, her legs crisscrossed beneath her. Night after night, Lydia, the young school-girl, had sat, exacting the same pose, waiting until someone tucked her in and kissed her goodnight. Her aunt came most nights, other times her uncle showed up. Regardless, someone always came, not just for her, but for all of them.

"Hey, Jessie, I'm getting ready to turn in. Do you need anything?"

"No thanks, Lydia, I'm fine. Goodnight."

"Goodnight, Jessie." Lydia went to her room and climbed into the hollow of his arms. He held her gently then rolled over and turned out the lights.

Before Lydia showed up, the guest Jessie expected made an appearance. "Hello, Jessie," she said, holding a blanket. "I thought you might need this. Sometimes, the night air gets a little nippy."

"Thank you, Mrs. Mayers."

"May I sit down, Jessie?"

"Of course."

Their eyes met.

"How long have you known, dear?" Regina asked.

"A long time."

"Any plans?"

"I'm not sure."

Regina stood up. "Jessie, we can't change the past. In a funny sort of way, it stabilizes the future. Some things are out of our hands. However, all is not lost. From a storehouse of our memories, we'll present to you the man we loved and his vision for our family. Under Lydia's restructuring, I expect real change. She has the heart, the right temperament, and, of course, our blessing."

Although her comment felt comforting, Jessie had no clear notion why this woman's very charged emotional summation should matter to her.

"Goodnight, Jessie."

"Goodnight, Mrs. Mayers. Thank you."

CHAPTER 6

The next morning thanks to a couple of speed demons, a parade of cars arrived at the venue in record time. The guys went about their male bonding while the women followed the delicious aromas permeating the air. Under a tent, housed at the farthest corner of the grounds, tables displayed all kinds of scrumptious treats. Danielle had found the perfect tailor-made setting. Her strategically arranged bales of hay made for the perfect seating. The DJ fused a sizzling mixture of the old with the new and hoped his musical playbook would satisfy all ages. Lydia watched a zealous group of line dancers perform the newest version of on old favorite. The entire affair resembled a scaled down adaptation of *The Wild, Wild West*.

"You've done a terrific job, Danielle."

"Thanks, Jessie."

"It's simply amazing."

"Thanks, Lydia, I'm hoping Aunt Regina likes it."

"Like it, I love it," her aunt said, appearing in time to hear Danielle's comment.

"Thanks, Aunt Regina."

Mark sneaked up behind Danielle. "That's our song."

She giggled then joined him in a slow dance.

Lydia and Jessie walked over to where Pauline stood sampling the goodies.

"Well, hello, ladies," Pauline said.

"Hey, girl," they said.

Their aunt joined them shortly. Then everyone gathered around and toasted another birthday. Each year, she appeared younger as if she'd signed a contractual agreement with Father Time. Instead of him moving forward, he moved backward. Although older numerically, none of them had any clear idea what that meant in celebrated years. The celebration had already begun when Patsy arrived. Even the rebels Pauline and Uncle Roy never disrespected this tradition. After showing up late, Patsy made a bold statement. An emergency at work needed her attention. She couldn't stay. Finally, her aunt let out an exasperated sigh. "Patsy, please, of all days isn't there someone else capable of doing your job?"

"No, today it's just me." Then Patsy kissed her cheek. "I love you always, Aunt Regina," she whispered.

Everyone tried. Reasoning failed. Sadly, they watched her drive away. The party continued with most guests unaware of the rift. After an incredible weekend, Lydia, Jake, and Jessie boarded a plane late Sunday afternoon back to Philly.

Jesse hailed a cab. "Thank you again, Lydia. What a real treat! See you later, guys," she yelled as the cab sped off.

Even Jake, the skeptic, admitted Jessie brought a different flair to the party.

"See what happens with a little faith," Lydia said.

Jake shrugged his shoulders. "I never said she wasn't fun."

Too many years had gone by since Jessie enjoyed the company of a real family. In a single weekend, she frolicked in the limited memories of her own childhood while enjoying games of tug of war, horseshoe, and many others. In their simplicity, these games revealed a more wholesome aspect of true happiness.

Still filled with excitement, Jessie arrived at work early. Mid-morning, she walked outside to the common area where doctors and nurses gathered between patients to discuss their day. With a cigarette wedged between her fingers, she watched ringlets mockingly circle overhead as she inhaled, then exhaled at the same steady pace. Her bad habit started at the awkward age of fifteen. After numerous failed attempts to quit, nicotine remained her downfall. The health fanatic had a weakness like so many others who enjoyed the euphoric feeling nicotine gave them. She puffed slowly. On her graduation day some years earlier, she recalled Lydia grabbing her arm firmly as she hurried by. Excited classmates had already formed a single line. She'd imagined this day from the first moment she stepped onto campus.

"Oh, hey, Lydia, you better hurry. It's time."

"In a minute, Jessie, I'd like you to meet my Aunt Regina."

Jessie turned then gasped as she stared into Lydia's mirror image. Jessie felt oddly aware of their connection.

"Hello, Jessie, It's so nice to meet you finally. Congratulations, you turned out beautifully, dear," Regina said as the image of a beautiful baby wrapped snugly in a pink blanket flashed in her mind.

"Thank you."

That's strange, surely not another secret. Lydia wondered if Jessie noticed her aunt's peculiar comment.

"Lydia darling, congratulations."

"Thanks, Aunt Regina."

After the ceremony ended, Lydia and Jessie met up once again. They promised to keep in touch. Fate stepped in when they accepted employment at the same hospital.

That time seemed so very long ago. Suddenly, the image of waiting patients jarred her thoughts back to the present. Jessie crushed the cigarette beneath her feet then went back inside. Shortly after lunch, she stood at the desk of his receptionist. "Is he in?"

"Sure, Dr. Cooper, let me buzz him.

"Thanks."

"Dr. Barnes, Dr. Cooper's here."

"Send her in."

"Dr. Barnes, please forgive the intrusion," she said as she stuck her head in the door. "May I speak with you, please?"

"Sure. Come on in, Dr. Cooper. Did you enjoy your weekend in Sweetwater?" His question startled her. He laughed seeing the mortified expression on her face. "Dr. Cooper, I don't keep tabs on my doctors. I've known Lydia's family a long time. I supported her Uncle Edmond in his bid for the Senate. Later, we all became good friends. I heard a little rumbling that you attended a birthday party. You know how it is in this place."

"Oh. I had a great time." Jessie smiled, rendering the initial shock of his question useless.

"Regina's a remarkable woman. Lydia reminds me of her. I'd love it if you shared the highlights of your exciting weekend, but I know that's not why you're here. What's on your mind, Dr. Cooper?"

"Dr. Barnes, I came to request a sabbatical."

His mouth opened wide forming a perfect, but silent "Oh!" She had caught him totally off guard. "Jessie, is there anything I can do to help?"

"No, I'm afraid not."

"I see." His concentrated gaze made her squirm like a bug under a microscope. Noticing her uneasiness, he decided not to probe. "When do you want to leave?"

"At the end of the month."

"So soon?"

She ignored his question and the tiny little wrinkles adding unintentional years to his face. He couldn't wait to ask the next question. "How long do you plan on staying away?"

"Six months, perhaps. I'm not sure of anything right now."

"*Hum*, that long." He stared at her over his red-rimmed trend setting glasses. The thoughtfulness in his eyes made her wonder if what she saw reflected his concern for one of his doctors in crisis or solely for the welfare of the hospital. In the stillness, questions rattled around in her head like pebbles rolling noisily from side to side in an old empty can. He sighed. "I'm sure you've given consideration to the placement of your patients while you're away."

"Yes, definitely. By the end of the week, it will be done."

He didn't doubt her patients came first. Evident in her work, her compassion shone like newly minted coins. Out of the hundreds of interns and doctors he'd had the pleasure of knowing, she displayed the most compassion. "We'll miss you, Dr. Cooper." Worriedly, he looked at her, "You do plan on coming back to us, right?"

"Of course, this is my home."

"Good." He breathed a sigh of relief then stood up, walked from behind his desk, and extended his hand. "Be safe. Hurry back."

"Thank you, Dr. Barnes."

She graciously accepted his outstretched hand. Over the years when their paths crossed, his attentiveness warmed her heart like the gentleness of a doting big brother. Today, his quick response brought relief and disappointment simultaneously. She felt grateful that he didn't deny her request, however, the thought of leaving her patients filled her with anguish. After a long day filled with mixed emotions, she went home, heated up a frozen dinner, and collapsed in front of the television. Shortly after midnight, she crawled into bed.

The next morning, she left her office and walked across the adjoining breezeway. Her patient, Mrs. Peterson, sat upright with her left leg elevated. She held a book in her right hand. The very spry elderly woman had taken a nasty tumble in her bathtub. Her age along with other health problems presented complications in a normally very simple operation. Jessie paused in the doorway observing the avid reader as she turned the yellowed pages of one of her favorite books.

"Hello, Mrs. Peterson, how're you feeling today?"

"Pretty good, under the circumstances, but I'm so glad you're back." She placed the book down on her breakfast tray.

"Thanks," Lydia said.

"You're welcome."

"I missed you this weekend."

"I attended a birthday celebration with a friend."

"A handsome young man, I bet."

Jessie laughed. "No, I'm afraid not."

"Don't worry, you'll find some nice young man one day."

Sadly, that happened a long time ago. Unwilling to share her thoughts, Jessie simply smiled. One of her best decisions happened the moment she removed her name from a list of eligible, sometimes desperate women. Generally speaking, romance only complicated her life. She and Dr. St. Johns enjoyed a strictly sexual relationship, but traveling down that road hadn't turned out the way she expected either. In the beginning, she'd secretly hoped for something more.

"I'll check in later. You're progressing nicely, Mrs. Peterson. Next week, your physical therapy will start. Pretty soon you'll walk out of here."

"Thank you, Dr. Cooper. Oh, did you enjoy the party?"

"I had a wonderful time. See you later." Jessie walked to the door then looked back over her shoulder as Mrs. Peterson opened the book again.

Dr. Barnes couldn't stop thinking about her. Jessie's request blindsided him, like her lifestyle choices had so many times. This complex young woman had the hardest time adapting to anything too permanent. Although she had impeccable work ethics, that didn't keep rumors about her private life from flying like a kite on a breezy summer day. He'd heard all of them. Despite all the trash heaped upon her, Jessie never let hospital gossip affect her work. No one worked harder, except maybe Lydia. Sometimes, he wondered what demons ruled her emotions as he watched her literally throw herself into her work.

He needed Jessie. No, the hospital and her patients needed her. In his private thoughts, for the very first time, he admitted his feelings for her. Quickly, he shifted the papers in front of him while envisioning the great team of Dr. Cooper and Dr. Giddens together in private practice. That association seemed like the safer bet. He wondered if they had ever considered such an incredible once-in-a-lifetime option. Then he shook his head and picked up the piles of work needing his attention.

Jessie kicked off her shoes then tossed her handbag and keys aside. Loneliness washed over her. Minutes later, she stood outside of Jacksons' listening as all things familiar whispered her name.

She wiggled her way through the crowded entrance, placed her name on an impressively long waiting list, and took a seat at the bar. The velvety tasting liquid felt soothing.

Jennifer spotted her and walked briskly in her direction, "Good evening, Dr. Cooper nice to see you again. Let's get you seated."

"Thank you, Jennifer."

Jennifer had an incredible gift of perception. Jessie rarely came alone. Tonight, Jennifer suspected she had and, out of politeness, asked, "Anyone joining you this evening, Dr. Cooper?"

"No, it's just me." Jessie had skipped lunch. Now, she sat wrestling with her dinner choices.

"May I bring you another drink?"

"Perhaps later." Jessie continued nursing the bourbon and water. Occasionally, she enjoyed a change in everything, which included her choice of drinks.

"Enjoy your evening, Dr. Cooper."

A few minutes later, Jennifer returned. "Still doing okay?"

Jessie raised her glass. "I'll take another of the same please."

"Coming right up. I'm a pretty good bartender." When Jennifer returned, she set the drink down in front of her. "How was your day?"

"Pretty good."

"You look distraught for a pretty good day. Is something wrong?"

Jessie picked up her glass and sipped slowly. "Just dog tired, I guess." To her surprise, she spoke her frustration out loud. "Jennifer, my life's a real mess. It feels like a runaway train. Frankly, I'm just not sure if I can get back on track." Immediately, she realized her blunder. "Forgive me, Jennifer. I'm making a big deal out of nothing much. When I'm overworked, I exaggerate."

"Well, I'm a pretty good listener if you change your mind."

"Really, I'm fine, Jennifer. Thanks for caring."

On her way back to the bar, Jennifer visited with another customer. No one fit perfectly any place in life like Jennifer. Her love for her job showed in the attention she gave to everyone.

Jessie sipped her drink and gave the menu a brief once over before putting it back down. Had she made the right decision? What would she say after all this time? Would they welcome her home? Surely, she wasn't getting cold feet. More than anything, she certainly didn't want Dr. Barnes thinking of her as ungrateful, since he could've easily denied her request or even delayed it. Questions devoid of answers came derailing her thoughts like a train on a collision course.

Suddenly, the waitress appeared. "Are you ready to order?"

Startled, Jessie announced, "Sure, the special please."

"Good choice."

A loud, ugly growl rose up from her empty stomach as the waitress walked away.

"May I join you?"

Jennifer doesn't give up, Jessie thought.

"Of course."

"Jessie, whatever's going on will work out. Problems, regardless of their size are only temporary. Enjoy the rest of your evening. See you next time." Then she got up and walked away.

Jessie ate very little. Her glass sat empty for several minutes, then she heard, "May I get you another?"

"No thanks, I'll take the check, please."

She glimpsed Jennifer engaged in playful chatter with a waiter as she strolled toward the door. Tonight, loneliness drove her out of her condo, but when she stepped back inside, the room felt inviting once again. She curled up on the sofa with a partially read book. Her eye lids drooped. Sleep crept in. Bam! The book slipped from her hands hitting the hardwood floor with a deafening thump. Jessie jumped. A numbing tiredness swept over her body. It pushed her deeper into unconsciousness.

The next morning, her heart raced as she stood outside Dr. Barnes's office. She covered her ears with her hands to drown out the sound of blood rushing back and forth like a tidal wave.

Dr. Barnes sat at his desk unaware that the seamless transfer of her patients needed only his approval. He kept hoping she would change her mind until she walked in with her assignment in hand. He glanced down at the paper. Already, he missed her.

"Are you sure about this, Dr. Cooper?"

"I'm sure."

"Then I wish you well. The hospital and I hope you return soon." He stood and extended his hand. "Hurry back."

"Thanks again, Dr. Barnes." She heard hope and sadness in the same breath.

The completed placement of patients left her with an almost nonexistent workload. Mostly paperwork remained with only one thing left to do. "Good morning, this is Dr. Cooper, is she in?"

"Oh, I'm sorry Dr. Cooper she's not here yet."

"Don't mention that I called. I'll call back. Thanks."

She forgot that, unlike her challenging hospital hours, Lydia occasionally enjoyed more flexibility. Her shift in gears came as a result of her deteriorating health. Jessie took a few minutes then busily plowed through a few other issues. Although somewhat risky, she decided she wouldn't sell her condo. That decision took one more thing off her "get it done list." By now, she worried the news of her sabbatical could stretch its tentacles out and touch Lydia before they talked. That rumor mill had eyes and ears everywhere. Anything could happen once the paperwork left Dr. Barnes's hands.

Quickly, she grabbed the phone. "Hello."

"Hey, Lydia, can you talk?" Hearing that familiar hello always gave Jessie a warm fuzzy feeling.

"Sure, Jessie, what's going on?"

"I'm going away for a while."

"Well, it's about time. I can't recall you ever taking a day off for anything."

"No, Lydia, I'm leaving the hospital for a while. I've taken a sabbatical."

"A sabbatical?" Surely, Lydia hadn't heard Jessie correctly? "Are you sure about this?"

"Who knows?"

"But why now?"

"Sweetwater." Surely, Lydia understood.

Lydia's birthplace, her very own magic kingdom had the healing powers of warm spring waters that only recently offered Jessie the same restoration. "Jessie, I pray you find whatever will bring you peace. Just remember forgiveness works both ways. I'm here whenever you need a little conversation. Be safe. Please don't leave without saying good-bye."

"I wouldn't dream of it. Can we meet for dinner Thursday night around six-thirty?"

"Sure, Thursday sounds good." Lydia noticed she side-stepped her comment about forgiveness.

ಐಐಐ

The days breezed pass. Jake declined Lydia's dinner invitation. "You guys need to say good-bye privately.

Please tell Jessie I'll really miss her." After their weekend in Sweetwater, he had a change of heart. Finally, he admitted he'd misjudged Jessie.

Jessie sat waiting. "Hello, Lydia."

Their hug lasted a very long time.

"I can't believe you're leaving me."

"I'm not leaving you. I'm leaving work for a little while. Justin will take care of you while I'm away. He's a great doctor and, of course, Tommy's only a phone call away, too."

Lydia laughed. "I know. And we'll all get along swimmingly."

Jessie began feeling more and more like family.

Lydia swore she wouldn't cry. She broke her promise. As the evening wore on, they both cried. When the tears stopped, Jessie got up to leave after several hours of shared memories. Lydia hugged her. "See you later, Jessie," she whispered. "Go with the blessing of God."

"Thank you."

When Jessie walked away, Lydia wondered if this might be goodbye forever. Certain aspects of the weekend they spent together in Sweetwater, and her aunt's baffling behavior, kept playing over again in her head. Finally, she chalked it up to her own overactive imagination. Even that weak explanation didn't settle all the questions rummaging through her head. She never considered until now that, perhaps, her aunt had a hand in Jessie's decision. How was that possible? she wondered and shook her head.

CHAPTER 7

Lydia picked up on the first ring.

"Hey, girl."

"Hello, Pauline, how's the wedding planning coming along?"

"Great, we've chosen a destination."

"Well, tell me where we're going, girl," Lydia shouted excitedly.

"Hawaii."

"Are you kidding me?"

"Nope, behind Paris, it's probably the second most romantic place in the world. Aunt B J always said Paris held the patent on romance. Don't you remember, Lydia?"

"Of course, I remember." How could any of them forget? Their Aunt B J's incredible spellbinding stories left everyone within ear shot in a trance. Decades later, her flushed cheeks glowed when she talked about her honeymoon.

"Well, does everyone know?"

"Not yet, you're the first."

Finally, Pauline had a wonderful man in her life. During her teenage years, she repeatedly tested her aunt's faith and her uncle's patience. Her drinking and drug abuse caused a rise and fall of her self-esteem like a rickety old roller coaster charging up the hill before descending sharply into a valley. Regardless, they never gave up on her.

"Child, family don't quit on one another. They see it through to the end," her aunt had said. The Mayers household, like many families, had its share of ups and downs. Five teenage girls under one roof brought trouble into paradise. Some of them made it through those adolescent years unmarked. Others survived with their secrets securely locked away forever. Danielle had physical scars from a botched abortion. Regardless, she survived with little if any emotional baggage.

Then Mark came along. Together these teachers dedicated their lives to the education of all children while watching their adopted son teeter on the brink of his unexplored teenage years. Keisha fell hard, risking everything for the love of a man she suspected still pined for someone else. Of course, Lydia continued to outwardly wage war against an incurable disease while inwardly wondering what her predecessors saw in her. Why not choose someone else? Perhaps they, especially her Aunt Regina knew something she didn't. None of that mattered today. Pauline's impending wedding filled her Aunt Regina's heart with joy.

Until that unforgettable weekend, none of them knew for certain why Patsy drifted in and out of relationships. Well, almost none of them. Just like the old Pauline, Patsy had trouble attracting the right guy. More times than they could count, she hung around with some real deadbeats. Her strong views on almost everything intimidated the good prospects. What remained left her floating in a sea of clueless predators. For that reason, her relationships quickly headed south. Sometimes, Lydia wondered where on earth she found these guys. Had they slithered from underneath a rock as she crossed the street? Jokingly, Lydia wished Patsy had run over a couple of them and kept right on going. Some of them couldn't hold an intelligent conversation if their lives depended on them nodding the correct response. Whatever happened to her intelligent, vibrant sister? After Elliott messed over her, she simply gave up.

Her cell phone rang. When she heard the sadness in Pauline's voice, her heart skipped a beat. "Lydia, I'm worried about Patsy."

"I know. So am I. Until we figure this out, I don't want to worry Aunt Regina."

"Okay. Let's talk later," Pauline said.

"Sure." How foolish of Lydia to think Elliott's closeted lifestyle and Mark's over-the-top money problem got past her aunt? One thing for sure, Elliott's betrayal set off a chain reaction that solidified the allegiance between Lydia and her Aunt Regina. Adamantly, her aunt decided she would handle Elliott. She strongly suggested Lydia place Mark on her watch list.

Patsy had purposely taken a back seat to the rest of them, as if her life no longer mattered. Their loquacious sister, well versed in politics and current events, loved sharing her views every chance she got. Lately, she avoided them. Patsy really had Lydia scared. Had anyone else noticed? Lydia wondered. Maybe, she and Pauline only imagined their sister's struggles. Undoubtedly, something had to be done. It was Pauline who decided the sisters needed to talk.

"Lydia, we're all here," Pauline said.

Then one by one they joined in with each echoing a very loud, clear response before proceeding to the stressful business at hand. Openly, Danielle admitted her fear. Because of her own struggles, Pauline readily recognized the ugly disfigured face of depression. Patsy became their priority. No one felt like participating in their usual foolish banter. Hours after they hung up, their grave, yet dutiful good-byes cast a shadow over each of them. Finally, Lydia decided to make a call. After several unsuccessful attempts, a sleepy voice answered.

"Hello."

"Hey, Patsy, you okay?"

"I didn't hear the phone. I'm just tried."

"Are you sure you're okay, honey?"

"For goodness sake, Lydia, I said I'm tired, that's all."

Lydia backed off. "We'll talk later, baby sister."

The buzzing pierced Lydia's thoughts. The annoying silence followed. After Patsy dumped Elliott or Elliott dumped Patsy, depending on how you looked at things, she went from bad to worse. Finally, she dropped out of the dating scene.

Several months later, while speeding through the treacherous mountains in California, a passerby watched in disbelief as a car appeared to leap upward and over a cliff. Then the flame engulfed car exploded with a loud bang. Elliott's death came as a surprise to almost everyone. Surely, Patsy wasn't mourning the loss of her unrequited love. According to the sergeant, the police found no skid or break marks before his car crashed through the barrier.

Along the singed tree-lined path, debris covered the roadway. From the charred badly mangled pieces, they located the brake line, but couldn't determine if the severed line occurred before the crash or as a result of it. Finally, they ruled the crash an accident, due to mechanic failure.

එකෙන

Jake had already gone to bed when Lydia got home. Along with his new responsibility came an increased work load. They dined out less. Most evenings, one of them picked up dinner. As Jennifer began following in Margie's footsteps, dinner sometimes found its way into their refrigerator. Lydia's appreciation for Margie ran as deep as her beloved mighty Mississippi River, but tonight even the thought of Margie's good deeds couldn't soften all her blows. Patsy really worried her.

The next day Danielle called Patsy's office. She learned her sister had taken time off for personal reasons. Danielle jumped into her car. Minutes later, she stood listening to the repetitive chime of her sister's door bell. Patsy peered through the peep hole then reluctantly opened the door. Her faded pink robe hung awkwardly off one shoulder. Hair like porcupine needles stuck up all over her head. Inside, the house looked like the aftermath of a fierce tornado. Dirty dishes filled the sink. Mounds of clothes lay strewn over the sofa, chairs, and floor. How could this room belong to her obsessively compulsive sister? "Patsy, are you okay?"

"Why won't everyone just leave me alone? I'm fine," she yelled.

Danielle hugged her tightly. "We can't. We love you."

Then she got busy cleaning up the chaos. Several hours later, on the surface, Patsy's home appeared orderly again. Danielle prepared two cups of hot tea. She sat down on the sofa next to Patsy. They talked or perhaps she did all the talking until Patsy yawned noisily. Danielle walked her to the bedroom and tucked her in. On the way home, she cried before calling Pauline, the one person who naturally understood.

"I wish I'd known that you were going to see Patsy. I'm afraid to ask about your visit," Pauline said.

"Her house looked like someone activated a bomb inside. She's in worse shape. Her self-loathing sticks out like an unwanted pimple. I don't understand why none of us saw this coming. How's that possible, Pauline?"

"The broken are masters at hiding their fragments. Take it from someone who knows. It's a choice. Some days, I still hide behind my mask."

In retrospect, Pauline wished she could take back the suffering she caused her family. Thanks to Dr. Maude, together they worked at rebuilding her deeply bruised self-worth. What she took away from their sessions helped in restoring a marred family trust. When Dr. Maude retired, her daughter Dr. Ada took over her practice along with Pauline's care. Pauline never forgot that Patsy protected her from some of the spineless men she hung out with early on. All of them had forgotten that, every now and then, even the strong needed a shoulder they could lean on.

"I'll call Dr. Ada." After three rings, the answering service picked up. Shortly after lunch, the nurse returned her call.

"Pauline, the doctor will see your sister at ten o'clock tomorrow."

"Great, thanks. We'll be there."

Danielle sat waiting anxiously.

"Her appointment's tomorrow at ten. I've tried several times, but Patsy won't pick up," Pauline said.

"Thanks, Pauline, "I'll keep trying." Who knows why she picked up Danielle's call. "Patsy, Dr. Ada wants to see you tomorrow morning. Pauline and I will pick you up around nine thirty, okay?"

She sighed loudly without offering any resistance. "Okay."

They drove downtown the next morning. The ordinary building stood two stories high, flirting with the clouds overhead. Its crusty red exterior walls leaned slightly while struggling with the weight of four over-sized windows. Her sister buildings stood timidly to the left and right of her, looking exactly the same. Patsy smiled. Inside this refuge, Dr. Maude had saved the lives of five very frightened little girls. Although their visits started out a little rocky, they spent some good times in her care. They had major hurdles to overcome. Each of them dealt differently with their parent's death. Their bi-weekly pilgrimages continued for several years. Nope, this was no ordinary place. When they stepped inside, everything looked just like they remembered. The recep-tionist smiled. She recognized Pauline from her on-going visits.

Then Dr. Ada stepped out of her office smiling, "Hello, everyone, you look well, Pauline."

"Thanks." Pauline then made the introductions. "Dr. Ada, meet my sisters, Danielle and Patsy."

Dr. Ada extended her hand. "Ladies, it's wonderful to meet you." She looked exactly like her mother. The petite natural blonde had big azure eyes with an unmis-takable pull. "Patsy, come on in, let's talk. Ladies, why don't you grab an early lunch. You can meet Patsy back here in about an hour.

Lunch sounded like a great idea. They could catch up on the family's goings and comings. A few months ago, their cousin Alan got married. Except for his sister Mia and step-sister Kellee, most of the family, along with a few close friends, attended their very private ceremony. Mia and Kellee's most recent Doctors without Borders mission pushed them even farther into one of the most remote violence-riddled third-world countries. No one could trace the last time either of them set foot on Ameri-can soil.

Pauline looked down at her watch. "We'd better go.

The session's over." Danielle ignored a couple of speed limits. They arrived just as Dr. Ada walked Patsy out into the waiting area.

"See you next week, Patsy."

"Thank you, Dr. Ada."

Danielle couldn't resist. She looked directly at Dr. Ada. "How did it go?"

Dr. Ada just smiled then turned to Patsy with a twinkle in her eyes. "Patsy, how do you think the session went?"

"Okay, I guess."

At this point, her saying I guess seemed a lot better than her saying nothing at all.

Patsy kept her appointments the first and second month. After that, she didn't bother. Her excuse—she forgot. Dr. Ada's plea fell on resistant ears. Nothing any of them said made any difference. Then she quit her job and dug a hold so deep, her seclusion scared them. That lethal combination left Lydia with no choice. When she told her aunt, mad barely described Regina's reaction. Her words felt like a raging firestorm. "Lydia, how dare you treat me as if I'm no longer relevant? What on earth made you think you could handle this situation alone? When I feel confident you can stand alone, I will gladly step aside. Until then, I'm sure, family decisions will not be entirely up to you. Not yet, anyway. Lydia, don't act like you know everything. You don't. I'm your mentor. I'm just getting started."

Her sharp reprimand bruised Lydia's ego.

"I'm so sorry, Aunt Regina." Lydia's decision hurled her like a human cannon into a pivotal power play. For now, her limited power required her aunt's blessing. Perhaps, some family business actually escaped her aunt, but Lydia doubted it. Somehow, Regina knew their premature thoughts and deeds. Although she felt the bruising,

Lydia hung up, relieved she'd escaped with most of her dignity still intact.

As soon as the ringing started, Patsy sighed loudly. She knew. Mostly, she dreaded hearing the caller's voice. "Patsy, I'm on my way."

Why won't they stop pestering me? Pasty thought. When she opened the door, the warmth of the western sun moved gently across her face.

"Hello, honey." Her aunt grabbed and held her close. Patsy smelled as fresh and clean as a newborn baby. "Planning to get dressed anytime soon?"

Pasty ignored her question as if rhetorical.

The entire house looked like Patsy had done some early spring cleaning. No evidence remained of any earlier turmoil. "Did you eat already?"

"I'm not hungry," Patsy snapped. Quickly, she realized she'd made a big mistake.

Her aunt's voice took on an authoritative tone. "This must stop, young lady. How dare you worry us like this?" Then as quickly as the anger came, her voice softened, the anger disappeared. "We love you, Patsy. Please let us help you get through this."

"I can't help how I feel," Patsy cried out through blinding tears.

"Then go back to Dr. Ada or come home with me." Regina's pleading fell on hollow ground. She walked away knowing she'd done all she could for her child.

CHAPTER 8

Two short months later, Lydia's world eroded like the earth crumbling into the sea. "Dr. G., it's your sister. She sounds very upset."

Lydia rushed to the phone. "Hello."

"Lydia, Patsy's dead," Danielle screamed.

Lydia's loud gut-wrenching scream sounded like a wounded animal's plea for help. It reverberated in her ears long after the phone slipped from her hand and dangled beside her like a wet noodle.

"Dead?" Lydia grabbed the receiver again. Maybe, she misunderstood. Even as her mind teased her with doubt, she knew. Lately, this same nightmare forced her from a deep sleep soaked in perspiration with her gown clinging to her body. "Please, God, not my baby sister."

She felt her body sinking downward into the earth swallowed up like quicksand. From somewhere deep inside a voice whispered a faint reminder. *You're not on foreign soil, Lydia. You know how to handle this.* Immediately, she straightened her back.

Quickly, she seized control of her emotions. "Danielle, I'll get there as soon as I can. How's Aunt Regina?"

"Not well. Please hurry home."

The warmth in her pleading melted Lydia's heart. "Patsy's dead," Lydia murmured and shook her head in disbelief.

"Oh, Dr. G., I'm so sorry," the receptionist said.

When Rebecca heard the commotion, she ran out of the back office. That awful despair in Lydia's eyes told her something had gone terribly awry. "Dr. G., what's wrong?"

Lydia raised her hand and covered her mouth. The pain mounting in her chest kept building up pressure until it felt like her heart would literally explode scattering tiny shards in all directions. Afraid weeping would publicly compromise her strength, she lifted her head high as her world unraveled. Even after the receptionist repeated those ugly distasteful words, she denied the truth.

"I'm so sorry," Rebecca said in a weepy voice as she pulled her close. "I'll cancel your appointments."

Where had her voice gone? The pain tore through Lydia's heart and then exploded in her head. She imagined her head lifting off her shoulders orbiting like a planet around the sun. "I've got to go. My keys, where're my keys?"

Miraculously, she walked to her desk under her own strength. She grabbed her handbag. Her hands shook violently. Somehow, she found her keys.

Rebecca grabbed them. "I'll drive. You're in no condition to go anywhere."

"No, I'm okay."

"No, you're not. Give me the keys, Lydia." Finally, Rebecca tossed formality aside. Then with assertiveness, she publicly addressed her friend, her benefactor, without all the fanfare of a title.

"Do whatever you want," Lydia snapped and then tossed her the keys.

Again, Rebecca assumed her role. She called Jake's

office. He'd already left. Nervously, she dialed his cell.

"Hello."

"Jake, it's Rebecca, Lydia just got some horrible news. Patsy's dead. I can't let her drive in this condition. I'll bring her home."

"No, I'm on my way."

Lydia's legs betrayed her with willful disobedience and forced her into the seat next to Rebecca.

"Bring me a wet towel," Rebecca barked.

The receptionist made a mad dash somewhere then returned with a damp towel. Rebecca bathed Lydia's forehead as gently as if caring for a sick child. At a half past eight, a few doctors arrived so they could prep before the morning rush. They inquired, offered their condolences, and then continued on their way. Moments later, the back door swung open. Jake rushed inside. Noticeably angry, Lydia ran into his outstretched arms. He held her close.

"I'll call with travel arrangements," Rebecca said. Jake grabbed Lydia's hand then led her out the same door.

When the purring engine stopped, Lydia jumped out of the car. She ran inside. Jake followed. He found her slumped over the toilet, coughing and heaving. Her body shook. No tears flowed. She splashed water on her face then rinsed the foul taste from her mouth.

"Why won't these nightmares stop, Jake? God, where are you?" she shouted.

Jake held her tightly. "I'll call my office. We can go to Sweetwater together."

"No! No! I'll need you later." Her sharp reply startled him.

Patsy's death knocked the wind out of her, but Lydia recovered very quickly. Her seemingly weak moment disappeared. In its place, an incredible resiliency rose up.

Then she walked into their bedroom. Haphazardly, she tossed clothes into her luggage. What a jumbled mess. She didn't care. Off in the distance, a ringing sound momentarily distracted her.

"Thanks, Rebecca," she heard him say.

He stood motionless and watched her from the bedroom door.

"How could this happen?"

He pretended that he didn't hear her question. Instead, he grabbed her cold, shaky hands and led her to the kitchen. "Your flight leaves in two hours. I'll drive."

She didn't protest. Thirty minutes later, the traffic welcomed her with considerable ease as she once again traveled that familiar route.

"Don't worry about me, Jake."

"Are you sure you're okay?"

"I'm sure. Every day brings a challenge to this family. It's just that some problems are larger than others."

"Then I guess I'll see you in a few days. Call me as soon as you arrive."

She ignored the disappointment in his voice, kissed him good-bye, and walked through the automatic doors.

Today, even the crowds seemed invisible. Keisha boarded her southbound flight just as Lydia took a seat on her own flight next to a stocky young woman with a small child. They exchanged a few polite words before she turned her face toward the window, hiding the sadness that she knew filled her eyes. On more than one unhappy occasion, the people she loved kept leaving her.

She struggled. Staying afloat took every ounce of her strength. Their personal problems kept pulling her under. "Why Patsy?" she murmured.

Her alarming whimper frightened the little girl seated next to her. The mother tilted her head and whispered into her child's ear. Lydia wondered what nuggets of wisdom she poured out into her daughter's mind. Deeply affected, the child rested her head peacefully on her mother's lap for the duration of the flight.

Just once more Lydia longed for the wisdom of two very special people. Their insightfulness always inspired and strengthened her. Most likely her discerning mother would've said voyagers destined for another time and place never stayed anywhere for very long. Her deeply philanthropic friend Jackson often said that it was the unforeseeable pain that caused the most damage. Oh, how she missed them. As the plane suddenly began its descent, the unhappy face of Patsy roused her from a zombie-like semi-consciousness.

Danielle pulled up to the curb and waited. Lydia suspected those fashionably dark sunglasses hid swollen blood-shot eyes.

"I'm so glad you're here." Danielle held her so tightly that Lydia felt the tension leave her sister's body. She unconsciously wrenched away.

The image of her aunt walking through the house humming and singing one of her favorite old Negro spirituals brought back poignant memories of Sunday morning praise and worship at Mt. Olivett, their home church. Regina's refusal to eat or sleep began with the death of her husband. No one sang, "Oh Lord, I Want You to Help Me," with more conviction. Over and over her beautiful soprano voice whispered sweetly unto God in a chant that grew louder and more passionate as she carefully plowed through every line of the chorus. "Oh Lord, I want you to help me. Oh—Oh—Lord, I want you to help me. Help me on my journey, help me on my way. Oh, Lord, I want you to help."

Those memories kept Lydia strong when she felt crushed under the weight of their expectations.

Her harnessed emotions remained in check until her

aunt's sad eyes greeted them. Makeup furrowed down her face. Lydia felt her aunt's strength seep from her pores as she rocked her back and forth. Regina's weeping stopped briefly only to ask one of her children why? Lydia wished she had an answer.

The steps of her exhausted suitor quickened when he saw the agony on her face. "Barton, you came."

He bent down and gently kissed her cheek. Their tender affection sparked a faded memory. Years earlier, as a stranger, he had laid devastating news at her feet. Now as her companion, they would face this life-altering moment together. The pain in her eyes mirrored nothing Lydia had ever seen before.

Lydia delegated, her sisters obeyed. Several hours later, Keisha arrived, looking frazzled from the inside out. Food and condolences poured in from sympathetic friends and neighbors. The same scene kept repeating itself—death, then food, in that order. Frank and then Jake called with flight updates. The phone rang constantly. More than once, Lydia considered tossing it into the trash. Every call demanded they relive the events that led up to that hour. She grew tired of helping outsiders understand what she had trouble grasping. Her body functioned on auto-pilot. Everywhere she turned felt cold and lonely. Her battle-fatigued family needed rest. Mark and Joe left first. The sergeant hoped Lydia would let him stay, but once she made up her mind, she stayed her course.

"Call if you need me."

"I will, Sergeant."

Her sisters wouldn't leave. They felt ashamed. The guilt sat on their sagging shoulders. It's weight pulled downward. Lydia glimpsed their heartache marching toward them in her nightmares. Why couldn't any of them stop her suffering? Before Patsy shut her out, they spent hours talking. Lydia thought they shared everything. Apparently, they had not.

The effects of too many prescription drugs and booze swooped down like a hungry scavenger to devour the spoils. Where had Patsy gotten the crazy idea they needed her help? Helpless! How absurd! Regardless, she obsessed over their safety.

Lydia hadn't given Patsy's last call very much thought. Without any warning, the conversation started playing over and over again in her head like a memorable love song. She recalled Patsy chuckling mischievously as if privy to a powerful secret. "Hey, girl. Sorry it's so early. I wanted to catch you before you left home."

"Something wrong, Patsy?" Lydia remembered saying because Patsy's voice sounded strange, but certainly not inebriated.

"Everything's fine. I've made some plans. I'm going away. Please check in on Aunt Regina and the girls in my absence."

Patsy hit a raw nerve. Lydia lashed out. "Patsy, good grief, you're not going away forever. You never could stay in one place for very long. I think I can manage a week or two while you're vacationing somewhere in the sun."

Patsy laughed. "I'm quite sure you can, my darling big sister. My apologies, I didn't mean to offend you."

"Oh, Patsy honey, forgive me, I'm just acting like a brat. You know what happens when I'm sleep deprived."

Patsy chuckled. "I know. You get a little rude."

"Of course, I'll check on them."

"Thanks, Lydia. I love you, big sister."

"I love you, too. Where're you going?"

"What?" Patsy sounded distracted.

"Where're you going?"

"Oh, away. I've got to get going, Lydia, I'll miss you."

"*Huh,* how odd." Right away, that unsettling feeling came back.

Now, Lydia walked into her old bedroom, tossed her limp body across the bed, and wept privately. "Suicide, God, please no."

Guilt kept taunting her. The brief escape helped, but when she returned to the room, the stifling smells and sounds brought everything back all over again.

On that particularly gray day, Regina stood on the steps of the church and stared up at the threatening clouds overhead. Her basic black pant suit matched her somber mood as she absent-mindedly twirled her three-strand pearl necklace around her fingers. Briefly, a ray of sunshine broke through the clouds. She smiled. Again, she clutched the pearls tightly to her chest. The sergeant gripped her hand. Together, they walked inside. The church overflowed with friends and family. Throughout the day, many of them gathered at the house. Regina stood poised as she greeted each guest. Another journey had begun. Unfortunately, the road back for most of them would take even more effort.

The sergeant stayed close, fearing she would fall apart if he left her alone for one minute. Wow! He hadn't caught up yet, Lydia thought as she watched her. Regina had an innate resilience. Most of them had no idea what culpable grief felt like until now. Death wasn't a stranger, but today something felt different. All of them stared at their guilt and realized it glared accusingly back at them.

"Lydia, I'm so sorry about Patsy, if you—"

Lydia interrupted her. "Thanks, Jessie. It's just a part of the cycle." Her much-too-business-like tone caused Jessie to shudder. "Oh, before I forget, I'd like you to meet my friend Dr. Tommy Calvin." Then she grabbed

Jessie's hand and pulled her along. "Tommy," Lydia called out. A tall very slender man turned to greet them.

"Hey, Lydia." His lips greeted her, but his rich coco eyes spoke directly to Jessie.

"Jessie, meet Dr. Tommy Calvin."

"Well, Well, I'm finally in the company of the famous Dr. Jessie Cooper."

"Don't you mean infamous?" Then Jessie laughed sarcastically."

He laughed softly. "That too, I guess."

Jessie's body language betrayed her. Lydia felt invisible caught in the middle of their game of "catch-me-if-you-can." She gladly seized the opportunity to disappear. An hour later, they found her.

"Lydia, I've got to get back. Take care," Tommy said, and then he leaned over kissed her cheek. "Where's my mother?"

"Over there."

"Excuse me." He then headed off in her direction.

Excited, Jessie grabbed her arm. "Tommy asked if I would share a cab with him to the airport."

Lydia smiled demurely. Again, things not even planned fell unexpectedly into place. She kissed Jessie good-bye. With the social grace of royalty, she walked off to thank yet another guest for coming. All afternoon people crowded around them offering hugs and condolences.

While Tommy visited with his mother, Jessie saw her chance. "Mrs. Mayers," Jessie called out as she walked over to her.

"Hello, Jessie, I'm glad you came."

"Mrs. Mayers, I'm extremely sorry for your loss. I heard some of the most wonderful things about Patsy. I hope you'll never forget that hidden inside of the heart is a secret door. Look closely. You'll find her waiting. We store the best of ourselves and of those we love there. It's not hard to gain access. We hold the key. If you believe, speak her name, the door will open."

"That's so beautiful, thank you."

Then Jessie stepped aside. The line kept getting longer and longer.

From across the room, Jessie watched Tommy kiss his mother good-bye and then whisper into her ear. No doubt he told her that he loved her. Minutes later, Jessie found him standing next to the open door of a waiting taxi. Her domestic checkpoint came first. "I enjoyed the conversation, Tommy. After all this time, at least, I can finally pin a face on my emails and phone calls. Perhaps, we'll meet again."

"Count on it."

He waved good-bye. He'd had the good fortune of meeting and sharing a cab with a strikingly beautiful woman. The possibility of missing his international flight or arriving late for his conference never crossed his mind. They talked about work the entire ride. It made him wonder if they had anything else in common. And, yes, her rather colorful reputation most definitely preceded her. Regardless, he couldn't stop thinking about her.

Early the next morning, Lydia and her sisters met at Patsy's house. Her beautiful, small two-bedroom house sat in the cul-de-sac of a quaint well-established community. Unimaginable pain flowed from their aching hearts. Tears ran down each of their faces. Standing there in her space magnified their suffering, but they couldn't leave this daunting task for their aunt. Slowly, they walked through each room searching for clues to the end of her troubled existence. They found nothing. Patsy left her affairs and her home in perfect order. They boxed up memories, shut the door behind them, and went home to their families. Her death quenched the fire in all of them.

For a moment, the atmosphere around them felt demonic. No doubt Lydia's belief in God's power to change circumstances kept her from wallowing in her pain.

A burning question kept gnawing at Lydia. What had Patsy said in her dying declaration? she wondered. Even if it meant dredging up heartache, she had to know. Alone, at last, she asked, "Aunt Regina, did Patsy commit suicide?" Her aunt's lips trembled. For the sake of one of her children, she faced her pain all over again.

Regina's voice trembled. "Patsy could no longer hide the mind-altering effect of her drug abuse. She chose her own end. I heard the resolve in her voice."

"Hello, Aunt Regina," Patsy had said in her last phone call.

"Hey, Patsy, sweetheart, how are you?"

"I'm good. Mama, Daddy, and Uncle Roy can't wait to see me. I'm so tired, Aunt Regina."

"Oh, no. Don't go, honey. We still need you. Please hold on a little while longer."

"It's okay, Aunt Regina," Patsy whispered.

"Then she thanked me for the gift of a mother's love. Tears of gratitude rolled down my face as one of my children spoke words so powerful, they melted my heart. I feared the worse and dialed Nine-One-One."

Although her head had trouble accepting what one of her children had done, her heart cried out with understanding. The EMS team pronounced Patsy dead upon arrival. On that awful day, the giver of life pried open her hands and plucked from them the treasure she had held so close to her heart. She relived for Lydia, a painful truth that once again split open two wounded hearts.

Had everybody buried their heads in the sand? Lydia wondered. Surely, some of them had figured out that the puppeteer and her apprentice orchestrated their lives. If not, in time, they would. When Patsy waded out into some pretty deep waters, Lydia and Regina were remiss in their obligation. Why didn't they prevent her from drowning? By the time they tossed her a life preserver, she had already gone under too many times.

Regina tried to shift the focus. "Would you like some tea, Lydia?"

"Sure, Aunt Regina."

Their family business demanded both toughness and shrewdness. Had they made the right decision? Every day knocked with urgency. Hopefully, Regina had done her job well because soon a reversal of roles would take place. The top only had enough room for one leader, one matriarch. But she couldn't step aside. Not yet, until she knew without any reservations that Lydia could handle the load.

"Lydia, do you remember my comment about the past?"

"Yes. I believe you said, let's talk after you've stepped back into the past."

Lydia never forgot the words that aroused her curiosity. In Regina's declining years, her role demanded she unlock the past for the new commander-in-chief even if it meant resurrecting some terrible secrets. As mentor, her responsibility required she acquaint Lydia with all the players whether beneficial or expendable. Lydia had a very long and curvy road ahead.

Regina spoke slowly, pronouncing her words carefully like a kid in a spelling bee. "Lydia, I loved your Uncle Roy with all my heart, but love's a tricky business. Rarely do we intentionally plan on hurting the people we love. Sometimes, stuff happens. It just ends up that way. Some betrayals require that we work harder at forgiving. Sometimes, we never set the record straight. Every day, I've wondered what if, but I've always cared more about the power. And because of that, I willfully destroyed the man I promised to love forever. Just like love, hate's a powerful emotion."

Lydia's body stiffened, her heart raced. She couldn't shake the words, *willfully destroyed*. "What had she meant?"

Before Lydia got the chance to ask, Regina changed the subject. "Did I ever tell you how Roy and I met?"

Lydia nodded. Oddly, their inspiring love story began and ended in a chapel. Its dusty ginger colored stucco exterior and discolored trim stood in stark contrast among clusters of flowering trees, waxed leaf hedges and lush green lawns surrounding it. The weathered outer shell with its beautiful stained-glass windows offered the same welcoming warmth and charm as her small country church. One afternoon, Regina sat alone in the chapel in deep concentration until someone touched her shoulder. She jumped.

"I'm sorry. I hope I didn't frighten you. Do you mind?" He didn't wait for an answer. Instead, he slid into the pew next to her. "I'm Roy Mayers."

"I'm Regina," she said, smiling shyly.

Roy had a raw yet, sweet profile unlike the freshness of her immature classmates. Their sharing felt like they once co-existed in another life time. His fascinating stories of life outside her small sheltered community filled her with wonder. The thirst for life she saw in his eyes awakened her own untapped desires. They fell in love. After college, they joined the staff of her local high school.

Six months later, they got married. She always had children on her radar. Unfortunately, destiny had other plans. A cruel diagnosis fractured her self-esteem. It almost destroyed their marriage. Piece by piece, she surrendered, first her heart, then her soul. Not long after, she sank into a deep depression. Then one day, she saw a completely restored future through the eyes of her students. Almost immediately, she adopted them into her heart.

Then a few years later, a tragic accident shook her world again. In the end, it gifted her with the most incredible blessing.

"I'm forever grateful to my sister Rachael for my girls."

CHAPTER 9

Lydia told Jessie that redemption's road required someone to take a first step. Jessie had only dreamed of returning home. After visiting Sweetwater, Jessie put her running shoes away. No more. Tiny beads of water rose to the surface of her wet, chilled skin. She wiped her nose with the back of her hand and dried off quickly. The freshly lingering memory of her first regimented trip to the place she once called home came at her fast.

It seemed, as if on a whim, her father uprooted his family and moved them to the Vineyard. The temperatures hovered in the low eighties with very little humidity as the plane bounced and skipped down the runway of Boston Logan International Airport. She squinted then shut her eyes tightly to ward off the blinding sun.

These novice travelers huffed and puffed as they raced through the airport, trying to keep up with his carefully organized schedule. With his ever present fear of forfeiting his place in line, her daddy pushed beyond the speed limit to reach his destination on time. He knew limited street lighting and a shortage of bike paths on the Vineyard made navigating the narrow tree-lined roads treacherous at night alongside bicyclers. Jessie pressed her face snugly against the window while she day-dreamed. Two hours later, he pulled into what resembled a huge stadium parking lot and got into a very long line. Rows and rows of cars and trucks snuggled next to each other in the massive hull of the ferry. The metal monster, docked at the edge of the ocean, looked like a replica of a creature ripped from the pages of a science fiction movie. He inched along slowly.

The engine stopped. Her excitement swelled as she climbed the stairs to the top deck. Jessie stood mesmer-ized, gazing out across the indigo waters of the Atlantic akin only to the Pacific in massiveness. Miles and miles of rippling water stretched out before her in all directions literally taking her breath away. The ferry rocked, sooth-ing her fear of the unknown that waited on the other side. Visible, yet far off, she caught a glimpse of a lighthouse. Honorably, these gatekeepers of the sea sat alone, watch-ing and guiding ships safely through the darkness with a single light illuminating their path.

Individually strung rows of steel coils separated her from the ocean's floor. She perched on her tip toes feel-ing the magnetic pull from an endless body of blue liquid. The waves thrashed and licked the sides of the ferry. Jes-sie closed her eyes, enjoying the moment she fell in love with the ocean and the tug she felt as it loved her back.

Shortly before the sun bowed down for the evening, her father drove into the township of Oak Bluffs. Weath-ered shingles covered the top of their small cottage-style house obscured from view among hedges of beautiful sweetly fragrant hydrangeas. The purring sound of the engine ceased. Jessie jumped out with wide eyed excite-ment.

"It's beautiful," Ginny screamed.

Loud cheers rang out. He unlocked the front door.

Their parents walked inside together. No one bothered with the drudgery of hauling luggage out of the car. Jessie and Ginny ran around to the back and down to a private dock leading to the water's edge. They watched the rays from the sun shoot from the sky and gingerly caress the water. It sparkled like bubbles glistening in a glass of champagne. The house sat all alone atop a hill overlooking a small meandering stream that moved slowly through a man-made cove. Rugged cliffs jotted off its sides. In less than twenty-four hours, Jessie had fallen in love again.

Now, many years later, a more mature woman, Jessie returned to Boston, draped in the comfort of Lydia's wisdom. "Jessie," Lydia had said, "man's sacrifice for God will never exceed His. Everything happens on His divine time table. Wait on him."

Jessie's rented cottage sat on a secluded section of beach in the township of Aquinnah—known as the end of the land. A priceless memory flashed across her mind of one sweltering summer day when she and Ginny toured the lighthouse at Gay Head. That beautiful time in her life seemed so long ago.

After two sleepless nights, she called her sister. Boxes stacked knee high all around the room heightened her unsettling feeling. Hurriedly, she hid them in closets and underneath the bed. Then she sat anxiously waiting with all the clutter out of sight. Why had the thought of her sister's visit paralyzed her? The minutes dragged on. An hour later, she stood in the open doorway unconsciously biting her lower lip. "Hello, Ginny."

"Hello, Jessie, I've missed you."

Jessie's stiff posture relaxed at the sight of tears streaming down her sister's face.

"Come on in." Jessie gave her a hug then pulled her inside. She nervously ran her fingers through her tightly woven hair. Her pinky ring got trapped in the curls. Then yanking, she broke free.

Ginny smiled as she inspected Jessie from head to toe. *Yep. It's the same old Jessie, all right. Poor darling! Still hasn't tamed her unruly mane*, she thought. "Jessie, you're still one of the most gorgeous creatures I know."

"Liar. You used to tease and call me a tomboy."

Ginny laughed. "Sure, but I never said you weren't beautiful."

"Oh, well! That's old news. Ginny, I'm really glad to see you."

"Me too, I've missed my little sister."

Reliving all those silly childhood pranks filled their afternoon with laughter. They especially remembered the time Jessie put a frog in her teacher's desk drawer. Boy, Mrs. Cartwright got so angry her lips quivered. Her nostrils flared.

"Thank you for calling me, Mrs. Cartwright," Jessie's father said. Before she started babbling, he quickly interrupted. His abruptness crushed her hysterical tirade. Eying her cautiously, he took a seat. The way she twisted and then pinned her hair high upon her head reminded him of his mean-spirited spinster teacher from decades ago. Except for the cat-eye glasses with thick lens framing her broad face, they looked alike. When he noticed the genuine fear in her eyes, he turned to his daughter with a no nonsense expression on his face. "Young lady, you've got some explaining to do."

Mrs. Cartwright smirked then turned and left them alone. She hoped Jessie would get a much deserved scolding or maybe even a spanking later at home.

Jessie's father leaned down close to her. "Jessie, that wasn't very nice. When life gets in the way, most grownups cash in their sense of humor. Sadly, that includes me. Next time, young lady, prank your classmates, not your teacher." Then he smacked her lightly on her bottom.

That gesture appeased Mrs. Cartwright, who stood listening outside the door. He silently admired Jessie's bold spirit. In this man's world, he knew one day it would serve her well.

Ginny laughed. "I loved my role of big sister. You, Jessica Jessie James, came here demanding your rightful place. I bet that hasn't changed."

Behind her soft, familiar laughter, Ginny sensed her sister's trepidation. The topic of their parents could wait. They had lots of catching up to do.

Whenever Jessie thought of home, mostly unpleasant memories surfaced. Sifting through the bad ones for a glimpse of the good took too much effort, so she stopped trying. She found physical relationships with no strings attached less painful. Not a single day went by that she didn't think about her sister. It was Jessie's subscription to their local newspaper that kept her in touch with her township. Despite the fact that a few fond memories kept drawing her back, she left home hating everything about her life. Every time the paper arrived, she quickly scanned it for an engagement or wedding announcement. No such luck. Ginny remained unmarried.

A short while later, Jessie read an exciting announcement. The caption: Local businessman, Jasper James purchased Jamison Veterinarian Clinic. A month before her graduation, Virginia "Ginny" James received her DVM and a thriving business all on the same day. The first time they brought their dog Penny in for her checkup, Dr. Jamison seemed old. Now on the upswing of seventy and struggling with crippling rheumatoid arthritis, his retirement seemed inevitable. Unfortunately, the right guy remained a figment of Ginny's imagination. The children of Jasper and Vivian James had too many battle scars. They resembled crushed or broken toys cast into a separate storage bin marked damaged goods. Ginny had no husband or significant other and, like Jessie, no children. The whole notion sounded like a family curse.

"Did you ever get another Weimaraner?" Jessie asked.

Ginny shook her head. "No. I could never replace my sweet girl. Penny's dying hurt too much. The day she died, I vowed I would never get that attached ever again."

A year into her practice, someone found a seriously injured brown and white beagle alongside the road. They brought him to the clinic. Ginny nursed him back to health with a less than enthusiastic search for the owner. Months later, Keeper, her new companion came home with her. The journey began all over again.

Too many years had gone by. Jessie and Ginny talked continuously for hours. "My goodness, look at the time. I'm late. Jessie, let's do lunch this weekend." Naturally, she assumed Jessie planned on staying in town for a while.

"I'd love to."

Jessie waved goodbye. She watched as Ginny pulled out of the driveway heading south toward the freeway. They got through an entire afternoon filled with laughter and happy tears. Overwhelming pangs of anxiety sprang up whenever Jessie thought about her parents. Despite the high cost of her therapy, she held tight to some of her pain.

The afternoon drifted into evening as she mundanely opened and discarded boxes. Her body ached all over. The pain forced her to set aside the rest of the unpacking for later. Total exhaustion swept over every inch of her body before very quietly subsiding. She'd heard the cliché "let sleeping dogs lie." Its meaning, once lost in a fog, seemed much clearer. Should she categorize her life as a bunch of blunders best left covered up? How could she explore a future with such an uncertain past? As always, she had more questions than answers. Sleep came quickly. Early the next morning, she swam out into the numbing cold waters of the Atlantic Ocean.

In what seemed like another galaxy, Jessie and Cooper once dreamed big dreams stretched out under the shimmering lights of a million stars. Regrettably, the wonderful life they imagined together had a short shelf life. As she lay wrapped only in the gentle breeze of the morning, she felt the rush of a painful memory like a stampede of wild horses charging toward her.

"Cooper, Cooper," she called out and then jumped straight up. Her damp body trembled. "Not now," she whispered.

His buddies dubbed him Coop. Everyone else called him Cooper, except his mother who preferred Reese, her maiden name. That first summer fields of sunflowers brazenly reached for the sun as they welcomed the arrival of a new romance. Almost immediately, life changed for Jessie James and Reese Cooper. Nearing the end of his freshman year, he missed days that stretched into weeks, then months. He missed so much time his parents hired a tutor. Then half way his sophomore year, his teacher made a starling announcement. "Cooper's very ill. He won't finish out the year."

Jessie had blamed the dark circles beneath his eyes on a lack of sleep until Mrs. Cooper stopped over a few days later and confided in her mother. "Cooper has leukemia."

Bravely, Mrs. Cooper poured out her pain coupled with a hopeful outlook for her son.

"He hasn't told Jessie. He doesn't want to burden her."

"It's okay. Let me tell her."

"Thank you, Vivian."

They hugged again, and then Mrs. Cooper walked out. Gravely, Vivian took the stairs one step at a time. When she reached her daughter's room, she took a deep breath then walked in and sat down. "We need to talk."

Jessie hated hearing those four little words. Lately, they fought about everything. Her mother called it her teenage rite of passage. Unfortunately, Jessie wasn't prepared for what she said next.

"Honey, Cooper's in the hospital. He has leukemia, a form of cancer."

Not Cooper. The thought of him dying scared her. Jessie ran down the stairs. She kept on running. At the edge of the steps, she stopped and gripped the tall white column supporting the veranda so tightly her arms ached. The door slammed temporarily interrupting the confusion in her head.

Her mother walked over and stood beside her. "I'm so sorry, Jessie."

This time they cried together.

"Why didn't he tell me?"

"I suppose he thought he could protect you."

"From what?"

"Sadness."

"Will he get better?"

"We hope so."

"I've got to see him."

"That's a good idea, sweetheart."

Her mother kissed her forehead and then went back inside. Jessie hung her head in the locks of her shoulders. She wept softly, fearing that if Cooper stopped breathing, she would stop, too.

"He will get better," she yelled into the encompassing air, and that's what she spoke into her spirit every single day.

On her first visit, she shuttered at the sight of his skeleton. His pasty skin blended into the colorless sheet. All things considered, his magnetic personality still shone through.

"Hey, Jessie." Straining, she leaned in.

"You look well Cooper," she lied.

"Not really, but thanks anyway. I appreciate the vote of confidence."

"How do you feel?"

"Not so bad."

"Liar." She watched him smile unconvincingly back at her.

He spent most of his junior year in and out of the hospital. A few weeks before their senior year started, Cooper received an amazing blessing. His cancer had gone into remission. Their love grew as prolific as flowers inundated with springs of water. When she told her parents they wanted to get married, her daddy literally hit the low hanging ceiling in their outdated kitchen.

"Young lady, I won't hear of such nonsense," he shouted.

"You're not serious! You're just kids." Perhaps to compensate for her daddy's loud outburst, her mother's muttered tone never rose above a soft whisper.

Her father loved Cooper. Naturally, he loved his daughter more. He worried her love for Cooper clouded her judgment. Knowing the struggle that lay ahead, her parents questioned her judgment. The news spread quickly. Surprisingly, like open season on wild game, people took pot shots at the personal lives of her parents. A few coveted secrets found their way out of the closet. Sadly, even a decade-old friendship like that of her parents and the Coopers' couldn't withstand those underhanded attacks. Rather quickly, the rumors and innuendos dismembered a solid friendship.

Privately, Jessie and Cooper moved ahead with their plans. Ginny voiced the same sentiment as her parents, but agreed she would keep their secret. They eloped two days after graduation. Disappointed parents cried. Immediately, the happy couple embarked upon an uphill battle many young couples would probably never face. They refused their parent's financial assistance, but freely accepted their moral support. The tremendous back-breaking stress of a part-time job along with his undergraduate studies weakened his body. The enemy returned with a vengeance. Four weeks before graduation, he died. While standing at his gravesite, Jessie wept bitterly. His death left her wretched with guilt. Early detection might've made a difference. They had spent more time in the emergency room than the classroom. A bleak hospital room felt more like home than their minimalistic one-bedroom apartment. The health of the man she loved declined rapidly. In a special ceremony, his parents joined her as the university presented her with his posthumous degree. She never spoke to his parents again.

When Jessie finally looked back, she regretted what she saw. They shared a fantasy world with lofty dreams of a non-existent future. Instead of tiptoeing in, their reality charged through the door trampling their hopes and dreams. Almost from the moment they met, Cooper knew that he would leave her. When he left, the loneliness terrified her. Had Ginny not moved in, she might've found going on entirely too difficult.

As if Cooper's dying wasn't disastrous enough, Jessie's world flipped upside down again two months later. It rained hard off and on all day falling in white rippling sheets from a sky filled with an abundance of saturated clouds. After an afternoon movie, Jessie and her sister decided they would surprise their mother. Their daddy's car sat in the driveway. With each step, the soggy earth beneath their feet made a swooshing noise. As they approached, they heard loud, angry voices coming from the house.

Not again, Jessie thought.

They rushed inside. Their mother stood in the middle of the room, fighting back tears that mimicked the falling rain. Still, they couldn't deny her beauty. No one could. She had gorgeous long, lean legs and skin so artificially bronzed everything about her screamed Hollywood sex appeal. Her manufactured tan looked like a coat of armor. No matter what, her soft curly black color-treated hair stayed anchored in its place. The veins in their daddy's neck pulsated. His clenched jaw made his acne sprinkled face appear distorted. Their escalating brawl had finally reached a climax. Many times Jessie wished for a physical confrontation in hopes the sight of real blood would draw a truce. Instead, their words left an indelible mark that produced uglier, longer lasting images. Every verbal attack drew imagined fresh blood with a couple of innocent casualties strewed about in its wake.

Their marriage had problems long before another man showed up. Her daddy refused counseling. He thought it made him appear weak. Despite what he thought, an outward change occurred. Time, along with their constant bickering, aged him less gracefully. Apparently, too late for them to retreat, Jessie and Ginny stood stone-faced, listening, as he spit venomous unthinkable accusations at their mother. Then he flung a handful of papers across the room that landed in a sprawled heap face up in front of Jessie. At the moment, Max Investigation Agency seemed insignificant until his next words sliced her fragile identity into tiny pieces.

"Did you plan to carry this lie to your grave, Vivian? I trusted you all these years. For God's sake, tell the truth for once in your life. DNA doesn't lie," he shouted and beat his chest. "Yes, Ginny's my daughter. Who's Jessie's father?"

Jessie felt the anguish erupting from the depths of his punctured heart as he yelled out her name. Horrified and helpless, Ginny watched the color drain from her sister's face.

"Tell me, Vivian, I have a right to know," he yelled.

The more she cried and pleaded, the angrier he got. "Please, Jasper, let it go. It's over. You love Jessie. I know you do. Why destroy her life now?"

Then she looked over at Jessie. She flinched when she saw hate fill the same eyes that once gazed at her with affection. Ginny wanted to strangle her mother with her bare hands. At the same time, she felt genuinely sorry for her father.

"What about my life? What about the truth?" he shouted again. His temples throbbed.

"Why now?" Vivian asked.

He remained silent, but his bulging eyes gave her cause for alarm.

"Go upstairs, girls." The frozen expression on their faces scared her. "Go now," she shouted.

The sheer panic in her voice shook them free. Ginny grabbed her sister's hand and pulled her upstairs into her room then locked the door behind them.

Rage consumed Jessie. She cried out, "I hate them. I never want to see them again."

Anger clouded his reasoning. Her father no longer cared who knew the truth or who it hurt. The shouting continued until they heard the front door slam shut and tires screeching. He made one stop. The sealed envelope contained no demands. In a day or two, the recipient, like him, would know the same humiliating betrayal.

Vivian knocked sharply. Without waiting for an invitation, she barged into an empty room. Across the hall,

Ginny's locked door stood as a barrier between a mother and her wounded children. "Jessie, please open the door. We must talk."

Jessie dreaded hearing those words. Her repeated pounding drowned out the clicking sound as Ginny unlocked the door and stepped back.

"Go away, Mother. You've done enough damage to last a lifetime," Ginny shouted angrily over her sister's whimpering.

"Ginny, leave us alone, please. You and I will talk later," Vivian said sharply. Then she peered over Ginny's shoulder at her daughter's limp body sprawled across the bed.

Mother! Ginny thought. *Who gave you permission to play God?*

Her betrayal affected not just her husband, but all of them. Regardless, her position in their lives remained unchanged. The affair and who had the rightful claim to fatherhood didn't matter one bit. Ginny loved her sister. That would never change. She looked over at Jessie. With her nod of approval, Ginny called out, "Penny," and then clapped her hands. Her adorable trusted companion rose up slowly. Those yellow eyes stared up at Ginny and obediently followed her command.

Vivian grabbed Jessie. "Honey, I'm so sorry, I'm so sorry."

Jessie struggled against her mother's grip. Vivian had never really thought about the consequences or that the people she loved might get hurt. Anyway, it happened. She had regrets, but they had nothing to do with her daughter. Roy, her very wise romantic partner, believed in the power of repentance. A concept, Vivian didn't fully understand. Her moment of weakness cost the loss of her dignity along with the respect of her family. The flirting that began at a business dinner between two unassuming strangers rearranged their destiny.

Jasper sat waiting with a gin and tonic in his hands.

"I'm sorry I'm late," Vivian said as she rushed in.

He stood and kissed her cheek. "No problem love. Vivian, I'd like you to meet Roy Mayers, my business partner."

Roy stood and extended his hand. "Good evening, Mrs. James, it's nice to finally meet you." He had a throaty voice.

She smiled. "Hello, Roy," This delightfully appetizing man stood tall in his dark mocha skin. They shook hands and then took their seats.

Before that evening, Vivian never knew her husband had a partner. As a matter of fact, he shared very few details about his work other than an occasional complaint about delayed or late shipments. He liked controlling everything and everyone. It made him feel powerful. She shuddered when she thought about her husband's exhausting mood swings. Suddenly, his phone rang. "Excuse me. I'll be right back." A few short minutes later, he returned. "There's a shipment problem back at the office."

Roy rose and pushed his chair back. "I'll come with you."

"No, let's catch up in the morning over breakfast. In the meantime, stay and enjoy the company of my beautiful wife. I've got this under control." Again, Jasper leaned over and kissed her cheek. "See you later love."

Vivian spent a quiet evening in the company of a perfect stranger who found her charming and perhaps a little irresistible. Almost immediately, their friendship blossomed into a passionate love affair. Unfortunately, the strain of lying and sneaking around took a toll on him. But, she suspected something more sinister than a possible divorce had him on edge. Whatever Roy feared kept him guarded. Soon, her gentle giant broke off an affair he felt would ruin many lives.

It was time. Jessie deserved the whole truth. Explaining the beginning of the story seemed easier than dredging up the painful ending. Jessie sat on the edge of the bed with her eyes almost swollen shut. Vivian cringed, watching her daughter in so much pain, but she couldn't turn back now. She once thought these words would never reach the light of day.

"Jessie," she said, "your father came along when I needed a good friend. Roy's death left me heartbroken and scared."

"Roy?" Jessie glared at her. Finally, she had a name.

"Yes, Roy Mayers was your father."

"Roy Mayers," Jessie repeated his name not believing the irony. "This can't be happening. Why didn't you tell me?"

Her unexpected rage startled Vivian. Perhaps, she hoped Jessie would welcome the news of her biological father, no matter when it came. Sadly, she'd misjudged her daughter. How could she possibly expect civility when she'd hidden her affair and the identity of Jessie's father?

Jessie sprang to her feet. Her whole body shook. Angrily, she stood toe to toe with her mother like a soldier in hand to hand combat. An emotionally battered daughter stared into the terrified face of the woman she once loved and trusted.

Vivian couldn't reason with her daughter. So, she stood quietly in a sea of hostility. Jessie pushed pass her then ran into the bathroom and locked the door.

"Please, Jessie, let me in," Vivian pleaded frantically as she pounded on the door.

"Leave me alone," Jessie yelled. Her sobbing grew louder and louder. Then through blinding tears, she hurled words that carried the sting of death. "I hate you! I hate you!"

As soon as they leaped from her lips, she regretted saying those awful words to her mother. Now, too late she couldn't reel them back in. Those three little words shouted in anguish brought her sobbing mother to her knees. A wall of separation sprang up between a mother and her daughter.

Again, her mother cried out. "I'm so sorry, I'm so sorry."

Stubborn pride got in Jessie's way. Heartbroken, her mother walked out of the room. Gently, she closed the door behind her. She leaned her head up against the wall and whimpered softly. When Jessie was born, Vivian briefly experienced a feeling of separation as she stood outside the nursery window. She peered through the glass watching as her beautiful baby girl kicked, stretched, and fought the confinement of her new pink blanket. Suddenly, her nostrils filled with the overpowering smell of a fragrantly expensive perfume. She turned around just as sunlight bounced off of the auburn streaks in a woman's dark brown hair.

Large gold hoops earrings adorned her ears and, as the woman shifted her body, at least a dozen tiny gold bangles jingled softly. They had never met, but intuitively Vivian knew those stolen moments and this adorable creature sucking eagerly on her thumb belonged to this woman's husband.

"She's very beautiful, what an exciting moment for you and your husband."

Vivian heard undeniable sarcasm in the woman's voice. "We're very happy." She squirmed under the scrutiny of the woman who stood uncomfortably close to her.

The woman sighed. Long ago, she realized she could never give her husband the one thing he desired more than anything on earth. She took a deep breath, shrugged her shoulders, and faced her adversary. "Roy will never belong to you, Mrs. James. Perhaps, I've lost the first round, but trust me, you're not equipped for this rather costly battle. You'll never comprehend the cost. I took those vows 'until death do us part' very seriously. I keep my promises. Jessie really is very beautiful." Then she flashed a wickedly sweet smile and walked away.

Although no physical punches passed between them, the woman's cold, revenge-charged words sent a shiver down Vivian's spine. The real sting of her threat came much later. Long before they stood together outside of the nursery, Roy had confessed his affair to his wife, a woman he promised to love exclusively. Admitting his unfaithfulness took enormous courage. Regrettably, pride bought her silence. Then one day the call she'd long expected came.

"Vivian, Vivian, did you see the news?" Sadly, her friend cried out, "Oh, Vivian, I'm so sorry."

"What? What?" Vivian yelled.

"Roy's dead, Vivian. I'm so sorry." Then in a loud shrill voice, her friend restated the facts as she'd heard them. "The assassination of a man now identified as Roy Mayers made the headlines this morning. His slain body lay face up in a deserted parking lot with his wallet, cash, and credit cards undisturbed. The keys remained in the car's ignition. Someone sent a strong message. The kill shot hit the center of his heart."

Numbness and fear swept over Vivian's entire body. The news she received unearthed a deeper dread. She knew Roy expected the arrival of this day. Somehow, she had too.

CHAPTER 10

Coming home undoubtedly proved the best medicine for a wayward soul. Jessie spent her days swimming and relaxing in fantastic weather. Friday morning Ginny called. "How about joining me for dinner this evening at La Belle Vee?"

"I'd love to."

Their family gathering place, La Belle Vee, seemed the perfect setting. For many years, it provided her with the same peace that Jacksons' gave Lydia. Her parent's best friends Henry and Lucy Bellavee owned the establishment.

Ginny quickly picked up on her fear. "They're out of town for the weekend."

Jessie felt relieved. "I'll meet you there."

As she entered the door a few hours later, she received a text. *Run—n—late—c—u—shortly.*

Jessie sensed someone watching her. She turned around.

"Oh my goodness! It's really you. Jessie, you look simply gorgeous. Child, how long has it been?" Mrs. Bellavee asked while holding her in that motherly grip.

"Too long I'm afraid. How are you, Mrs. Bellavee?"

"I'm well, honey." Mrs. Bellavee then turned and beckoned for her husband.

"Jessie," he called out with his arms stretched wide open. "You're still as beautiful as I remember."

"Thank you, Mr. Bellavee." Neither of them said anything about her parents. Just as she announced, "I'm waiting on Ginny," her sister walked in and not a minute too soon. Jessie felt a little awkward knowing her parents' close friends shared their family's secret.

Ginny gave Mr. and Mrs. Bellavee a quick peck on the cheeks and blew her a kiss. "Hello, everyone!"

"Hello, Ginny. It's wonderful to see you," they said.

"I know you're excited that your sister's home. You girls got a lot of catching up. Enjoy your evening," Mrs. Bellavee said. Then they walked away.

"Wow! You clean up nicely."

"Thanks and so do you," Jessie said.

They ordered drinks then settled in. All evening, Jessie noticed her sister make an attempt and then stop short.

Finally, Ginny couldn't stand it any longer. "Jessie, do you plan on seeing them?"

"Of course."

Ginny sighed. "I haven't told them you're here." Then, looking over her shoulder, she said, "I'm sure they'll know real soon."

Jessie laughed. Right away, she picked up the menu, decided, and then closed it. Nothing would satisfy her taste buds more than a gigantic bowl of steamed mussels. The first time she ordered this incredible dish, her lips tingled like the innocence of her first kiss.

Ginny raised her glass. "Welcome home, little sister."

Choosing between the lasagna and Mrs. Bellavee's prized winning meat loaf had Ginny in a quandary.

"Well?" Jessie asked.

"The meat loaf, silly," Ginny said and then took another sip from her glass. "Jessie, please call them. I'm sure they've already canceled any future plans. They've probably booked the next flight home."

Jessie looked nervous. "I will."

"Just tell them what's in your heart. Isn't that why you came back? Don't chicken out now."

Jessie laughed. "Chicken out, that's your mature advice?"

Ginny laughed, too. "It's all I've got right now."

Finally, they called for the check. Mr. and Mrs. Bellavee had paid the tab and already left for a prior engagement. On the back of her business card, Jessie wrote: *tonight felt just like old times. Ginny and I thank you for your generosity, the James girls*. Then they walked out together.

"Jessie, they've had the same numbers for a lifetime. Call them. The load won't get any lighter."

"Great advice this time, big sister. I promise I'll call them." Then she gave Ginny a hug and said goodnight.

Jessie locked her car door. Then she sat there, deeply troubled, before starting the engine. A single porch light lit the pathway leading up to the front door of her rental. The whole place looked totally different than a few short days ago. Soft melodious music streamed from the radio. A bottle of wine sat chilled and waiting.

The next morning, an empty bottle sat conspicuously on the counter. She knew that wasn't the answer. Then she remembered Lydia telling her once that "fear drowns us, we don't drown it."

Her mother clearly expressed remorse that day so long ago, but Jessie didn't know where her father stood. Perhaps, she had misread his feelings. Had he rejected his daughter or his wife's affair?

Jessie lost her nerve after only one attempt. She hung

up. Nervously, she redialed then panicked when her finger accidentally hit the wrong button. The phone tumbled
from her shaky hands. Then she picked up and dialed
again.

A familiar voice answered. "Hello. Jessie, is that
you?"

"Hello, Mother."

"Oh, Jessie, it's so good to hear your voice. How've
you been?"

"Well."

"I've missed you. We couldn't believe it when Lucy
called with the news."

Jessie and Ginny figured as much. Had Jessie heard
her correctly? Had her mother really said she missed her?
Now, that's pretty funny! She never received one call or
letter in all those years. Just as well. She probably spared
her mother more rejection.

"Mother, I came back to see both of you, if Daddy—
uh—Jasper wants to see me."

"Jessie, he loves you. You ran away without giving
your father a chance to apologize. That ugly time in our
lives still haunts us."

"My father," Jessie mocked.

Her mother ignored the sarcasm in Jessie's voice.
"Please come to dinner. Jasper's already here. Okay?"
She sounded excited.

"Okay, Mother."

When Jessie left home, she hit delete and temporarily
erased their big emotional scene. "I can't do this, it's too
hard," she had said out loud. She immediately started
manufacturing excuses. None of them seemed plausible
for the strong woman who came home in search of restoration. Back when she needed someone, Lydia helped her
understand the importance of developing a personal relationship with God. Lydia had said, "When you cry out to

God, you want Him to recognize your voice and then you must trust Him with your request."

Here goes, Jessie thought. "God, I can't do this without your help. I once held my parents in high esteem. Help me find the words that will bring closure then finally peace."

Located in the same township, the drive should've taken only a few minutes from her rental. Instead, it seemed like a thousand miles. She wrung her hands. Beads of perspiration formed on her forehead and surprisingly under her armpits. Several uncomfortable minutes passed as she peered through clusters of trees and discovered beautiful houses hidden from view. After a few close calls, the James girls could calculate within minutes the distance home from just about any point on the island. Forget about divide and conquer. Her parents formed a united front when confronted with unacceptable grades and a breach of curfew.

On each side of the long sidewalk, large hedges of overgrown purple and white hydrangeas in full bloom stood at attention. Jessie stopped, looked down, and laughed. She knew the exact number of bricks in the sidewalk leading from the garage to her front door. One hot lazy summer day, she sat nervously counting each brick while waiting for her daddy's declaration of punishment for missing curfew. Instead, he prolonged her agony with a lecture. The sting of his words lingered painfully longer than any punishment he could've meted out. She took that hauntingly familiar walk up to the front door. Before she reached the last step, the door swung open. It surprised her how easily she fell into her mother's arms. Their cheeks touched, and tears merged running swiftly like streams into a river.

"You look terrific, Jessie." Then Vivian pulled her inside.

"Thanks, Mother, you look great, too."

Except for a few more definitive lines here and there, her amazingly thin mother looked exactly the same. A quick glance around the room found every stick of furniture in the exact spot. Nervously, Jessie's eyes zipped from one corner of the room to the next in search of someone other than the presence or absence of things.

"Sit down, Jessie. Dinner's almost ready. Give your father another minute."

My father, she thought. Jasper James didn't share her DNA. Jessie noticed the twitch over her mother's left eye. During their silly teenage years, she and Ginny made fun of her imperfection. Her mother's heightened nerves had her babbling excessively. The smells flirted with Jessie's senses. They increased her hunger pains. A German chocolate cake sat on the countertop. Next to it, lay a stack of letters tied neatly together with a delicate piece of pink ribbon. Jessie picked up the bundle of stamped letters. She stepped back with her mouth agape. Still reeling from the initial shock, she proudly placed them into her handbag and then wrapped her arms around her mother's waist. Her mother's tears said everything and, for the first time in a very long time, Jessie heard every word.

Slowly, she turned around. The enormousness of his presence filled the room. He looked old, his acne seemed less noticeable. Complete baldness replaced a receding hairline. Unsure of what to do, Jessie extended her hand. Despite their marital troubles, her parents remained married. Happily? Who knew for sure? At the sight of her outstretched hand, he let out a thunderous clamor that caught her off guard. He no longer looked strong or powerful like she remembered. Now, he appeared approachable.

"I've missed you, sweetheart."

"I've missed you too, Daddy." She ran into his arms. While she clung to him crying, she watched the annoying twitch over her mother's eye disappear.

"I acted like a complete fool. Honey, I'm so sorry. I never meant to hurt you."

"Dinner's ready." Vivian's cheerful voice interrupted their joyously tearful reunion.

They dined on great food while getting reacquainted. The James girls always enjoyed their mother's great home-cooking. Their daddy rarely reaped the benefits of her cooking classes. Somehow, he always showed up after they cleaned up her mess. Her trial and errors had their place, too. Many days Jessie wished some mythical power would swoop down and clean up their messy marriage. After dinner, they moved into the family room. Some things still needed saying. He wasn't about to waste this moment.

"Jessie, I'm so ashamed. My foolishness caused lasting repercussions. Before I shoved that report in your mother's face, we knew our marriage needed some serious overhauling. I'm equally to blame for what happened. My anger came from a place of desperation. Fear will make you do crazy things. I couldn't bear the thought of losing your mother."

Jessie figured the difference in their ages affected his judgment. On one of her fishing expeditions, Ginny found their birth certificates. Being twelve years Vivian's senior gave him a legitimate reason for his battered look. Gladly, Jessie pushed the lost years aside, prepared to make new memories as all the pain and anger melted away like unwanted calories.

Her mother re-entered and sat down next to her. "Jessie, please forgive me for not listening to my heart."

"All's forgiven, Mother."

"Please spend the night, sweetheart."

"Not tonight, Mother, perhaps another time." Fear of jeopardizing their new start gave Jessie the courage needed to decline her offer. Besides, she had some plans already in the works. "Goodnight. I love you both."

"We love you, too."

Then Jessie hugged them and walked out of the door. The sight of her daddy's arm draped lovingly around her mother's waist warmed Jessie's heart. Lydia was right. The power of forgiveness could change those who asked and those who received. Her emotionally charged night started with a superb dinner. It ended with an honest discussion.

Except for the sound of the ocean, her beach cottage felt strangely quiet until the phone rang.

"Hello."

"Oh, hello, Ginny."

"The suspense's killing me. I called home. Mother said you'd already left. What happened?"

"Daddy showered me with an expression of his love more powerful than I dreamed possible. Until tonight, I never realized that my greatest gift came that day Mother reopened a painful door so I could discover the blessing behind it." Jessie had personal memories of a man she loved and called her daddy, but only a snapshot from her mother's memory of the man who gave her life.

"I'm so happy, Jessie. I've prayed for this day for so long. Finally, I've got my family back. Goodnight."

"Goodnight, Ginny."

Her parents loved her. That's what Jessie had longed to hear. She sat down, opened her handbag, and hesitantly took out the pile of letters. Immediately, her eyes zoomed in on the dates. Her mother wrote the first letter the day Jessie left home and one every year on her birthday. When she tore open the first one, her mother's sorrowful words sprang from the pages and leaped into her heart.

Jessie, I love you, and I'm sorry. It seems like I've paid a thousand times over for my sin. It has swept over everyone I ever loved like mighty flood waters while indiscriminately destroying everything in its path. What matters now is that in some other place far from here, you've started over. Roy knew he would never be your daddy, but he proudly accepted his role as your father. One day he hoped I would share the truth with you. If so, he wanted me to tell you that he'd never seen a more beautiful little girl. Roy loved you, Jessie, Jasper loves you, and I love you too.

Emotionally wrecked, Jessie's hands shook. Her heart beat like a warrior's drum. Each letter captured the true love of a repentant spirit. When the tears stopped, she placed the letters back in her handbag then crawled into bed. As soon as her head hit the pillow, she fell asleep and slept through the night without libation. No more demons chased her. Her biggest regret—her sister suffered as a casualty of their war. At the break of dawn, Jessie ran a couple of miles down the beach. She hoped the fresh ocean air would clear her head. It worked. After returning to the house, she called and invited her family to dinner.

℩℩℩

Ginny waved to Jessie as she entered the restaurant.

"Mom and Dad late?" Jessie asked.

Ginny shook her head and pointed to a door at the back of the restaurant. The large block lettering on the door read *Private Office* and underneath in a smaller print the names *Henry Bellavee and Lucy Bellavee, Proprietors.*

Jessie grinned. "Some things never change."

Ginny nodded.

"May I get anyone a drink?"

Jessie jumped. She didn't realize the waitress stood so close behind her.

The waitress smiled. "Excuse me."

"Not a problem. For now, just water please."

"Two please," Ginny said.

Their parents and the Bellavees walked up behind them. When Jessie heard her mother's infectious laughter, she turned around.

"Hello, girls," they said.

Jessie and Ginny stood in line like commoners in the presence of nobility. Trace evidence of Mrs. Bellavee's makeup left tiny furrows on her cheeks.

"Enjoy your dinner everyone." Then the Bellavees walked away.

Their waitress appeared carrying two complimentary bottles of wine. She filled their glasses and left the second bottle on the table. The room brimmed with conversation and laughter as if time had stood still. Jessie had missed her sister's witty sense of humor. She even missed the odd relationship her parents' labeled a marriage. Even with all their battle scars, she could see they loved each other.

"Mr. James, would you like another bottle of wine?"

He eyed two empty bottles and then glanced at his slightly inebriated family. "No thank you, young lady."

Jessie had personally made the reservations, but it looked like someone else controlled the evening. A long procession of a healthy heaping of salads started the evening off as several waitresses entered carrying heavy trays on their shoulders.

Jessie gorged like a pig in a sty. Looking the way she felt, her daddy pushed back his chair. Her mother and Ginny ate the least. At some point in their lives, they'd tried every diet on the market.

His cell phone rang. "Couldn't it wait? Nothing moves until I say it does." His abruptness transported them back in time. Immediately, the call shifted their focus. "Forgive the interruption." Then he got up and walked away.

Jessie gleaned from his annoyance that the business remained unchanged. Minutes later, he returned.

"Is everything okay, Daddy?" Ginny asked.

"Never better, sweetheart." His tone sounded light-hearted, despite the slightly miffed look on his face.

An early morning run along an isolated shore had helped Jessie sort things out. For days, she'd fretted over what she would say to them. As soon as he took his seat, a sudden lull presented her with that dreaded opening. She seized the moment. He knew before she spoke.

"Everyone, I'm glad I came back," she said. I've enjoyed these last few weeks." Jessie cupped her hands together to prevent them from shaking. "I'm leaving in three days."

Ginny sprang to her feet and ran out of the room.

Her father sighed. "Jessie, whatever makes you happy will make me happy, too. I'm sorry you carried around all that old baggage all these years. I love you. I never meant any of this. Go," he said, shooing her with his hands. "Get on with your life. Just don't leave without saying good-bye."

"I won't, Daddy, I promise. I love you both."

Her mother sat quietly. Finally, she asked, "Jessie, what about your job?"

"I took a sabbatical."

"Where will you go?"

"Around the world...well, not the entire world, just a small portion of it." She pushed her chair back. "Please excuse me." Then she went searching for her sister. She found Ginny leaning against the bathroom sink. Jessie dampened a paper towel and dabbed Ginny's moist eyes.

"Please don't go."

"I've no reason to stay. All is well. Besides, I'm excited about seeing the world."

"The world?"

"Yes, I'm going abroad."

"I'll miss you, Jessie."

"I'll miss you, too."

After they returned to the table, her leaving never came up again. When dinner ended, they said goodnight. He had plans. Their mother developed one of her famous migraines.

"The night's still young," Ginny said. "Let's party for old time's sake."

Jessie hated the thought of spending the rest of her night in the company of sweaty strangers. Reluctantly, she agreed. They attempted unsuccessfully to crash several popular bars until a bartender with a fondness for a crisp Andrew Jackson had a change of heart. He commandeered them a table. They ordered drinks. Jessie talked, Ginny listened.

The evening wasn't a total loss. Guys flocked to them like flies to honey. After a couple of drinks, Ginny sashayed around the dance floor, oblivious to the presence or absence of a partner.

Jessie looked down at her watch and then up at Ginny. "Oh, my goodness! Ginny, it's late. We should go."

"Oooooo—kkk—aay." Ginny slurred and spit like a two year old. Her incoherent chatter stopped the minute Jessie tucked her in and kissed her goodnight.

Early the next morning, Jessie checked in. "How did you sleep, Mother?"

"Not very well, that darn headache kept me up most of the night."

"I'm sorry," Jessie said.

"Oh, honey, it's not your fault."

"Did you take your medication, Mother?" Jessie asked.

"Yes, and it helped a little. Ginny called on her way to pick up her car. I guess you girls had a good time."

"We did."

"Jasper got home pretty late last night and left before dawn. I suppose he hasn't resolved the problem from last night."

"Perhaps. I'll talk to you later, Mother. I've got to start packing. The first leg of my journey starts day-after-tomorrow in London." Giddiness swept over Jessie. As soon as she hung up, the ringing started again.

"Hello, Jessie."

"Lydia! Girl, I've missed you. How's my city?"

"Still your city and waiting with open arms."

"Philly's got a little wait, I'm afraid."

"Oh?"

"I'm going abroad for a few months."

"Sounds wonderful, Jessie, I hope you have a good time."

"That's the plan. So, what's going on?"

Lydia breezed through all the latest gossip and then casually threw out a strange comment. "Whenever Dr. Barnes drops by the restaurant, he never fails to ask if I've heard from you."

Jessie ignored her comment. Surely, the chief of medicine didn't miss her. But, it warmed her heart, knowing he thought about her.

"Hurry back, Jessie."

"I will. I promise."

Jessie hung up and walked hastily down to the water's edge. The soothing back and forth sway of the waves calmed her spirit. On the walk back to the house, she paused then giggled, feeling the wet sand between her toes.

"James Import—Export."

"Mr. James, please?"

"Who's calling?"

"His daughter, Jessie."

"One moment please."

"Jessie, I'm glad you called," his exuberant voice rang out.

"Daddy, any plans for lunch today?"

"No, sweetheart, what do you have in mind?"

"I'm around the corner from the office. I'll grab a couple of sandwiches."

"Sounds good."

A few minutes later, Jessie walked in.

"Hello, sweetheart." His large smile greeted her and then came his inviting hug.

"Hello, Daddy." Jessie hugged him back and then sat down.

He studied her face for a hint. *Lunch or goodbye*, he wondered?

"Daddy, it's time for me to go. I'm finally happy again."

He didn't say anything for a few minutes. Then he grabbed both of her hands and held them gently. "I love you, Jessie. Your old man can't handle any more regrets. At the end of the day, I want more than an old man's pride. Finally, my daughter has come back. I'm not letting her go." Then he joked, "Watch out for the locals, sweetheart."

Laughing, she squeezed his hands. "I love you too, Daddy."

"Send lots of pictures. One day, I'll carve out some time for me and your mother so that she can see the world."

They finished lunch and said their goodbyes. Early the next morning, Jessie made the first of two calls.

Ginny sniffed. "I expect a text or an email every once in a while."

"You got it. Goodbye, Ginny, I love you."

"Ditto, little sister."

It took a more conscious effort to make the next call.

"Jessie, you're up early."

"Yes, Mother. I'm calling to say goodbye."

"Oh, Jessie, what about—"

"We've talked." Jessie heard a sigh of relief. Over a few short weeks, the power of forgiveness not only transformed, it brought her family closer. Lydia was right. "Goodbye, Mother, I'll miss you."

Then she picked up her bag and walked out of the door.

CHAPTER 11

These days the crushing weight of Patsy's death pounded Lydia and her family with such force it started to weaken their foundation.

"Enough." Lydia remembered the promise she made at the funeral.

All of them understood their aunt's suffering. Jake got home earlier than usual. Until she heard him fumbling around in the kitchen, she'd forgotten about dinner. Quickly, she dialed the number.

"Jacksons," a young man's voice called out.

"What's today's special?" Lydia asked.

"Oh, hello, Dr. Giddens, it's chicken and dumplings."

"Sounds terrific, I'm on my way, thanks."

"We'll have everything ready, Dr. Giddens."

She and Jake shared a late dinner and something vaguely resembling polite conversation. Physically, she sat across from him while her mind courted memories of a small Mississippi town hundreds of miles away.

"Lydia, what's wrong?"

"Aunt Regina needs me. I'm taking a few days off."

"Sounds like a good idea. Go on to bed. I'll finish up in here."

"Thanks." He got no argument from her. She slept soundly.

"Good morning, sleepy head." Lydia woke to the sound of his voice. You've got a few hours before your flight. Would you like breakfast?"

"Nope, perhaps I'll grab something at the airport. Thanks for driving me."

"No problem."

Lydia's airport experiences always started out a bit unsettling. It drove her crazy just thinking about how bad things had gotten before the improvements. Suddenly, the sights and sounds of the traffic fighting for entrance into the busy terminals jarred her back to those maddening years. Pot holes, like small craters, took over the only straight route from her house. The ravished roads constantly needed repairs. Unexpected detours popped up overnight. Back then, road rage happened so frequently on that crowded stretch of pavement leading into the terminal she renamed it "rage alley." Thanks to the passing of a new bond, she hardly recognized some of the intersecting streets.

Jake pulled up to the terminal and got out. He held her tightly and kissed her lips passionately. "Babe, I miss you already. Come home soon. Give Aunt Regina my love."

"I promise."

She breezed through security and ignored the ache in her stomach. When she reached the gate, she opened up her laptop. Several messages sat in her inbox. The clinic's administrator advised the reassignment of her work for the week and ended with *Enjoy your stay*.

Lydia responded *Thank you* then scanned over a few other messages before finding one from Jessie.

Hey, Lydia! I'm having a great time. The first leg of my journey is behind me. Of course, I checked out a pub or two before leaving London. No surprise there, right? It's a short hop from Heathrow to Charles De Gaulle. Wow! I'm officially a tourist. I never saw it coming. What an enlightening adventure so far. Love, Jessie.

Currently-boarding rows flashed repeatedly on the marquee. Lydia quickly stuffed the laptop back into her carry on and got in line. Passengers maneuvered the narrow aisles while their eyes roamed in search of their assigned seats. Her seat belt clicked as it locked into place. Then she glanced out of the window, watching two workers carelessly toss baggage from a cart on the tarmac into the cargo area of the plane. *What luck*, she thought. The seat to the left and right of her remained vacant which guaranteed her a small piece of solace. Shortly after take-off, her head began bobbing back and forth until the sound of the landing gear lowering for a final descent woke her.

The carrousel stood still, as if it expected her arrival, then it slowly started turning. Bags flew pass her like seconds of time. She yanked her bag up and over the ledge before dropping it to the floor. As the automatic doors opened wide, she spotted Danielle's car pulling up to the curve.

Danielle waved. "Hey, Lydia, get in."

"Girl, you look terrific!"

Danielle looked like a new improved version of the old model. Lydia couldn't stop staring.

Danielle laughed. "It's all that pool time. We spend so much time around the pool the neighbors think I've hired my own personal lifeguards."

Lydia laughed too.

Danielle drove straight to the storehouse of their enduring childhood memories. Once old and weather-beaten, the front door wore a fresh coat of paint.

"Mark painted it last week," Danielle said noticing Lydia's surprise. Then she unlocked the door. They walked inside.

Their aunt stepped out of the kitchen and greeted Lydia with a big hug and kiss. Danielle stood speechless, not even moving when Regina planted an adorable kiss on her cheek, too. Lydia smiled. Besides their strikingly similar physical attributes, they had other common denominators.

"I'll just finish up in here. You girls can eat. Hungry, Lydia?"

"Yes, I'm afraid I skipped breakfast. I'll just need a minute."

Danielle followed Lydia into the bedroom and closed the door behind her. "Lydia, yesterday she acted like a total stranger."

Lydia laughed. "I believe you."

None of them understood her like Lydia. Their aunt thought sifting their lives like flour would get rid of the unwanted lumps. Did it do any good? Lydia wasn't sure. Danielle probably had no idea their fiercely independent aunt co-managed two totally different worlds. Danielle shook her head as she walked out. Lydia went into the bathroom and washed her face. The guilt-fueled reflection of her aunt stared back at her.

A tuna casserole and a pan of freshly baked bread sat cooling on the counter. Danielle stuck her spoon in the casserole. "Aunt Regina, this casserole's delicious. I'd love the recipe."

Aunt Regina laughed. "It's yours, sweetheart."

They turned around as Lydia walked in.

"Don't look at me. I have a personal chef and a capable young woman who manages my business from the front door to the back. I'm not interested in cooking or learning how. Not now or ever."

They laughed.

"And how is Jennifer?" Aunt Regina asked.

"Marvelous. She sends her love."

"What a terrific gal. Margie knew a good thing when she saw one."

"That's for sure," Lydia said.

Danielle stood up, "I've got to pick up Joe from school. I'll see the two of you later this evening."

Lydia helped her aunt clear away the dishes, and then they sat down.

"So, what's this I hear about you quitting on us?" Lydia asked.

"Sweetheart, I'm not a quitter. I had no idea losing a child hurt so much. It feels like someone ripped a piece of my bleeding heart right out of my chest."

Lydia saw the pain in her eyes. "I'm so sorry, Aunt Regina."

They talked for a while longer then Lydia went to her room to unpack. They prepared for an evening of lively conversation with Danielle and her family and then later, maybe just the two of them.

Lydia hoped she would learn what her aunt had previously left unsaid. She barely had time to mull over the thought when she heard—

"Hello, where is everyone?" Danielle yelled out.

"In here," Lydia shouted over the whistling noise of the teapot. Where had the time gone?

"I'll take one of those." Danielle grabbed a cup from the overhead cabinet.

"Hello, Mark! Good to see you."

"It's good to see you too, Lydia."

Joe settled for a hug. Those days of twirling him around were now long gone.

"Oh, Mark, I hear you've got a new toy. Congratulations."

For a brief moment, he looked bewildered. "Oh, you mean the pool. Yep. It's our baby, mine and Joe's."

Danielle frowned. "Your baby, gee thanks, Mark, for officially replacing me with a big hole filled with water."

Taking her cue from Danielle's noticeable annoyance, Lydia dropped that hot topic. Then she glanced over at her nephew with glee as she remembered those days of old.

Mark's earlier glitch almost put a damper on their evening.

An hour later Danielle announced, "Guys, we'd better get going. Tomorrow's a school day."

"Danielle, why don't you and Joe go ahead? I'll drop Mark off shortly."

Danielle didn't look surprised. Perhaps, she expected an intervention. "Goodnight everyone. Mark, I'll see you later at home." She blew them a kiss, Joe waved. They walked out together.

Regina stood up. "I think I'll turn in now, goodnight, Lydia, Mark."

"Goodnight, Aunt Regina," they said.

"Anything wrong, Lydia?" His voice sounded unsure, yet cool.

"Mark, let's go outside, the night air will do us both good."

They walked outside and sat down in that familiar old squeaky swing. The air felt crisp, the sky clear. Their eyes locked.

"Mark, how can I help you solve your problems? I've heard some disturbing news. Anything that affects my sister and nephew affects me. Family means everything to us, you know that, Mark."

Alarm quickly displaced his earlier self-assurance.

He looked like an inexperienced matador staring down an angry bull.

"Mark, gambling away my sister's financial stability and my nephew's college fund concerns me. When I get worried, it's time you rethink your lifestyle choices. I hope we understand each other."

"Lydia, I'm sorry. Everything's under control, I promise."

"I certainly hope so. Nobody should get more than one reminder. Don't you agree, Mark?"

Still in shock, he didn't respond. Mark looked like a deer caught in the blinding headlights of a speeding car. Lydia couldn't believe how much she sounded like her aunt. Trapped in her fixed stare, he shivered noticeably.

"It's beautiful out tonight, Mark. Come on, let me drive you home."

Mark stood up and then stumbled backward as if the floor beneath him pivoted slightly. Long before he married Danielle, he'd heard some bizarre tales about her family. Anyway, he had convinced himself that jealous people told tall tales. Of course, he always pictured Lydia as the no-nonsense sister. After their talk, he no longer had any doubts about the family or Lydia's commanding role.

She shook her head hard. Lydia had actually seen fear in Mark's eyes. When she finally pulled into her aunt's driveway, exhausted, she went inside and fell into a deep sleep.

℘℘℘

A pungent smell drifted into her room, her nostrils. Still clad in pajamas, she followed the sizzle of bacon.

"How did Mark receive your message last night?" her aunt asked as she sipped her tea.

"It shook him up a bit. I don't doubt that he understands the alternative. Danielle will soon see a new man."

"Good."

Lydia cleared away the breakfast dishes, went to her
room, and called her sister. "Danielle, you sound sleepy."

"A little."

"I told Aunt Regina we're having lunch. I've got an
appointment with Dr. Ada this morning. Will you cover
for me?"

"Of course. Oh, Lydia, by the way, when Mark got
home last night he seemed pretty shaken up. Is everything
okay?"

"Sure, everything's great."

Danielle didn't say another word. The authority in
Lydia's voice halted any further questions. One thing for
sure, Danielle didn't get much sleep either. Whatever
Lydia said spooked him. Mark tossed and turned for
hours. Finally, Danielle fell asleep. Sometime during the
night, she rolled over into an empty space where he once
laid. She jumped up, tripping over the tangled bed sheets
lying in a heap on the floor and followed a faint whisper
to an open doorway. Mark sat humbled, his head and torso bent downward.

☙☙☙

"Good morning, I'm Lydia Giddens. Dr. Ada's expecting me."

"Good morning. Please take a seat." The young
woman picked up the phone, spoke briefly with someone
then looked back in her direction. "The doctor will be
right with you."

Lydia's eyes darted around the room. The office
hadn't changed one bit. Sunlight flooded the room and
whitewashed the brightly colored walls.

Dr. Ada stepped out. "Dr. Giddens, please come on in."

The receptionist's jaw dropped. Her eyes danced in her head. When she made the appointment, Lydia intentionally omitted her professional title since it had no bearing on her visit.

Over the rush of happier childhood memories she heard, "Dr. Giddens, please sit down."

Lydia had an impressive reputation and the skill set to cleverly present Dr. Ada with a hypothetical scenario that wouldn't cross the line of ethics. "Dr. Ada," she said, "here's the problem. Sometimes, powerful women engaged in emotional battles question their own wisdom. Desperately in need of help themselves, they ignore their own needs over the cries of others. Hopefully, when faced with such predicaments, they seek out qualified professionals. What advice would you offer?"

Dr. Ada smiled. She wished her mother could've witnessed Lydia's shrewd approach. Her prideful eyes would've overflowed like a river before reaching its crest. Just like Lydia, Dr. Ada, like her own mother, Dr. Maude, devoted her life to the wellness of her patients, too.

The oath she took protected her patient's privacy. Her love for humanity assured them that restoring their wholeness meant everything to her as well.

"Dr. Giddens, I'm sure the patient's aware of their importance. When the ground beneath them started crumbling, they grabbed a branch. My advice—stay close. Sometimes even rocks crack or break under pressure."

"Thank you, Dr. Ada."

"You're welcome. Perhaps, Dr. Giddens, we'll meet again under different circumstances."

Lydia smiled politely. On the drive home, she prayed

then called her sister. "I'm heading back to Aunt Regina's."

"Well, what did Dr. Ada say?"

"We should stay close."

"So it's' true. Aunt Regina's her patient."

"Perhaps." Lydia gave her characteristically short reply. Danielle accepted it without any further discussion.

Minutes later, Lydia stood outside of the house ringing the doorbell. "Lydia honey, where's your key?" her aunt asked.

"It's probably at home in another handbag."

The truth, she'd lost it. The day of her uncle's funeral it slipped from her hand. It made a loud clanging sound as it fell down the drain of the kitchen sink. Why should she care about some old key? She'd lost someone more valuable and irreplaceable than a shiny piece of metal.

"Don't worry about it. I've got a spare." Then Regina made a mad dash to her bedroom. When she returned, she handed Lydia a key.

Lydia dropped it inside the zippered compartment of her handbag.

Her aunt then spun around and ran back to her room as if she'd forgotten something. "Did you enjoy lunch?" she yelled.

"Yes, very much," Lydia yelled back.

"Where did you girls eat?"

Lydia went blank. "Think," she said out loud. "Oh, that new barbeque place you told me about.

"*Hum.*"

"Aunt Regina, can I grab a quick shower?"

"Yes, we'll eat at six."

Lydia's whole body felt sticky caught in the grips of another typically hot muggy summer day. After a quick shower, she squeezed into the same pair of jeans she'd worn to her aunt's birthday party. She laughed. They fit like paper on the wall. As the never-ending fitness battle persisted, her weight continued to move up and down like a seesaw. She finished dressing then sat down on the bed and opened her laptop.

Jessie's note began, *Hey girlfriend how's work these days?* Oops! Jessie didn't know she'd gone home for a few days. *Lydia, the London countryside's now behind me. Paris begins the second leg of my journey. I arrived in Paris a few days ago to slightly cooler than expected temperatures for this time of the year. I'm so enthralled with this city. The weather hasn't minimized its romance or beauty. I walked until the bottoms of my feet developed big oozing blisters and still missed seeing the ornate gargoyles. The next day, I strolled through The Louvre. Later that same evening, I took a magnificent sunset dinner cruise down the Seine River. Am I dreaming? Say hello to everyone.*

"OMG!"

The answer to Lydia's prayer stared back at her. Jessie had copied her family on the email. Lydia closed her laptop and headed to the kitchen. This evening, Danielle's family had a little league game. Finally, they would get some uninterrupted time. On her last visit, her aunt's unfinished conversation left her mystified. Lydia hoped this time Regina would finish what she started.

"Sit down, sweetheart."

Lydia sat down on command.

Regina let her words marinade slowly before she spoke. "Lydia, never forget that, crouched angrily between years of good will and hard work, old enemies lay in wait. Be careful. I don't deny chaos helped shape our colorful family, but strong leadership kept it from falling apart."

Lydia sat quietly. The unusual and trusting friendship between her uncles, their wives, and best friend had a long-lasting effect on all of them. Sometimes Lydia wondered if her sisters truly understood the depth of their predecessors' love for them and especially the measures that kept them safe. Who knows what prompted her Aunt B J to record in code their human frailties along with their justifications. Dear sweet Aunt B J strongly believed in the healing power of truth. Perhaps, she supposed God could use a little help deciphering their cryptic deeds. How funny and contradictory since this faithful woman understood better than any of them that God didn't need their help. Unlike her Aunt Regina, her Aunt B J had an impenetrable faith. She believed faith capable of the impossible and that same faith didn't require an understanding of the answer, only a belief in the possibilities. Her Aunt B J said God understood their hearts, but their heads frustrated him.

The fire that burned the little black book destroyed all records of their shortcomings, except for the inescapable fragments confined to Lydia's memory. Perhaps, she wasn't the only one. Something tormented her Aunt Regina, too. Had she broken a vow or betrayed a confidence?

Her aunt paused briefly then in a slightly muffled tone she began again. "Lydia, no one loved their families more than these men and, what they did, they did for love. Despite his moderate salary, your Uncle Roy loved his job. He took his responsibility as the high school principal very seriously. His vested interest in a lucrative import-export business boosted his income. It also fed his lavish taste for the finer things in life. He threw good money after bad at the race track. His appetite for fancy cars grew increasingly lustful. The five-year-old Bentley had fewer miles than his one-year-old silver Jaguar. I defended our choices, and I accept full responsibility for them. Your Uncle Roy's endeavors supported our family. The land he acquired stretches as far south as Gulfport and north to Holly Springs in our home state of Mississippi. Other parcels reached as far west as California and then eastward up to Massachusetts. His dirty money reentered mainstream America through legitimate businesses up and down the eastern seaboard."

Lydia felt as if she'd thrown up her hands for the last time before drowning in her own disbelief. Regina's echoing words hit hard, knocking Lydia over like bowling pins as they tumbled, split, and crashed wildly about.

Finally, she saw the truth about the man she adored. He wasn't just this life-size hero with a heart of gold who provided for and protected them, but another flawed human being.

"Lydia, who knows how this life will end for any of us? Unlike Roy, your Uncle Edmond grew up in a place and time where he didn't belong. He ignored the problem way too long. The absence of the truth plunged his children deeper into his masquerade. Eventually, he spoke the truth and gave his damaged children a choice. One chose truth, the other chose the only life she knew. No one blamed Mia. Her grandmother's lie paid for her first class citizenship. She wasn't about to throw that away. Edmond tried, but he couldn't shake the burden of his mother's sin."

Lydia watched her shift gears. Light streamed through Regina's eyes, they twinkled and lit up her face.

"Lydia, I'm proud of my African-American ancestry. I don't blame Edmond for denying his roots. He'd built such a powerful, successful life until turning over that leaf so late in his career would've ruined him politically. It wasn't his fault. Color got in the way. His mother created his nightmare. In the end, it destroyed her."

Lydia's spoiled and privileged cousins Alan and Mia never followed the norm. They behaved like children born into wealth, power, and position. What else did they need? Alan's internal struggles rose out of trying to fit his uniquely crafted life into an ordinary existence. After all, he had his biological mother's passion for life. Nobody bothered guessing where Pauline got her bull-headed attitude. In a short period of time, Regina covered a lot of ground and yet, it felt like she left something more chilling untouched.

"Tea?"

"Yes, please."

Regina set the two piping hot cups of tea down. "Where did I stop? Oh, our beloved friend Jackson, I believe. Poor man, he had many demons."

Lydia remembered all the wonderful things Jackson taught her about life. Not until she opened a little black book did she know how dangerous or exactly how much power any of them wielded. The complexity of their love for family astounded her. Later, she learned these typical hard-working, civic-minded leaders and parents covertly manipulated, even destroyed, the lives of other people for their greater good.

Her aunt kept talking, speeding up the tempo as if she saw her time running out. "Dear sweet Jackson turned a blind eye. Like those around him, he lusted after position, money, and power. Hopefully, in his later years, his philanthropic ventures brought him comfort and atonement for his transgressions. However, I can't help thinking his earlier deeds still kept him up at night."

"Why risk everything?" Lydia asked, even though she knew the answer. She wanted confirmation—no, she needed confirmation from a member of their inner circle.

"For love, my darling Lydia, for love."

"Aunt Regina, what aren't you telling me?" Lydia asked bravely.

"You're very perceptive, sweetheart. You've always had the gift, child. Let's take a break. I'm tired."

Reluctantly, Lydia agreed. So far, her aunt's confessions and Lydia's suspicions followed a parallel path. *Will Aunt Regina's remaining disclosures shock me?* Lydia wondered. From the window, she watched her aunt carefully inspect roses cascading over a trellis fashioned in every hue of the rainbow. She stooped and smelled their sweet fragrance then pulled a lone weed before walking back inside.

"I think I'll take that nap now," Regina said. "Do you mind, Lydia?"

"No, Aunt Regina. I'll catch up on my emails."

A well-documented email from Jessie, outlining the third leg of her journey, stood out *among the junk mail populating her inbox.*

Hey, girlfriend! I've spent an exhausting thirteen-plus hours aboard a flight from Paris to Hong Kong. Can you imagine an old fishing village so affluent it boasts of a thriving culture where the east now meets the west? By the way, the night life's terrific. Yesterday, I joined a group of backpackers traveling the world like me. In four days, we'll begin the fourth and final leg of a journey through Southeast Asia from Hong Kong to Thailand. Wish me luck~

With her world seemingly moving faster than the speed of light, Lydia took a few minutes to reply.

Jessie, I'm in Sweetwater visiting my aunt. I miss you, too and I'm so happy you've closed some gaps. Remarkable!

Then she stretched out across her bed and fell asleep until a light tap on the door woke her. "Lydia, may I come in?"

"Yes, ma'am."

"That nap did me a world of good. Let's take a walk."

Lydia recognized the drill. She put on her sneakers and left her cell phone behind. Fondly, she remembered those promenades. In a house full of problematic teenage girls, her uncle constantly needed some fresh air.

"Ready, Aunt Regina?"

"Sure." They strolled down the sidewalk hand in hand and ended up on a park bench in the rear of the community.

A gloomy shadow skipped across Regina's face.

"What's wrong, Aunt Regina?"

"It's complicated, child."

Lydia chose not to pry. Instead, the two comrades sat quietly listening and watching the beauty all around. Birds chirped sweetly as bees jumped from one flower to the next in search of sweet nectar.

"Lydia, we should head back."

As they reached the door, they heard one final ring and then silence. Lydia rushed in, checked the caller ID, and immediately every muscle in her body tightened as she hit redial.

"Lydia." Alan's shallow voice bared his heartache and destroyed her supposition with an unexpected announcement. "B J died. Her heart stopped beating."

"Oh, my God," Lydia shouted.

Her aunt grabbed the phone. "Hello!" Hello!" she shouted as if the caller had trouble hearing her. Then her body slumped down into the chair, clothed in silence, as Alan repeated the sad news of her best friend's home going.

At her annual checkup a few weeks earlier, Lydia's jovial aunt had chatted about the family. As almost an afterthought, she mentioned an occasional shortness of breath and recurring nausea. These symptoms prompted Lydia to run a few additional tests as a precaution. She found no arrhythmia, clogged veins, or abnormality.

"It's just age, sweet girl," B J had said.

"Perhaps, Aunt B J, but let's see what Dr. Martin thinks."

Aside from his arrogance, he had a reputation as one of the best cardiologists in the nation. When Jessie had challenged his technique, she never doubted his skill. From time to time, Lydia consulted with Dr. Martin on a few of her patients, but this patient meant everything to her. After a thorough examination, he found nothing a little rest wouldn't cure.

The news of B J's death shocked everyone. Her husband barely had any life left in him and continued fighting for every breath.

Grief-stricken and weepy eyed, Lydia prepared to mourn the loss of one aunt while in the middle of discovering more truths from another. The following evening, they boarded a plane to Philly. Two days later, Reverend Kettle delivered the eulogy. She thought she saw a teardrop slide down her uncle's face as he stared blankly at the casket. Had he remembered? Alan, Mia, and the children of her aunt grieved openly. Even with a heavy heart, Kellee looked like a younger version of her beautiful mother. Her handsome dependable brother Danny hung his head. Midway through the celebration, her aunt's first husband Adam slid quietly into a pew in the rear of the church and whispered goodbye to his first love. After her service ended, he visited privately with his children.

In her Uncle Edmond's world, her beloved Aunt B J became an astute student of politics, too. After the interment, family and close friends gathered at a place Mia no longer called home. She seemed perfectly content living estranged among strangers. Like her father, Mia's awe-inspiring work brought her great joy, but unlike him, she let the real pleasures in life slip through her fingers.

Off in a corner of the room, a lost and confused young woman stood alone. Her Aunt Regina touched her gently on the shoulder. "Mia, honey, are you okay?"

Puffy sleep deprived eyes stared up at her. "I can't believe she left my daddy."

Regina gasped. What happened to the young woman who gladly accepted necessary and often risky work so she could improve the lives of others? Day in and day out, her sweat and sometimes her blood poured into assignments that kept pushing her deeper and deeper into the most dangerously isolated areas of the world.

"Mia, I know you stare death in the face every day. Our hearts bleed more profusely when the attack's personal. B J knew your brother would see his father through the rest of the way. We're all on this amazing journey. Like B J, when the ride's over, we must get off. I'll miss her, too." She hugged Mia then walked over to a wheel-chair-bound, frail, unresponsive man and kissed his fore-head.

Alan and Elaine stood next to him. "Day or night, please call me," she said, smiling into their sad eyes.

Alan kissed her cheek. "Thanks, I will. Goodbye, Aunt Regina."

She turned back around as Mia sat down on the floor next to her father and reached for his hand.

As soon as Lydia dropped her family off at their airline checkpoint, her cell rang. "Hey, babe! I'm sorry I missed the funeral. The boss called an emergency meeting two hours before my departure. I missed my flight and couldn't get another one out in time."

"It's okay, Jake. I'll see you at home later tonight."

It really didn't feel okay. Work always got in the way of life. Now, it seemed like it got in the way of death, too. She'd walked away from enough food that a small country could enjoy its reserve for a year. Lydia stood staring into an empty refrigerator. At that moment, food wasn't a priority. She changed clothes, grabbed an unfinished book from the top of her dresser, and settled in comfortably on the sofa. The words blurred. Tears and ink merged then evaporated before her eyes. Like Mia, Lydia couldn't believe her Aunt B J's earthly life ended so abruptly. Several weeks before she died, Lydia had driven out to the country. Maria greeted her with a little less bounce in her steps.

"Mrs. Stein's outside in her garden."

Elaine heard the door bell, too. "Hey, Lydia."

"Hello, Elaine. How's he doing today?"

"Sadly, no change."

Lydia took that long familiar walk. He sat alone with his eyes fixed on nothing in particular, looking like a breakable plastic toy. Her heart longed for those important talks. Overcome with emotion, her eyes watered when she saw the shell Alzheimer's left behind. The disease crippled his body. Slowly, it began erasing his dignity. For now, she expected no real change. Personal research and reflective conversations with other doctors produced very little in the way of hope or treatment. However, she remained hopeful a new breakthrough would come in time. She kissed his cheeks. "I'll see you soon, Uncle Edmond."

Lydia didn't remember walking outside until she heard, "Lydia, darling, I'm happy you came. You look well," her Aunt B J said.

"Thanks, I'm feeling well. How're you feeling, Aunt B J?"

"Splendid. Come join me."

They hugged. Then B J bent down and picked a straggly weed from among her bouquet of beautiful flowers. Lydia smiled. She didn't know the difference between a weed and flower. They sat underneath the shade of a blooming overgrown wisteria that crisscrossed over a pergola.

"Lydia, I'm a blessed woman, regardless of some poor choices. Repentance and forgiveness often produce great rewards." Her aunts took great pride in delivering profound messages. Lydia wasn't sure if she fully understood, but she expected more would come. She pulled in a deep breath and listened carefully as her aunt continued.

"Do you remember the first time you came to dinner?"

Lydia nodded. "I walked away, regretting all those wasted years apart from my uncle."

That evening, the cleanup of a badly contaminated past got under way. Behind the scenes, B J's, tireless unifying efforts built an unwavering relationship between the two people she loved. People like her Aunt B J flavored the earth. Lydia had no doubt she left this world unburdened. Would she ever say the same about her Aunt Regina? she wondered.

CHAPTER 12

If necessary, the sergeant decided, he would move heaven and earth for Regina. Then a few weeks after the funeral, Regina made a surprising announcement. She'd sought the care of Dr. Ada. Imagine that. Where had Lydia and her sisters gotten the notion that no one deserved more than one love affair in a lifetime? Perhaps, they never understood that the heart's a much bigger gateway. Certainly, she and Jake could benefit from such an astonishing bit of information. A big gaping hole created a void in their marriage, but they kept trying to hold things together.

In the middle of the afternoon, her last two patients cancelled. Lydia couldn't wait. She called Jake. "Hey, babe, you'll never believe what happened." Before he could guess, she spilled the exciting news about her free afternoon. "I've just pulled out of the garage. What time will you get home?"

"I'm heading home too. Let's grab a movie and a late dinner."

"Sounds good."

Her commute took less time than his collision course route to and from work. Jake hated fighting south bound traffic on a Friday evening. Getting a head start didn't necessarily mean an early arrival. The road stayed congested. An encore performance of horns honking and people swearing filled the air waves. When he stepped inside the door, she stood freshly showered. Her naked skin glistened like early morning dew on tender blades of green grass. He quietly wrapped her in the comfort of his arms as a beautiful symphony played in her head.

Then the words she missed hearing flowed from his lips once more, "I love you, Liddie."

Everything felt right again. Later, they dressed and headed across town for the showing of a steamy love story and then dinner.

Jennifer looked up and waved as they entered. "Hey, guys."

"Hey, Jennifer, nice crowd tonight," Jake said.

"It's wonderful." They started pouring in as soon as we opened the door this morning. It's exciting. I love crowds. Follow me," Jennifer said.

Lydia, Jake, and Margie met quarterly to evaluate the restaurant's bottom line. Since its doors opened more than two decades ago, it remained in the black. Jennifer waved her hand.

A chubby face young man with a plump belly appeared, looking like the baby brother of the Pillsbury Dough Boy.

"Good evening Lydia, Jake. Meet Matt," Jennifer said.

"Good evening, I'm Matt. I'll take care of you this evening."

"Hello, Matt, give us a minute."

"Yes, sir."

"Enjoy your evening guys," Jennifer said. Then she and Matt walked away.

"He looks so adorable. I'd love to—" Lydia said and

giggled. She imagined tickling and squeezing him until he chuckled.

Jake read her mind. "I hope you behave yourself, Lydia." He smiled at her then waved his hand. Matt returned.

Matt looked at Lydia. "May I take your order?"

"Yes, please, a glass of merlot."

"What may I get for you this evening, sir?"

"I'll take a very dry, very dirty martini."

Oops. Lydia's antenna shot up. They rarely changed drinks. Sometimes, she drank a different kind of wine, and perhaps Jake drank beer. They stayed away from the really hard stuff. Tonight, she took notice of a troubled man sitting across from her. His shoulders drooped. His eyes looked sad.

So, she asked, "Slow or busy?"

"Busier than ever. The office's under-staffed. I'm guessing there's no more money in the budget." Jake chuckled sarcastically. "Maybe, I should've checked the fine print before I signed on the dotted line."

Perhaps he intended it as a joke, but it came out very grave. His long-awaited and coveted promotion increased his salary, his hours, and his responsibilities. Free time became a luxury.

Not wanting to further dampen the evening, he raised his glass with a glint in his eyes. "Here's to my beautiful, passionate wife. I love you, Lydia."

The glass on glass sound created a crescendo of soft, beautiful musical notes.

"And I love you more."

The look in his eyes brought back an unforgettable memory...

Jackson's encouragement and wisdom had always calmed her shaky nerves during those hellacious weeks of very little sleep and too many hours on her feet while interning at the hospital. She took a seat and glanced across the aisle at the soup of the day scribbled on a chalkboard. Minestrone. Yuck! Then disappointed, she turned toward the kitchen as the swinging doors flew open. He stepped out with a dishtowel draped over his broad shoulders.

"Hello, I'm Jake. Uncle Jackson had a meeting across town. He left me in charge. And you are..." She looked up. As he gazed into the intoxicating warmth of her big brown eyes, her bewitching smile immediately stole his heart.

She extended her hand and smiled. "I'm Lydia."

His milk chocolate skin looked as soft and smooth as butter.

"Well, hello there, Lydia. My uncle said a pretty young woman might drop in. I'll forgive his mistake," he said and paused. "I'm shocked, he forgot beautiful."

Her face suddenly felt hot, her throat tightened. His undeniable charm made her blush. She found herself at a loss for words.

"What can I get you?"

"A nutpnut—no, I mean a peanut butter and jelly s— sandwich please," she stuttered.

That sweet, sweet memory seemed so very long ago.

"Would anyone like another drink?" Matt asked.

"No, we're good here, man."

Almost immediately, he felt her temperature rise. *Big, big mistake, Jake*, he thought. He hoped she would blame his presumptiveness on his new drink of choice since he'd already downed two. After Matt took their orders, she momentarily ignored Jake's flub hoping to bait him into engaging in her favorite pastime. The women in her family had a spirit of discernment. The accuracy of her gift gave Jake goose bumps. He preferred they spend the evening discussing current events and not pry into their patron's private lives. He talked, she listened. Thank goodness dinner came just in time. As soon as Jake took a man sized bite of his sandwich, Jennifer appeared.

"How's dinner?"

Jake nodded.

"Where've you guys been? Everyone missed you."

"Working," Lydia said.

"I'm glad you're back. I'll check on you later." Jennifer walked away.

Jacksons' had come a long way. Every weekend, Jennifer showcased smooth jazz and soulful, down-home blues that had large crowds flocking to the restaurant. Her vision created a phenomenal change that improved the overall ambiance of the restaurant. Brunch, another exceptional change, had the local food critics printing fantastic reviews.

They finished dinner. Even though she never drank excessively, Lydia just couldn't let it go. She beckoned for Matt. "I'll take another merlot."

Under that sweet smile, Jake felt the sting of defiance.

"And what can I get for you, sir?"

"I'm good, man, thanks."

The waiter felt the tension as he set down her drink. He turned and quickly walked off. Winning meant everything to Lydia even if it frustrated her sometimes. Of course, she blamed those control issues on her genetic makeup.

She sipped slowly. When she finished, she set the glass down. After all, she'd proven her point.

ᥴᨣᩬᔆ

"Good morning, sleepy head. How did you sleep?"

"Soundly," Lydia lied. No way would she admit two glasses of Merlot pushed her over an imaginary cliff.

She'd foolishly stretched her limit and for what? "Any coffee?"

"Yep. Just made a fresh pot." He poured up two cups, his second. "What's on the agenda today?" he asked.

"I'd love a picnic," she said.

Jake's quick scan of the refrigerator took all of a split second. A half empty carton of orange juice sat alone on the top shelf. One of its side doors held a jar of strawberry jelly. The pantry was almost bare, except for a jar of creamy peanut butter. Most couples had a special song or favorite restaurant to remind them of their first date. Lydia and Jake had a peanut butter and jelly sandwich. All things considered, it was going to be another peanut butter and jelly day.

At the crack of dawn, they hopped onto a couple of rented bikes then took off down a winding pathway and up the slightly sloped terrain. A short distance later, they settled down comfortably under a cluster of tall, powerful oak trees. They waved with renewed enthusiasm as people rode or walked leisurely pass. Time flew by like birds on a winter pilgrimage. Then as the sun slowly drifted westward, they rode back down the hill, dropped off the bikes, and drove home.

Sunday morning, Lydia sat in deep reverence as her pastor delivered to every parishioner the promise of forgiveness for their past with a welcoming glimpse into a glorious future.

Monday morning, she left the house ahead of Jake. She feared her early escape on Friday left some fallout.

"Good morning, Dr. G."

"Good morning." Lydia nodded and walked briskly pass her receptionist.

As she turned the corner, she literally bumped into Rebecca.

"Good morning, Dr. G., how was your weekend?"

"Amazing! And worth every muscle ache from those uphill climbs."

Work and family concerns had gotten in the way of their personal time. Too often Lydia took Jake for granted. "What about your weekend, Rebecca?"

"Terrific! Thanks for asking."

Except for her bulging inbox, her early departure didn't leave any disasters behind. As soon as she arrived, a constant flow of patients strolled in and out of exam rooms. After a busy morning, Lydia ate a quick lunch at her desk then replied to her e-mails. Most of them came from her sisters. Pauline had wedding fever. Every email started and ended with the beautiful island of Hawaii and of course, the very handsome and athletic Rick. Lydia wasn't totally surprised that her pastor, Reverend Kettle would officiate her sister's wedding. Who wouldn't, with all expenses paid? Pauline's ailing pastor couldn't tolerate such a long flight.

In contrast, Danielle talked about the great weather back in Sweetwater, and their aunt's new beau. Her email ended with, *She's okay now, Lydia, thank God.*

Where in the world had Jessie gone? A month and not a single word from her and then as if Jessie had read her mind a message appeared.

Hey, Lydia, what's going on? I miss everyone and can't think of anything else these days, but family and home. I can hardly wait. The final leg of my journey's winding down. Until I set out on this extraordinary adventure, my little knowledge of the world could fit into a thimble. I'm in awe of the cultural diversity of Southeast Asia. The ex-pat's favorite city Chiang Mia felt so alive and comfortable, I hated to leave. I'm a little more adventurous these days, but cautiously chose curry, rice, and noodle soups while touring Thailand. The air's hot, humid, and infested with lots of thirsty mosquitoes. Despite all that, I've fallen in love with the largest port in Viet Nam, the city of Ho Chi Minh, formerly the old Saigon. Bangkok, my least favorite city, bustled with literally thousands of noisy motor bikes spewing thick black smoke into the air. Not only that, this sleazy city reeked of prostitution like the ungodly cities of Sodom and Gomorrah. Back home in America, we take clean water, air conditioning, and air quality for granted. Here, the air's so polluted, it a bad joke. That's it for now. I'll save the rest for when I return home.

Had Lydia missed something? Whatever happened to her friend? Not too long ago, she had trouble getting Jessie away from work for a weekend. Look at her now, eagerly exploring another continent.

CHAPTER 13

Lydia hoped Jessie would surprise her and pop in from some place across the ocean. Rather quickly, she learned from Dr. Barnes that wasn't going to happen. Jessie remained clueless. She hadn't figured out that Dr. Barnes's interest in her went beyond any employer and employee relationship. Approximately four months ago, she left the hospital with one agenda that turned into something spectacular.

The countdown had begun. Lydia got chills every time she heard the excitement in Pauline's voice. Alan hired extra help for his dad. Two weeks later, Alan, his wife Elaine, along with Lydia and Jake, headed to Hawaii. They arrived early then took a shuttle to a beautiful hotel sitting at the edge of the ocean.

Lydia stepped out onto the twenty-ninth floor balcony and looked out across an endless body of sparkling blue water. The white sand glistened against the sun's rays like diamonds in a showcase.

Jake's body moved in closer and then he kissed her tenderly on her lips, her neck, and in the hollow between her breasts. "I love you, Liddie."

Passion swept her away until a soft tweet interrupted

the moment. He reached into his pocket and pulled out his cell phone. Slightly annoyed, she moved away and stood listening to the waves as they crashed against the shoreline.

Quietly, Jake sneaked up behind her. His touch was gentle. "We're meeting Alan and Elaine in fifteen for a light lunch and swim."

The couples sat out on the terrace. They talked while admiring an incredible sun-kissed view of the ocean. Waves rose up as if to swallow the sky and then fell face down in disappointment. Alan's cell phone buzzed. Suddenly, their rapidly firing chatter came to a screeching halt. "Thanks Maria for the update."

"Is everything okay, Alan?" Elaine asked. She prayed nothing had gone wrong back home.

"Everything's fine," Alan said.

Already, the therapeutic powers of the island started transforming Elaine as she watched blissful couples stroll leisurely along the shoreline. Their contagious joy energized her. The guys jumped up. She and Lydia grabbed their bags and followed them down to the water. Lydia rarely put her feet in the ocean anymore. Jake's near-death experience still conjured up nightmares. His lifeguard training proved useless the day Rick had snatched him from the jaws of death on a beach on the other side of the world. Shortly after that harrowing experience, Jake swam back out into the deep blue waters. His dance with death hadn't deterred him.

A thousand miles from home, the guys swam under the watchful eyes of their wives. Today, her cousin's wife shared snippets of admiration for her now deceased stepmother-in-law.

"Mrs. Stein really loved her husband. She loved all of us. I really miss her," Elaine said.

Her voice sounded tearful. Lydia nodded her agreement. She feared if she spoke, her words would expose her sorrow, too. The kindness of Lydia's Aunt B J touched all of them.

The guys came ashore twenty minutes later and stretched out on blankets under a clear blue sky. Earlier, Lydia had spoken with the concierge who bragged about an irresistible dinner club called The Centerpiece. Before heading to their rooms, Lydia stopped at the concierge desk. She made reservations for four. Until dinner, they had several hours to relax.

Jake preferred soaking up the beauty of paradise wrapped in her arms. She enjoyed the surge in their romance.

Later that evening, the couples met in the lobby. Lydia giggled inside. She wondered if Alan and Elaine felt the island seducing them, too. More than anyone, they needed something that would rekindle a spark in their love life. The couples took a cab to the dinner club where a culture hodgepodge of superb food and sizzling music waited. One thing for sure, the concierge knew his island hot spots. Immigrants from as far away as China, Japan, America, Portugal, and Korea brought traditions that left a permanent unforgettable mark on the island. They dined on huli' huli' chicken, turnips kim chee, mango bread and a list of foods they couldn't remember or pronounce.

After dinner, they moved into a partitioned section of the dinner club only minutes before the band took to the stage. Brightly colored lanterns hung from the ceiling over an oak laminate parquet floor. Elaine's dance moves surprised Lydia, but not Alan's. The night exceeded all of their expectations.

Early the next morning, the hotel shuttle took them to the big island of Waikiki. A crowded beachfront appeared as the driver rounded the bend in the road.

Lydia's cell phone rang.

"Hey, big sister, where are you guys?" Pauline asked.

"We just arrived at the beach in Waikiki," Lydia said.

"Oh, that's wonderful. We're checking in now. See you guys later."

Tomorrow afternoon, Pauline and the man of her dreams planned to stand at the edge of a constantly changing ocean under an indigo sky and pledge their love for one another. Again, Keisha and Frank's late arrival had Lydia overly anxious. Unconsciously, she bit her nails. Silently, she prayed that nothing would delay their flight. If Keisha missed her sister's wedding, their sibling squabble would create such a powerful ripple, Lydia feared her family would never recover.

Like always, the cool strikingly blue ocean called out to Jake. He willingly obeyed. Alan followed dutifully behind him. Like Jake, he had a love affair with the ocean, too. Lydia purposely ignored its call. Instead, she and Elaine found a spot on the white silky sand. Like squatters, they staked their claim. Not even their oversized umbrellas offered enough protection from the scorching sun and sweltering heat. When the guys came out of the water, they hurriedly gave up their seats.

"We won't be long," Lydia said.

Underneath her sugary façade, she had no intentions of rushing through what remained of her day. They strolled through the market looking and occasionally buying. Two tours later, they stumbled upon some shops in a hotel along the shoreline. There they enjoyed the comfort of air conditioning. Elaine looked so happy, strangers probably assumed she'd discovered a tantalizing fountain of youth. Lydia watched her resurrect the art of bartering. Had Alan realized how much his wife needed this getaway? She hoped this trip would unearth his passion for life again for Elaine's sake, if not his own. Somewhere between the deaths of his mother, then his step-mother, and now watching his father slowly vanish before his eyes, Alan had lost his zeal.

The couples enjoyed an eventful day, but once back at the hotel Alan and Elaine opted for a quiet evening alone. This time the concierge steered Lydia in the direction of a Luau happening on the beach later that same evening. It sounded like so much fun she invited her family. Danielle especially loved the idea.

Before hanging up, Danielle asked, "Can you believe Aunt Regina and the sergeant paid for separate rooms? Does she think we care what consenting adults do privately?" She didn't wait for Lydia's response. "Surely, Aunt Regina can't still think of us as naïve little girls."

"Of course not," Lydia said.

But she pondered her question. What had Danielle expected her to do about it? Thanks to Pauline dropping in unexpectedly, everybody knew they shared the same bed sometimes, so why not in paradise? Her aunt's absolutely ridiculous behavior made Lydia wonder what happened to the fiery woman she knew when they were growing up.

After a very long and exhausting day, the idea of entertaining her aunt's foolishness could wait. Lydia and Jake went back to their room in search of a little solitude. About dusk, they met everyone in the lobby then walked the short distance down the beach to the Luau. Flames flaring from an exaggerated number of Tiki torches in concert with a multitude of stars lit up the pathway leading to the Luau.

Several long tables stretched out across a neverending beachfront with brightly colored table cloths flapping loudly as a chilly breeze blew in off the Atlantic.

The festivities began with folk music, hip shaking hula dancing and then a parade of food. This new, exciting experience baffled them, but they graciously embraced the Polynesian culture.

Lydia recognized poi, Kalua pua'a—Hawaiian pig— poke, and a few other items on bountiful trays. By the time Rick and Pauline arrived, the party had begun.

"Hey, everybody," they said.

"Hey, guys." The group's harmonious greeting echoed through the joy-filled open air.

Aunt Regina winked. "Nervous?"

Pauline responded with a quirky smile. Her aunt's powerful wink magically erased her discomfort. Instantly, an obvious calmness lifted Pauline's shoulders and her spirit. A smile parted her lips. Then she and Rick joined the excitement. Everyone got so caught up in learning the hula dance, time quickly sped pass them. Midnight arrived. The time had come to bid their amazing evening farewell.

Lydia grabbed Jake's arm. "I'll see you back at the room. I want to speak with Aunt Regina."

He gave her a curious look then walked over and stood next to the sergeant. They spoke briefly and then together Jake, and the sergeant walked back toward the hotel.

Lydia and her aunt held hands and walked in silence for a few minutes. Regina shivered as the chilly night air crept into her bones. Lydia removed her wrap and draped it around her aunt's shoulders.

"Thanks, sweetheart."

Lydia came unprepared but prayed for divine inspiration. Her Aunt B J told her many times that if she spoke the truth only then could she live that same truth. Their Aunt Regina's choice became their choice the minute she chose the sergeant as her companion.

Lydia wondered why her aunt would spend a miserable weekend pretending she and the sergeant shared a merely platonic relationship.

"Aunt Regina, we accept the sergeant as your companion. We get it."

Regina's grip tightened. A sharp stinging pain shot through Lydia's finger tips. She suppressed a cry as her wedding ring dug into her flesh. Had she overstepped her boundaries? she wondered.

Her aunt stopped and then faced her. "I'm not ashamed that Barton shares my bed. I'm not a prude, Lydia," she said very curtly.

Evidently, another troubling issue had her rethinking their relationship.

Ah ha! A crack in the armor, Lydia thought.

Her aunt took a deep breath and sighed. "What scares me has nothing to do with sex. I'm afraid he might ask me to marry him. I'll never do that again. Even now, I feel like I'm publicly flaunting Barton while debasing the memory of a man we all loved."

Finally, Lydia saw it. Regina had put her life on hold to preserve her husband's memory. If that meant giving up her happiness, she didn't mind making that sacrifice.

"Aunt Regina, I understand the magnitude of the power and position I now hold. You have my blessing whatever you decide."

Regina took Lydia's face and held it between her hands, "Thank you, sweetheart. Now, let's go inside."

The elevator door opened onto the tenth floor. She stepped out then turned and blew Lydia a kiss.

Jake looked up as soon as she entered the door. "Hey, babe, any luck?"

She leaned with her back against the door and religiously kicked off her shoes. Everything's all good."

"The sergeant and I had a long talk, too. He plans to ask Aunt Regina to marry him."

"Well, he shouldn't. She told me she'll never do that again."

"Seriously?" Jake asked.

"Seriously."

"Pleasant dreams, babe," Jake said.

Not possible, Lydia thought. Long after he turned out the lights and tucked her into the folds of his arms, her aunt's words swirled around in her head until sleep came.

They woke to the sound of tapping. It came softly, then loudly. Jake opened the door. "Join us for breakfast?" Alan asked.

"No thanks, Alan, we'll grab something later."

"Okay, we'll see you later."

Jake dialed room service then crawled back into bed and pulled the sheet up over their heads.

Lydia threw back the sheet and sat straight up. "What time is it?"

"Eight o'clock."

They had plenty of time with the wedding at four. She fell backward onto the bed, pulled the sheet up over her head, and turned over. A half hour later another knock forced Jake out of bed. He stood face to face with a short moderately obese man carrying a large tray upon his shoulders.

Discounting his stature, he had a rather handsome round face with a tiny handlebar mustache.

"Good morning, sir."

"Good morning," Jake said as he watched the man set the tray down on the table and uncover the dishes. Jake thanked him properly and closed the door.

Lydia and Jake sat out on the balcony eating and watching the sun play tag with the ocean. A sudden vibration shook her mind free.

When she picked up, the caller asked, "Lydia, where are you?"

"Good morning to you too, Keisha."

"Girl, I don't have time for games. Pauline's falling apart."

"Where is she?"

"In her room, please hurry." Keisha sounded beside herself with worry.

Noticeably, Lydia's role as the big sister or perhaps their new go-to-person started evolving rather rapidly. Now, with Keisha here, she had one less thing to worry about.

"I'm on my way." Lydia hung up and turned to Jake. "I gotta go, Pauline's having a meltdown."

Jake looked puzzled. She ran into the bathroom, splashed water on her face and brushed the foul taste from her mouth. Then she scooped up the clothes lying in a pile on the floor from the night before and dressed quickly. With her ear glued excitedly to the voice of a new caller, she rushed out.

"Hey, Lydia, I'm sorry I won't make the big day. Give Pauline my best."

"Jessie?"

"Yes, it's me."

"I've missed you. Your last email came weeks ago, where are you?"

"Heading home."

"Philly or Boston?" Lydia asked.

Jessie laughed. "Both. I've given Dr. Barnes my return date. See you later and don't forget to give Pauline and Rick my best wishes. I'm very happy for her."

"Wait! Wait!" Lydia shouted over the sound of a click and then a buzzing. The elevator door closed behind her then quickly reopened. She rushed out. With one sharp knock, the door swung open. Pauline ran into her arms looking simply gorgeous. "When I'm scared, I'd like to still look this beautiful," Lydia said. Pauline smiled. Lydia studied her. "What's wrong?"

"I'm not sure," Pauline said and kept wringing her hands together.

At any minute, Lydia expected them to dispel water. She grabbed Pauline's hands. Then she looked directly into her eyes. Today, her sister would begin the rest of her life as someone's partner. That scared her to death.

"Do you love Rick?" Lydia asked.

"Yes, of course."

"Does he love you?"

"What a silly question," Pauline said.

"Then what's the problem?" Lydia asked.

Pauline stared blankly at her but never answered.

"Today, you've given Mama and Daddy another proud moment." The magic in those words caused Pauline's shoulders and her breathing to relax. Her eyes regained their sparkle. Another memorable moment happened as her sisters watched, in awe of Lydia's persuasive power. Then she gave Pauline a big hug and turned to them. "I've got to go, ladies."

Each of them had a part to play. In memory of her twin sister, Pauline chose a single white rose over the traditional bridal bouquet. She wore a simplistic white gown and, although she chose a glitzy rhinestone studded veil, it lacked the power to diminish her flawless features.

Lydia stood gazing at her own reflection in the mirror. The woman staring back resembled her aunt more and more each year.

When Jake walked into the room, his eyes filled with unbridled desire and then came. "OMG Lydia, you're beautiful. You look just like—"

"I know." Lydia threw her hands up into the air. Their likeness improved with age. Once when her sisters taunted and dangled the slight possibility of her as their aunt's illegitimate love child, Lydia's blood got so hot her nose started bleeding. "Liars!" she shouted.

They quickly backed off. Lydia loved deeply, but, like their aunt, she had a get even philosophy.

Jake swung her around and halted her thoughts with a kiss. "Never leave me."

He held her so tightly she felt every beat of his rapidly pulsating heart.

Where did that come from? Lydia detected a hint of guilt in those words. Immediately, a tiny bit of fear flickered in his eyes. Her mind swirled as bits of this and that came into focus. Already, Lydia suspected what this moment confirmed. Yet, she vowed to let nothing spoil her sister's day.

Abruptly, Lydia pulled away. "I've got to hurry. Pauline will kill me if I'm late."

Maybe, she'd forgotten Rick had chosen him as best man or maybe not.

"I'm sure Rick wouldn't appreciate me showing up late either." Jake's tension-filled remark hung in the air long after he walked out to finish dressing. Lydia slammed the door behind her and blotted out that split second of hostility. As planned, the ceremony took place at the edge of the ocean with the waves crashing about as tiny sprays of water dampened their attire, not their spirits. Blue ribbons, fastened to rows of white chairs, swayed blissfully in the breeze. Her sisters presented each guest a colorful umbrella as they accompanied them to a seat.

Some guests tossed them up into the air to filter the sunlight, while others twirled them about playfully. Reverend Kettle, Rick, and Jake stood at attention like soldiers guarding a military post. Mark proudly took his position. When the music changed, he escorted Pauline down the aisle. Lydia caught the glimmer in her aunt's eye. Then a smile moved quickly across her face. As Rick placed the ring upon Pauline's finger, it happened again. Magically, tiny flakes of sawdust fell from the sky and landed on Rick's shoulders.

෨෨෨

Lydia and her sisters adored their father. Every day, he toiled in a saw mill while their stay-at-home mom cared for them. Their extraordinary parents lived ordinary lives and, even in death, their spirits had the power to jazz up the lives of their children. The first blessing showed up on Lydia's wedding day. It arrived again at the double wedding ceremony of her sisters Danielle and Keisha. Those tiny particles of sawdust that stole most of their father's good days, and eventually his life, became symbolic of their parents' approval of the men they chose.

Pauline's attempts to steer clear of an overly impressive wedding failed as candlelight bathed the ballroom in soft shades of a matchless sky and ocean. Everyone stood to their feet. A hush fell over the room. Pauline entered wearing a short red form-fitting dress with a plunging neckline and ruffles flowing like a peacock's plume off the back and down to the floor. No one moved. Even the air stilled. Then Jake stood up. Loudly, he announced the arrival of Mr. and Mrs. Richard Martin amidst thunderous applauds and ear shattering cheers. The lights dimmed on command. The music took a long deep breath then swelled to a flaming hot tempo. Her damp skin glistened under the dim lighting as their seductive bodies moved in sync.

"Sweet." Jake's voice boomed as he held the microphone up close. Actually, too close.

Pauline had a knack for delivering the unexpected. The guys whistled. The women applauded. Lydia glimpsed the remnants of her aunt's lingering grin. She even caught Danielle swaying to the beat of a foot tapping melody. Swollen and miserable, Keisha looked like she'd bitten into a sour apple. Her unmistakable frown corrupted her stunningly beautiful features. In her defense, what could they expect?

ತಿ.ುೋೆ.ು

Except for the band, almost everyone had gone. Elaine stood up and floundered. Alan, with Jake's help, propped her up. Finally, they got her to the room. Across the hall, Lydia kicked off her shoes at the door and undressed in the middle of the floor. Jake kissed her tenderly. They clung to each other.

"I love you, Liddie."

His touch ignited a rapidly burning fire before it slowed to a passionate spark. Periodically, hot spots reignited throughout the night until the uncomfortable weight of his arm resting on her chest woke her.

ತಿ.ುೋೆ.ು

"Good morning, sleepy head," Jake said.

"Good morning."

"After last night, I thought you could use some extra sleep." He laughed. "Girl, you partied like it was 1995."

What in the world got into her last night? Her body felt like she'd gone a round or two with a featherweight boxer. Regardless, she had no intentions of broadcasting her distress. She grabbed her purse, closed the bathroom door, then rummaged through all her stuff until she found a seltzer clinging to the very bottom. Plop! Plop! She

watched as it fizzed. Then she gulped it down quickly
and climbed back into bed. Except for Jake's touch, her
hazy memory left no clues that two unlikely party goers
got pretty wasted. In a seemingly perfect evening should
she remember that Elaine bared their sorrows? Elaine
rambled on and on like a "Chatty Cathy" doll all night.
Lydia already suspected Alan harbored guilt about ac-
quiring his father's prestigious practice. He blamed himself for what he couldn't control. Alan looked happy last
night. For a moment, he probably forgot about the frus-
trations awaiting him back home.

She and Jake walked across the hall. Alan and Elaine
sat packed and waiting.

"We'll miss you guys. Last night was so much fun,"
Lydia said.

The guys looked at each other and then at their
wives. They laughed. Their laugher was so contagious,
she and Elaine laughed, too.

Then a knock at the door announced their time in
paradise had come to an end. Alan opened the door. The
bellman picked up their luggage. Everyone followed.
Alan closed the door behind them.

"Call me when you get back," Alan said.

"I will and thanks for listening, man."

She and Elaine hugged.

*Well, well, perhaps Jake finally decided to trust
someone with his secret*, Lydia thought.

ოჯოჯ

The next day, a chartered helicopter and its distinguished guests set down on the less densely populated
island of Kauai. Pauline and Rick hoped to experience the
beautiful cliffs and waterfalls found along the North
Shore.

These outdoor enthusiasts had an adventurous week packed with early morning horseback rides, hikes along the scenic Kalalau trail and lazy afternoons at Hanakapiai beach.

Their Aunt Regina invited the rest of the group to brunch. The very pregnant Keisha wobbled in behind her husband, greeted everyone and sat down.

Frank walked over to Lydia with the manly glow of a proud expectant father on his face. "Hello, Lydia. How're you feeling?"

"Good. What about you, Frank?"

"I'm good," Frank said.

"Congratulations, I'm very happy for you and Keisha."

"Thanks."

Keisha strolled up behind her husband and rested her hand on his shoulder. She loved her sister, but it didn't lessen her insecurity. Keisha wished she never knew Lydia and Frank had once shared the same bed. They met in college a very long time ago. Their relationship ended amiably. After college, they went their separate ways. Lydia's feelings for Frank had felt more like admiration for a courageous leader rather than the fiery passion she felt for her husband.

"Lydia, you really kicked it last night!" Keisha said. "Frank and I left you partying. You reminded me of the old Pauline. I looked again to make sure my eyes hadn't played a trick on me."

"I had a ball. Anyway, I couldn't pass on a good time. I guess that old saying holds true. People never let you forget your past."

Embarrassed, Keisha looked away.

Jake winked at her. "I'll tell you what a good time got her. She woke up with a hangover. Yep. I noticed."

She laughed then jabbed him playfully. "Stop it, Jake, and stay out of my business."

"Hey, everybody." Danielle and Mark arrived in the middle of their playful banter. Joey slept in. The simultaneous chatter sounded like a swarm of bees had taken up residence overhead.

After brunch, Regina and the sergeant decided to do a little sightseeing. The guys went for a swim. Lydia and Danielle reclined under a couple of beach umbrellas. They watched. Jake swam like a fish. It looked like Mark's new training ground had paid off, too.

Danielle looked puzzled. Her forehead had a cute little wrinkle just above her eyebrows. "Lydia, did you see what happened at the wedding?"

"Perhaps," Lydia said.

Danielle sat up and looked her directly in the eyes. "Get over yourself, big sister. You know what I mean."

The sharpness in sweet little Danielle's voice surprised Lydia. Finally, her sister was showing a little backbone.

Lydia lifted her sunglasses with one hand, eyed her sister carefully and fired back. "What do you think happened?"

Danielle looked pleased. "Those tiny flakes appeared again."

Lydia didn't deny or confirm her suspicions. She simply smiled then dropped her sunglasses over eyes overflowing with pride. Her aunt always said forcing the truth upon someone didn't help unless they arrived at it on their own.

After the guys came out of the ocean, they headed back to the hotel. Danielle and Mark stopped at the bar. "Lydia, please don't forget to call me before you leave tomorrow."

"I won't." When they reached the elevator, she

turned to Jake. "I need to visit with Aunt Regina before dinner."

He didn't say anything. They got off on the tenth floor. He knocked. The door opened wide.

"Hey, guys," Aunt Regina said.

Lydia hugged her aunt and Jake gave her a quick peck on the cheek. Her aunt's guest sat comfortably in an oversized chair near the window.

"Hello, Sergeant."

"Hello, Jake."

The sergeant walked over to Lydia. He extended his hand. Interestingly, during the entire time they'd known each other, he never attempted to hug her. Perhaps, he sensed he had to earn that honor. "Hello, Lydia, enjoying this beautiful tropical paradise?" the sergeant asked.

"Yes."

Her aunt gave her a soothing wink. "Sit down, sweetheart," she said as she patted the bed. Lydia sat down next to her and waited. Jake stood next to the sergeant. "Pauline had such a lovely wedding."

Lydia's face looked flushed. Her strained attempt to hold an intelligent conversation surprised Jake. That so-called mature attitude about her aunt's relationship had a serious defect.

Secretly, Lydia wrestled with the thought of any man becoming her aunt's partner. She began babbling about their early flight then jumped up and rushed to the door. Jake followed. Lydia's apparent nervousness cast a shadow too wide to ignore.

"I'm glad you came, Lydia. Barton and I decided to stay on a few more days. I'll call when I get back home."

"That's wonderful, Aunt Regina." Then Lydia kissed her aunt goodnight and nodded in his direction.

Who could resist the incredible ocean views, white sand, and temperatures worth bottling up and taking home? Unfortunately, Lydia's spontaneous visit felt to her like an intrusion into a private moment. "Stupid mistake," she whispered softly as she stood outside her aunt's room.

"For whom?" Jake asked as he laughed out loud.

Oh, how he enjoyed seeing her squirm. Annoyed, she pushed him aside and got on the elevator.

"Lydia, give her some credit. Aunt Regina is not a demure flower wilting under the heat of a passionate affair."

Momentarily, Lydia stood still. Finally, she actually listened to a voice of reason, even if it came from someone else for once. Jake's non-judgmental comment made her see pass a strong maternal relationship born out of the misfortune of losing her parents. After she almost spoiled their last dining experience in paradise, they returned to their room where they sat out on the balcony looking up at the stars.

"Lydia, it's time to go in. We really do have an early flight." He laughed. She laughed too.

The next morning they boarded a flight for home.

It was late, but shortly after they arrived home, Jake received a text. He looked annoyed. "I've got to go into the office. I'll call if I'm going to be very late," he said as the door closed behind him.

After one quick look in the refrigerator, she knew a little grocery shopping had to happen very soon. A couple of hours passed. She hadn't heard from him, so she decided to check. "Jake, is everything okay?"

"Everything's fine. I'm sorry I meant to call you. It looks like I'm here for the duration of the night. See you in the morning. Sleep well."

"I'll try."

Lydia didn't feel sleepy and thought re-reading *The Great Gatsby*, an old favorite might curve her restlessness. Gatsby, a complex man like her Uncle Roy, lived a fascinating life. At a half past midnight, she filled the tub with bubble bath and lit some candles. A nagging personal problem needed her attention real soon. She would never concede defeat. While stretched out in a body of warm, soothing bubbles with soft music swirling around her, she made that most important decision. Then she climbed into bed and slept soundly throughout the night.

Jake shuffled through the door. He blew her a kiss then headed straight to the shower. Lydia picked up her cell phone as the caller's cheerful greeting rang out. "Good morning, Lydia." Keisha was bursting with energy.

"Good morning, Keisha." Lydia listened. She even pretended she cared as her sister rated diapers and formulas. Although Keisha loved kids, plainly Lydia could see that time and maturity had plenty of work left. That virtue known as patience somehow escaped Keisha. Not Danielle, she had enough for all of them. Sadly, Lydia knew she would never experience the biological thrust of motherhood.

Keisha's early morning call started the whole thing. Lydia's cell phone rang continuously. With each ring, Lydia envisioned it literally jumping out of her pocket and into her hands. Alan called next to say that he and Elaine had a terrific time. Next, her aunt called with an update. Her excitement filled voice told Lydia more than she willingly shared. Finally, Danielle called with her mind reeling from the shock of Pauline's exhibition. Although, in the same breath, she asked Lydia what she thought the next chapter of their lives would reveal about them. Her rhetorical question had Lydia wondering if perhaps Mark found the courage to share with his wife the content of their earlier conversation. Danielle never confided Mark's weaknesses to any of them. Maybe, her question hinged upon their generation succeeding their aging predecessors. Not surprisingly, each of them got a little something innately different from their parents. In differing degrees, they proved themselves resilient, strong and capable of surviving the worst of times. However, by observing their predecessors, they developed fortitude. It helped them press onward through even more tough terrain. Both of these channels permitted intrinsic value worth treasuring. No wonder it effectively shaped their lives. When Danielle hung up, Lydia couldn't believe how all those exercises in family sharing left her drained.

Before arriving at work, Lydia had already used up too much energy on the maybe's and what if's of life. At work, she spent her time making intelligent decisions about the health of trusting patients. Again with lunch an afterthought, she finally took a break and ended up in the cafeteria where she gobbled down a tuna sandwich before heading back to her office. Several messages waited in her inbox. Right away, she clicked on the one from Jessie.

Lydia, I'm heading home. Boy, saying that felt good. I'll arrive in Boston next week. I'll spend a little time with my family then head to Philly. I've missed you. Guess what? I've heard from Tommy. He's flying out to Boston for a conference in a few days. Interesting, wouldn't you say? Oh, I called Dr. Barnes again. He now has my official return date. I can't believe how extremely pleased he sounded. Gotta go, girl, love you.

Her friend would soon be coming home. Lydia wished Jessie had taken a more personal interest in Dr. Barnes. That girl! Sometimes Jessie acted a little blonde. Somehow, Lydia knew Jessie's life was about to change, although she never dreamed it would drastically alter her life, too.

CHAPTER 14

Jessie's father stood waiting. His solo appearance surprised Jessie. Her arms encircled him. "Hello, Daddy, I've missed you."

"Welcome home, sweetheart. I've missed you too." He hugged her back. "How's that big old world out there treating you?"

"Wonderfully."

He laughed. With excitement in his voice, he began highlighting all she'd missed. Then as he approached the entrance ramp to the interstate, she felt it coming. "Jessie, the Coopers asked to see you."

She remembered the pain in their eyes as they stood alongside her at his graveside. What could they possibility say now that would change the past? Initially, she blamed them for turning their back on her until Lydia helped her see that his death turned their world upside down, too. Jessie got so caught up in her thoughts, she didn't realize they'd arrived home until the front door swung open and her mother ran out.

"Hello, Mother."

"Hello, darling, welcome home," she said holding Jessie ever so tightly.

"Sweetheart, Ginny's on her way."

Jessie's great escape worked. The woman who stood in her mother's kitchen had grown into many shades of different. The house looked the same. No surprise there. Amazing aromas filled her nostrils. Her mother's culinary skills far exceeded the average homemaker.

"Sit down, honey. You look exhausted. Dinner's at seven. Would you like to freshen up?" her mother asked.

"Later, perhaps."

Her father carried her luggage upstairs and then returned just as his wife pulled another pan from the oven. "Being on holiday seemed to agree with you. You look terrific Jessie!" His use of the European term holiday made her laugh. Home felt good, familiar once again just like her mother's infectious laughter.

"Hello, where's everyone?"

"In the kitchen," her father yelled back.

Ginny walked in and threw her arms around her sister.

"Gosh, you look stunning."

He smiled. "I couldn't agree more," her daddy said.

"Working hard, big sister?" Jessie asked.

"Not really. It feels more like I'm enjoying a very long, rewarding hobby."

Jessie knew exactly what her sister meant. They could've talked for hours about their careers. Instead, Jessie followed her daddy into the family room where they sat and peered through some old picture albums.

"Remember this?" he asked.

How could Jessie forget the worse day of her life? A very frightened little girl cried and clung to her daddy's leg while her mother sat in the car dreading the moment she could no longer hold onto her. Some of her earlier pictures looked like she'd escaped a prison for dwarfs. Before Jessie learned size didn't minimize the person, she felt small and insignificant. Then one day, she stepped into her own just as her daddy predicted.

"Dinner's ready," her mother called out.

It seemed amazing that Jessie returned from a world tour to experience the most incredible foods in her own home. Nothing she ate abroad compared to her mother's cooking. Although not born in the south, her mother raised Southern cooking to new heights. For sure, the Southern gentlemen who stole her mother's heart for a short time contributed to that.

Before her daddy left for work, he asked, "Will you come with me to the zoo?"

"I'd love to, Daddy," Jessie said.

How odd, she thought. Even as a little girl, he never took her on field trips and certainly not to the zoo. He arrived shortly before noon and drove them downtown. The rugged face man wearing a dark blue suit with a gun bulging from beneath his jacket was nowhere in sight. The sights and sounds uncovered wonderful memories of those times when she and Ginny came there in the company of their mother. The zoo seemed out of character for him. It surprised her that he knew the different species of reptiles and mammals and even more shocking when she learned he came there often. None of that mattered now. Finally, Jessie had him all to herself.

Jessie grew more anxious at the close of each day. Shortly, she would return to a place she felt more connected to than any other place on earth. Lydia and the hospital had become her surrogate family.

Tommy called a few days after she arrived home. "Hello, Jessie, how've you been?" He hoped the excitement in his voice wouldn't reveal his real motive for attending a conference in her home state?

"I'm good," Jessie said.

"I'm in town for a conference. I'm staying at the Waterfront Hotel. I can't wait to hear all about your travels. I'm free the rest of the evening. Can we get together?"

"I think I can arrange that." Her voice shook with anticipation.

They dined in the city the first two nights. On their third date, Jessie arrived at his hotel and drove out of the city toward the ferry. They boarded and stood watching the city fade behind them. She knew her mother looked forward to meeting the young man who'd put a noticeable twinkle in her daughter's eyes. An hour later, Jessie opened the door. Her smartly dressed mother stepped out of the kitchen, makeup applied perfectly with every strand of her color treated hair in place. Her daddy stood anchored at his wife's side. "Mother, Daddy, I'd like you to meet Dr. Tommy Calvin."

Tommy extended his hand. "It's a pleasure to meet you, Mr. and Mrs. James."

Her daddy held his gaze and grasped his hand firmly. "It's our pleasure, Dr. Calvin."

"Please call me Tommy."

Her mother smiled politely as she shook his hand. "Tommy, we're so happy you could join us for dinner." Then she turned and hurried back to the kitchen.

"How do you like our city?" her father asked.

"I like what I've seen so far, sir."

The door opened. They heard footsteps. "Where's everybody?"

"We're in the family room," her daddy yelled.

Tommy stood up. Jessie quickly made the introduction. "Tommy, meet my sister, Ginny."

He extended his hand. "Hello, Ginny."

"Well, hello, Tommy." When their hands touched, Ginny felt a surging current. Quickly, she pulled back. Tommy stood momentarily speechless staring into the eyes of a gorgeous creature with lightly toasted skin and hair as black as a moonless night. They sat down and stared in every direction except directly at each other. Everyone noticed. Jessie felt deflated like a football unable to rise to its potential. From the moment Lydia introduced her to Tommy, Jessie had high expectations. Now with her hope squashed, an uncomfortable feeling settled over her and the evening. Her parents took note of the commonalities between Ginny and their guest. They fared poorly on board games, talked passionately about their love of animals and their work. The physical attraction seemed a moot point. Fate had a sense of humor. When the evening ended, Tommy thanked her parents for dinner and reluctantly said good-bye to Ginny. Thoughtful quietness filled the air on the ride back.

As soon as they arrived at the hotel Jessie asked, "Tommy, will you join me in the bar?"

"Sure thing." He seemed a bit anxious as he grabbed a table. "Jessie, may I get you something to drink?"

"Nothing for me thanks." He waved the waiter over and hurriedly placed his order.

"Jessie, I had a great time this evening. Your family's terrific."

Interestingly, he discovered in a few short hours what it had taken her years to appreciate. Tonight, she watched again as fate called the shots. "Tommy, my sister's a very charming, intelligent woman. She likes you. I think you like her, too. The two of you should stay in touch."

He stared up at her from his half empty glass of Hennessy. "I'm sorry, Jessie. I hope I haven't offended you."

"Not at all, see you around, Tommy."

He stood and kissed her cheek. "You bet."

She smiled sweetly and walked out. Lydia had once told her destiny's the end result of what no one can change. After what happened tonight, Lydia was right again.

When Jessie opened the door, her mother rushed out of the kitchen with that old evidence of her frustration showing. "Jessie, are you okay?"

"Never better, Mother."

"Ginny's waiting upstairs in your room."

Jessie went upstairs. She found her sister lying across the bed. Puffy red eyes looked up at her. "Ginny, what's wrong?"

"I didn't mean to hurt you. I'm so sorry, Jessie."

"For what?" Jessie asked.

Ginny whispered embarrassingly and looked away, "Your boyfriend, Tommy."

"Don't be silly. Tommy's not my boyfriend, he's just a friend."

"I thought—"

Jessie interrupted. "Tommy's a nice guy and a very good-looking friend. No more, I promise."

Ginny jumped up and hugged her. "Oh my goodness, I'm so relieved."

"Everything's good. Oh, by the way, I talked to Tommy tonight. He likes you. You should give him a call sometime."

Then she jumped up and raced Ginny down the stairs.

Fearing a wonderful evening had gone south, her parents sat at the kitchen table waiting fretfully. Her father tapped his foot to a rhythm heard only in his head. The worry her mother often carried like a banner had reappeared over her left eye. Losing Jessie again and the risk of distancing Ginny had them worried until they heard the sound of giggling.

"Ginny's got a crush on my good friend Tommy," Jessie teased.

Knowingly, her mother smiled. She knew. Jessie perpetuated a lie the moment she explained Tommy as a casual acquaintance. Initially, Jessie had hoped for much more than friendship but made a sacrifice for someone she loved.

After Ginny ate the last slice of apple pie, she finished off the last drop of milk. Then she said goodnight and went home.

⸱⸱⸱

The Coopers' large ranch-style house sat lodged between a tennis court on one side and a pool house on the other. When Jessie ran away, she took the guilt bottled up inside and never stopped to say good-bye. Her hands gripped the steering wheel as she sat staring at the house on Ashton Street. Fear formed tiny beads of perspiration over her brow. Her hands felt sweaty. She came because her daddy said they asked to see her. After all this time, she couldn't shake the feeling that they had let each other down. Cooper's parents loved him and welcomed her as the daughter they never had. Under imperfect conditions, she had found the perfect guy. All of a sudden, Mrs. Cooper stepped out onto the porch then looked across the street. She waved. Jessie felt trapped. In this unscripted moment, she got out of her car and walked slowly up the sidewalk. Mrs. Cooper stood waiting.

"Jessie, it's so good to see you. Welcome back." Her hug felt comforting.

"Thank you."

"Come on in." Then she grabbed Jessie's arm and ushered her inside. "Would you like some tea?"

"Yes, please." Everywhere Jessie turned, she felt his presence and his love. Her eyes filled up quickly. Water ran down her cheeks.

"Milk and sugar?" Mrs. Cooper pretended not to notice the tears as she set the tray down in front of her.

"Just sugar, please." Through a large picture window, natural light filled the room. The freshly painted space appeared larger, more perfectly suited for entertaining. Jessie wiped her eyes with the back of her hand. When she looked up, Mr. Cooper stood in the open doorway.

"Hello, Jessie. It's so good to see you. How've you been?"

She stood up. "Very well sir, thank you."

He stepped forward wrapping her in a long, cumbersome embrace.

She cleared her throat. Mrs. Cooper sensed Jessie's nervousness. "Please sit down dear," Mrs. Cooper said then sat down next to her. "Jessie, we regret that we never said good-bye. Cooper's death struck us so hard we struggled every day. No one ever told us how difficult it would be to break free of the pain. We thought turning our backs on you would make it easier. But we forgot about your sacrifice, about what you gave up for him. He loved you with all his heart. We acted poorly. He never would've condoned our behavior. You gave him a reason to fight. Your strength kept him going for almost four years. We owe you a debt of gratitude. Please, please accept our apology."

The tears kept coming. Jessie could no longer speak.

Mr. Cooper stood quietly with his eyes fixed upon his wife. Then he turned toward Jessie. "My boy died a happy man. A father couldn't hope for any better outcome. Thank you, Jessie."

They lost him to an enemy none of them could defeat. The longer Jessie sat there, the more the memories came rushing back. She remembered her promise. Cooper's unselfishness and his love for humanity fueled her decision. In part, she became a doctor because of that promise. The tears flowed as they talked about a wonderful young man who taught them the meaning of love and, for a little while, shared his love with them. Her visit lasted a long time. When she walked away, guilt no longer occupied any part of her.

Jessie got into her car and drove back to her rental. Time kept advancing. Soon, she knew she had to return to her life. Two days later, she packed her bags. Her mother cried. Her sister begged her to stay.

"Please stay, Jessie. Our hospitals need good doctors too."

"I'm where I belong. Besides, Philly's my home now."

☙☙☙

Lydia screamed when she recognized the caller. "Jessie, where are you?"

"I'm heading home." This time she didn't need to ask. "My flight's scheduled to arrive late this afternoon."

"I'll pick you up."

"Nope, I'll grab a cab."

☙☙☙

"I'm home," Jessie yelled as she walked into her condo. The excitement of her homecoming seemed overwhelming. Then something strange happened. She picked up her handbag, walked out the door, and drove to the restaurant. Right up front, a perfect parking spot waited.

Jennifer approached her with a big grin. "Dr. Cooper, it's good to see you. Let's get you seated. When did you get back?"

Jessie felt the genuine excitement in her voice. "Just a few hours ago."

"Lydia worried about you traveling alone like that. You look amazing. I'm so glad you're back. Enjoy your evening." Then she turned and headed to the back of the restaurant where a woman resembling Margie waited.

Jessie waved then turned around and focused her attention on the menu in front of her.

"Good evening, may I get you something to drink?"

"Just ice tea and the special please."

"Good choice."

Jessie sat alone, enjoying a delicious meal. The crowds started to arrive just as she paid her tab. "Perfect timing," she said. Then she waved good-bye to Jennifer and the woman seated across from her.

Except for the sudden ringing noise, her sanctuary felt quiet. *Why not let the answering machine intercept the call?* she thought.

From across the room, she heard, "Jessie, it's Lydia. I'm glad you made it back safely. Call me. I left a message on your cell earlier, but thought it a safer bet to leave a message on your personal answering machine, too."

All of a sudden Jessie's heavy eye lids flirted with sleep. Until the sound of her neighbor's barking dog alerted her to a new sunrise, she slept soundly. On the way to the kitchen, she noticed the flashing light on the answering machine, hit play, and stopped in her tracks.

"Dr. Cooper, it's Barry—Uh—Dr. Barnes. Glad you're back. We've missed you here at the hospital. Call me when you get this message. Look forward to seeing you next week. Oh, I couldn't leave a message on your cell phone. Your voicemail's full."

Dr. Barnes actually took time out of his busy schedule to welcome her home. Lydia thought Jessie hadn't paid attention. Any female in close proximity to this man had to be blind not to notice his perfectly molded six-foot frame, chiseled face, and skin that looked as smooth as rich dark chocolate. Whether single or married, doctors and nurses drooled over him. Maybe, she'd call him later. Business could wait. Besides, she knew Lydia had gotten the news of her return.

∽∾∾

When Jessie opened the door to the clinic, the over-crowding surprised her. "Good morning! Please tell Dr. G., that Dr. Cooper's here to see her."

"Yes, Dr. Cooper," the receptionist said, still holding the receiver in her hand when Lydia ran out.

"Jessie!" she shouted with her arms outstretched. "Girl, I've missed you! How've you been?"

"Terrific, now that I'm back. I see you're busy. Let's talk over dinner tonight. My place, I'll cook. Is seven o'clock okay?"

Lydia nodded. "Seven's fine."

Then Jessie waved and walked out.

Lydia had four remaining patients. The day had gone well, and then panic gripped her when the last exam took longer than expected. She hated showing up late for any occasion. She called home.

"Hey, babe," she said when he answered. "Jessie invited me to dinner at her place. I'm rushing home to change. Can you manage this evening?"

"Sure. I'll make a quick stop over at the restaurant. Say hello to Jessie for me."

With a few minutes to spare, Lydia made another call. The ringing went on and on. "Don't panic," she said out loud before she nervously redialed.

Finally, her aunt picked up.

Lydia gave a sigh of relief. "Aunt Regina, anything wrong?"

"No honey, I didn't hear the phone. How are you, Lydia?"

"I'm well."

"Great! I'm doing well too." Regina gave her an update on her sisters then paused long enough that Lydia got in a few words.

"Jessie invited me to dinner this evening."

"Are you ladies dining at the restaurant?"

"No, Jessie offered to cook."

"Enjoy. Tell Jessie it's about time. Call me later."

"I promise."

"Hum." *It's about time* sounded like her aunt felt qualified to question Jessie's domestic skills.

Regina had always managed to stay one step ahead of them. Some things she said made perfect sense, and others didn't. Much of what Lydia learned on her last visit still had her head in a fog. Her family had some trust issues, even though they put a lot of stock into honesty. Frankly, they didn't think telling the whole truth applied to them.

☙❧

Promptly at seven, Jessie opened the door looking like a younger Lena Horne. Her tailored long white shirt hung below her buttock hiding a perfect figure melted into a pair of tight leather pants. The oil over acrylic on canvas and the watercolor and ink on paper of an unknown artist hung slightly askew on barely beige walls. These brightly colored works of art helped define the sparsely decorated condo.

"Red or white?" Jessie waved two bottles in front of her.

"Red please."

Jessie poured up two glasses. "Your timing's perfect.

I'm starved." A couple of grilled steaks rested on the counter alongside a freshly tossed salad.

Jessie grabbed two plates and passed Lydia one.

They shared food, drinks, and stimulating conversation. Jessie drank way too much. The more she drank, the more she relaxed. Lydia usually kept to her limit. She had a personal reason for not overindulging. When she thought about her unaccompanied twenty-five minute drive tonight, it gave her another reason to drink more responsibly. The mangled bodies and broken hearts of the family members she saw almost daily when she worked in the hospital left a lasting impression. Jessie moved her conversation away from the thrill of traveling the world to denouncing the sin that ripped her family apart. What she said next took a lot of courage. "Lydia, my mother had an affair. There's no biological connection between me and the man I've called Daddy my entire life."

"Oh, Jessie, I'm so sorry."

"Don't be. None of us can change the past."

Nothing in life surprised Lydia and certainly not Jessie's confession. Lydia prided herself on understanding human nature. Jessie's eyes looked glassy. Her slurred words fell thickly from her lips. From the looks of things, she couldn't last much longer. At a half past eleven, Lydia put Jessie to bed, loaded the dishwasher, and drove home.

Her aunt's catty remark, "tell Jessie it's about time," made Lydia wonder if she'd missed the real meaning behind that comment. Her aunt had a sly way of concealing her agenda until it served her purpose. Tunneling beneath the surface to understand her riddles demanded persistence like miners digging for gold.

Lydia checked in. "Hey, Aunt Regina."

"Lydia, I'm so glad you called. Did you enjoy dinner?"

"Yes, Jessie's a great hostess."

Actually, they had a blast! Certainly, she didn't want to insult Jessie. What was the point in repeating her aunt's cockeyed message? Obviously, her aunt wanted all the details. Lydia had never exploited a friendship, not now or ever. Why would she tell Regina that Jessie got so drunk she passed out? Who would benefit from Lydia saying that she hoisted Jessie up and literally dragged her dead weight to bed? Instead, she said they spent a boring evening dissecting various medical mishaps. Lydia felt the intensity in her aunt's prolonged silence and knew her answer didn't suffice.

"Jessie's a sweet girl. Keep an eye on her." The compassion filling her aunt's voice triggered a strange feeling.

სოტო

Filled with pretty high-strung teenage girls, Roy and Regina's house had more than its share of visitors in those days.

Lydia's uncle and aunt valued those quiet late nights under the stars in that old swing. This priceless commodity gave them their one escape from all the teenage hoopla that kept them on their toes. Although, a school night, everyone had some kind of activity. Lydia had forgotten her English Literature book. She planned to study for an upcoming test. Since the library was only a short distance, she came back. When she entered the foyer, she overheard a loud, heated exchange.

"Roy, how could you do this to me? I gave you all I had. Wasn't my love enough? I hate what you've done." Her aunt's yelling sounded more tension-filled than her usual blowing off steam.

"I'm sorry. Please forgive me, Regina. I never meant

to hurt you. I love you." Then his voice dropped to a murmur as if he sensed someone listening.

Whatever he said next caused even more distress. She cried out, "Roy, you're not serious! That's a ridiculously insane idea. He's your partner and your friend for God's sake. You'll sign your own death warrant. If you're not careful, that woman will find herself six feet under alongside you." Then her strongly authoritative tone softened. "We'll move forward, but I'll never forget your betrayal. If you do this, neither will her husband."

"I've got no choice anymore in the matter, Regina. I must make this right."

"You foolish, foolish man, how much is the truth worth?" her aunt asked.

It bothered Lydia that she never mentioned forgetting. It seemed even more baffling that her aunt stood firm on not forgiving. Lydia panicked. When she heard footsteps moving in her direction, she hid in the hall closet. She had long ago suspected that her aunt held many trump cards, including one that kept even the powerful Roy Mayers in line.

CHAPTER 15

That long sabbatical made Jessie finally realize how much she missed her hospital and her city.

"Good morning, please tell Dr. Barnes I'd like a minute of his time," Jessie said.

"Of course, Doctor." The receptionist buzzed him and announced Jessie's presence. The door opened wide. Dr. Barnes stepped out. His perfectly aligned teeth sparkled against his dark complexion.

"Hold my calls," he said as he turned to the receptionist.

"Yes, Doctor."

The receptionist stared in disbelief as he grabbed Jessie and held her affectionately. She'd never seen him react to any woman that way and certainly not another doctor.

Oh no, Jessie thought. Like hot coals, his touch seared her clothing, her flesh.

"Come in, Dr. Cooper, it's good to have you back. Now, let's hear all about your travels."

His exuberant reception literally knocked Jessie off of her feet. She could barely catch her breath.

A brief overview of her travels took all of ten

minutes. That's all she could manage and keep the icy barrier around her heart from melting. Before this sexy, hot-blooded man took her into his arms, she owned her life. Totally shaken now, she sat on her trembling hands while he explained some administrative changes. Her mind continued to spin making anything he said impossible to remember. She kept reliving his touch. The feeling scared her. Had she sensed something more reflective than a casual friendship taking shape?

"Welcome home."

For a second time, the sincerity in his greeting caused her skin to tingle all over.

"Dr. Barnes, thank you for the time off."

"No problem."

They stood up. When their hands came together, she felt more alive than she had in a very long time. *What to do, what to do?* she thought. Had she imagined his touch? No, it felt too real. Suddenly, a buzzing noise redirected her thoughts.

He picked up the phone. Annoyance registered in his abruptness. "I've got to take this," he said.

Jessie closed the door then returned to her office. Despite the mounds of paperwork on her desk, her mind kept racing. Clearing away papers could wait. She left work early. Would he make another move? The shoes came off the minute she stepped inside her condo. Ironically, she and Lydia shared that trait, too. The flashing light grabbed her attention. She hit play.

"Jessie, I'm sorry about our short visit. If you're free for a late dinner tonight call me."

His sexy voice pierced her reasoning. She tried, but she couldn't disband the memory of his touch. Only one other man had ever caused the same emotional stirring. After all these years, she hadn't figured out how to completely let him go. After Cooper's death, Jessie engaged

in too many unhealthy affairs. Her reason—they prevent-
ed her heart from taking any more shocking blows. It
worked—until now.

All at once, a wave of embarrassment swept over
her. True, she flaunted all those meaningless affairs. A
fabrication of half-truths created most of her infamous
reputation, but she didn't bother setting the record
straight.

Dr. Barnes had heard all the rumors coming out of
that gossip-filled breeding ground. Spies lurked around
every corner then reported back to him. One day it happened.

"Sit down, Dr. Cooper." The authority in Dr.
Barnes's voice raised her stress level a notch. Had she
unknowingly jeopardized the wellness of one of her patients? Oh God, she hoped not.

"How're the rotations going?"

"Very well, sir." Her voice trembled slightly.

"Dr. St. Johns is a great teacher. How's that working
out for you? Any problems?"

She unconsciously shifted her body as his eye's
searched her face for an answer.

"No problems," she replied bluntly. What had he
heard? She thought she saw disappointment in his eyes.
The idea of involving her boss in the intimate details of
her life felt too weird. She wanted to get out of there fast.

"Very well then, you may go, Dr. Cooper."

"Thank you, sir."

His uncomfortable inquisition worried her. He tried.
Jessie wouldn't let him help. Although he respected the
legendary Dr. St. Johns, he never liked the man.

↷↶↷

Perhaps, her mind was still a little foggy from her

trip abroad. Had Dr. Barnes really asked her out on a date? Jessie couldn't wait to get Lydia's reaction.

"Dr. G's office."

"Is she in? It's Dr. Cooper."

"Oh, hello, Dr. Cooper, just one minute please."

"Hey, Jessie, what's up?"

"Are you free for about an hour?"

"Sure. I bought tickets to a local performance tonight, but I can certainly spare an hour for a friend."

Like a monsoon, the rain came down hard all day only breaking momentarily. Then it started up again. Jessie stared out her window, watching a dark, ominous cloud form. Raindrops slowly trickled down her windowpane. Like a child, she traced the water droplets with her fingers. "Oh my goodness, I'm supposed to meet Lydia." Almost in a state of panic, she rushed out. Minutes later, Jennifer took her raincoat then showed her to Lydia's private booth.

By now, her rapidly climbing fear increased her agitation. For years, her guarded feelings presented the one constant in her life. Suddenly, she wasn't sure if her feelings needed protecting anymore. An internal emotional struggle raged with the thought of his caress—*Stop it!*

Jessie looked up as Lydia walked in, wet from head to toe. She and Jennifer chatted briefly, then Jennifer tossed Lydia's wind-shredded umbrella into the trash, hung up her raincoat, and walked off.

Lydia ran her fingers through her wet tangled mane, looking a little rattled, and then slid into the booth across from Jessie.

"Hey, Jessie, I just told Jennifer some nut almost sideswiped me on the way over here."

"You're kidding."

"Nope, came within inches."

"Rainy weather brings out the crazies like a full

moon. Glad you're okay." *Ah ha.* That accounted for her mood and her late arrival.

"Thanks, girl."

"May I bring you the usual, Dr. G.?" one of the regular waitresses asked.

"No, just water, with limes please."

"Dr. Cooper what can I get you?"

"The same please."

Jessie was different after her trip abroad. Then after their late night dinner, things changed between them. Jessie avoided her for a week. Perhaps, she regretted telling Lydia about her mother's affair. Unlike the colorful memories Lydia and her sisters shared, their friendship had no connection to their collective past experiences. Lydia believed real friends made great sounding boards and that the sounds they made bounced all around them without ever leaving the room.

"Lydia, Dr. Barnes left me a message on my personal answering machine. He asked me out on a date." The thought of calling him Dr. Barnes on a date seemed too formal. Like a school girl, she giggled.

"Jessie, that's wonderful." Lydia avoided the urge to say I told you so.

"Lydia, I'm scared."

"Of what, am I missing something? The man of every woman's dream asked you out on a date, and you can't decide? Jessie, he's a solid guy with the respect and loyalty of his colleagues."

Surprisingly, the rumor mill filtered only sketchy information about his private life through their pipeline. Lydia knew he always showed up at social functions with the same woman. That's the extent of what she could accurately pass along without arousing contempt for her colleagues' investigative techniques. Jessie allowed fear in without realizing it threatened the start of what Lydia saw as a beautiful partnership. She worried Jessie would do something dim-witted, like brushing him off.

Finally, Lydia grew tired of watching her hide from her fears. "Jessie, stop whining. You've spent most of your life running away from your past. Stop feeling sorry for yourself and grow the hell up!"

Jessie felt her friend's indignation, although she hadn't expected Lydia's sudden blast of fury. After soliciting her advice what did she expect?

"Go out and get to know him before deciding he's a waste of your time."

Her sulking lasted a few short minutes. "You're right. I'll call him when I get back home."

"No. Do it now." Still annoyed, Lydia got up and walked away. She read people very well and especially their motives. Dr. Barnes had made the first move. The next move belonged to Jessie.

Nervously, Jessie counted each ring, and then the ringing stopped. "Hello, Dr. Barnes, it's Dr. Cooper."

"Oh, hello, Dr. Cooper, I'm guessing you got my message."

"Yes, thanks for the invitation. Dinner sounds great. I look forward to it. I'll meet you this evening around seven o'clock at Jacksons', you know the place?"

He chuckled. "Yes, I'll see you then!"

How stupid, she thought. Everybody in town knew Jacksons'. Even after she fumbled the ball, the moment felt right.

"Done," she said looking up as Lydia approached the booth. They didn't bother ordering. Lydia grabbed her raincoat and left the remnants of her umbrella in the trash.

Lydia laughed. "Enjoy your evening. Call me later. I want all the dirt."

Jessie smiled. A few minutes later, she walked out.

Later that evening crowds filled the entrance, the patio and then spilled over into the bar. The hostess greeted a couple in front of Jessie and informed them of a twenty-five-minute wait. They didn't seem bothered.

Jessie looked across the room. Her date sat waiting at the bar. He nodded. Minutes ahead of Jennifer, he walked in her direction. The woman took Dr. Barnes's vacated seat. Her date squeezed in next to her.

"Good evening, Dr. Cooper." Jennifer smiled at her and then greeted the gentleman who stood next to her. "Good evening sir."

"Good evening," Dr. Barnes said.

"Dr. Cooper, it's wonderful to see you again. Dr. Giddens asked me to show you and your guest to her booth. They're out for the evening."

"Thanks, Jennifer, that's really very sweet of Lydia."

Jessie knew they had gone into the city. Lydia had her fingers crossed Jake would appreciate a little opera.

☙☙☙

The next morning, Lydia waited anxiously for Jessie's call. It happened three patient exams later.

"Girl, I'm dying to hear about last night. How did it go?"

Jessie hesitated then decided Lydia had waited long enough. She answered quickly.

"We had a wonderful time. He's a sweet, gentle man." After she satisfied Lydia's curiosity, learned the highlight of Lydia's evening. It came from an enjoyable highly acclaimed performance of Porgy and Bess. After the play, Lydia and Jake stopped for a light dinner. They got home pretty late.

"Any plans to see Dr. Barnes again?"

"Yes, Barry wants to take me to the theater."

Lydia teased. "Oh, it's Barry, and so soon."

"Well, I couldn't sit around all evening calling him Dr. Barnes, now could I? He cleared that up at the beginning of the evening. Thanks for the special seating."

"You're welcome. Hope Jennifer took good care of you guys?"

"Of course, you know Jennifer."

According to Jennifer's play by play, Dr. Barnes arrived several minutes earlier and took a seat at the bar. When he spotted Jessie, he made his move.

"Hello, Dr. Cooper," he said, extending his hand.

"Hello, Dr. Barnes."

"Please call me Barry."

Her voice trembled. "I'm Jessie," she said as she reached for his hand.

"Yes, I know." His lips formed a sexy little smile. They both laughed.

At work, he respectfully referred to her as Dr. Cooper except for that one time when her name rolled sweetly off of his tongue. The name Jessie sprang up from her daddy's fascination with the bad boys of the old west.

He derived immense pleasure from watching his beautiful daughter enter a room then totally dismantle a young man's conventional idea conjured up simply from her name. It was the name he had chosen.

"I'm glad you had fun, Jessie."

"I had a terrific time." Lydia heard the joy in her voice.

"Great, see you later."

The hospital rumor mill spread the news of their date all the way over to the clinic where Lydia worked. Rebecca heard through the same grapevine that he broke off his relationship with his long-time companion the next day.

త్రోల్

As usual, Jake got up early on a beautiful Saturday morning and went to work.

Elaine answered the door. "Hey, Lydia, you came alone?"

"Yes. Another project needed Jake's attention, again. Where's Maria?"

"Maria works too hard. I gave her the day off. I'm glad you made it."

"Me too. I'll see you in a minute." Lydia strolled down the long hallway and peeked into a room at the far end. "Hello, Uncle Edmond."

Barely blinking, he stared straight ahead. His tiny body looked unbelievably fragile. Those arms that once held her so lovingly hung down like twigs on a dead tree. Lydia feared if she breathed too loudly, his limbs would snap into microscopic fragments. She felt the weight of his sadness pulling her down. The misery was so heavy it stifled her breathing.

She gasped then kissed him good-bye. Her most enjoyable visits were now only a memory. When she walked out onto the deck, Elaine sat waiting with a glass of ice tea in her hand.

"Sit down, Lydia." Elaine saw her sadness. Most days when she looked into her husband's eyes, she saw a similar despair. "How's Jake?" she asked, hoping that a shift in the conversation would break the spell.

"Busy all the time."

"What about Alan?"

"Busy, too. Thank goodness, he finally hired another lawyer."

"Poor Alan! I can't imagine how difficult that decision was for him."

"Quite difficult, I'm afraid."

Then rather quickly Elaine changed the subject. "Lydia, tell me about the Alan you first met."

Lydia wasn't about to compartmentalize Alan's past. If she'd told her everything she knew, Elaine might start second guessing the man she married. Back then, Alan and her sister Pauline's outrageous shenanigans kept them in trouble. The thought made Lydia laugh out loud.

Elaine looked at her strangely. "Gee, what've I missed?"

"Oh, a little of this and a little of that." She laughed again before she spoke. "We met Alan and Mia shortly after our parents died. In his last year of college, Alan's motorcycle collided with a tree. He ended up in the hospital with a couple of broken bones, a mild concussion, and a cracked rib that punctured a lung. After his almost fatal mishap, he made a few minor adjustments."

"Thanks, Lydia."

"You're welcome." Lydia stood up.

"Will we see you soon?"

"Of course." Lydia hugged Elaine. Then she got into her car and drove back to the city.

CHAPTER 16

"Good morning, Dr. G."

"Good morning, Rebecca, how was your week-end?"

"It was wonderful. Rob and I officially moved in together this weekend."

"So soon, do you think that's wise?"

"I hope so."

Sensing her tension, Lydia asked, "What's wrong, Rebecca?"

"It's Rob. Some days I'm not sure if he wants a committed relationship and then other days he makes me wonder if it isn't all in my head. Don't get me wrong, he's a terrific guy, Dr. G."

Lydia understood. Sometimes, Rebecca saw him as a helpless patient and herself with limited power to ease his suffering. "For most of us, a failed relationship's our greatest fear. Just relax and take it slow."

"Thanks, Dr. G."

"You're welcome."

That tiny whisper of wisdom coming from someone she respected helped Rebecca put things into perspective. Lydia finished with her last patient then called it a day.

After her last hospital stay, she'd adopted a more modified work schedule.

When she got home, Jake had dinner on the table. "Hey, babe, anything exciting happened today?"

"You could say that."

"Oh?"

Lydia shared the highlighted portions of her conversation with Rebecca. He listened increasingly shocked at her unbiased insight. After dinner, she curled up in his arms. They watched a movie.

The next morning, Rebecca waited ready to share the most current hospital gossip. Once again, Jessie had everyone speculating about her love life. Rumors flew off shelves like sweets in a candy store. Someone saw Dr. Barnes in a jewelry store looking at rings. Lydia shook her head and walked off. As she headed in the direction of the first exam room, the receptionist lifted the phone in the air, "Doctor, it's for you."

"Dr. Giddens."

"Hey, girl, I'm dying to try on this cute dress I saw in a magazine. I showed it to Barry last night. He loved it. Feel like a little shopping in The Big Apple?"

Lydia didn't love shopping, but what girl wouldn't want to try it every once in a while. "Let me make sure Jake didn't plan anything. I'll call you back shortly."

The phone rang and rang and rang then finally she heard, "Jake Giddens's office."

"Is he in?"

"Hello, Dr. Giddens." His secretary, a feisty young grandmother, still enjoyed the party scene. "I'm sorry he's in a meeting. I've got two out sick. I'm swamped and fighting off a nasty headache." Then jokingly she said, "I partied way past my bedtime last night. I'll give him the message as soon as he's out of his meeting."

Lydia laughed. "Thanks. Be careful out there.

Among other things, those late nights will kill you."

"I'll do my best." Then she laughed too.

A half hour later, Jake called. "What's up, babe?"

"Jake honey, any plans for this weekend?"

"No, as a matter of fact, I may need to work."

"In that case, I'm going to New York with Jessie."

"Tell Jessie she's a life saver. I won't feel guilty leaving you alone all weekend."

She and Jake put a lot of effort into appearing happy, but they had a long way to go.

"Jessie, I'm in," replaced the customary hello.

Besides, who didn't love the energy of that city? Jessie arranged everything from transportation to hotel accommodations. Lydia refused to let Penn Station, her least favorite gateway, stand in the way of a shopping adventure. Very early Saturday morning, they boarded the train. Shortly before lunch, they stood in the lobby of their hotel. They put away their bags and walked around the corner to a nearby deli.

"Thanks for coming with me, Lydia."

"Are you kidding? Girl, I couldn't miss a trip to one of the most energetic cities in the world with my best friend."

Their laughter boomed like a loud clap of thunder rolling quickly across the sky. After a light snack, they hit the streets, dashing in and out of stores, stopping only long enough to catch their breath. They didn't break a sweat in weather so perfect it seemed unnatural. Dr. Barnes had an eye for beauty. The coral colored strapless dress with its matching cropped jacket against the backdrop of her dark complexion and toned body made Jessie look like a million bucks. Of course, she bought the outfit along with several other fun items which included a gorgeous lambskin satchel in a dark brown. Unlike Jessie, Lydia seldom splurged—until she tried on a pair of red bottom leopard-print heels that made her legs look out-of-this-world sexy. She couldn't resist.

All total, they spent an insane amount of money in a short amount of time. On the way back to the hotel, they purchased theater tickets for the evening performance.

The play and its talented cast of characters exceeded their wildest expectations. Following a late night dinner, they went back to the room. They enjoyed some keeping-it-real girl talk. Lydia believed women spending quality time together created a nurturing environment responsible for building a powerful free-spirited coalition. She jokingly said that she and her sisters stayed up many nights solving the world's problems while others took credit. Tonight, she and Jessie talked until the wee hours of the morning about everything.

"Do you love Barry?" Lydia asked then smiled, thinking it a bit too presumptuous to address the chief of medicine, the man who secured her position at the clinic even privately in such an informal manner.

"Yes. I've only experienced that feeling once before and just like Cooper, his touch awakened desires that make my heart flutter."

Wow. Lydia heard affirmation of love and lust in the same tone. "Jessie Cooper, you're insatiable. You do know that right?"

They laughed.

Then the laughter faded. Finally, Jessie confessed the ache she carried. Her husband's death broke her heart, but the unconditional love of two other men made her look closely at their sacrifice. One lost a daughter, and the other endured the disappointment of never knowing his child. "My heart loved the man I called Daddy. My head told me that the man responsible for my existence deserved the same love. I had to ask myself, how do I miss what I've never had?"

Lydia didn't respond. They slept late, ordered room service, and late Sunday afternoon boarded the train for home. During their fun-filled weekend, Lydia felt a strange pull toward her friend.

ɞɞɞ

Those early morning and late night calls always caused a chill to creep up Lydia's spine like a vine draping its tentacles unsuspectingly around an old willow tree. She'd just sat down to her first cup of coffee when her cell phone rang.

"Lydia! Lydia!" Danielle shouted.

"Danielle, what's wrong?"

"Aunt Regina's very sick. Pauline and I rushed to the hospital. The sergeant really looked worried. The doctors aren't saying much yet."

Jake picked up immediately as if he expected her call. "Hey, babe, is everything okay?"

"Aunt Regina's in the hospital. Danielle said her condition looks pretty serious. After I make this last call, I'm heading out. My flight leaves in a few hours."

"I'll come with you."

"No, I'll call if I need you."

"Lydia, are you sure?"

"Of course, I'm sure," she snapped.

"I'll check on you later. Call me as soon as you arrive," Jake said.

"I will."

Dr. Charles answered his page. He called Lydia back, immediately. After hearing his unbelievable prognosis, she moved quickly. The last time she saw her aunt, Regina looked like a mature poster girl for a healthy living magazine. Lydia's phone rang again. She froze, afraid the ringing meant more bad news.

"Hello, Lydia." Frank's jubilant masculine voice rang out. "Keisha just had the baby."

"What?"

"Keisha had the baby." He repeated those same words. "My baby girl gave her mother no choice." Then he excitedly reported mother and baby doing fine. "At six pounds ten ounces, Stormy Regina came here with her mother's attitude."

"God help her." They laughed. "Congratulations! Frank. Give Keisha my love. I'll share the exciting news with everybody."

At precisely that moment, Lydia exerted her authority. Not only that, she took ownership of the situation. The other news could wait. Anyway, Keisha couldn't travel today.

The cab driver dropped Lydia at the curb then placed her bags on the sidewalk in front of the airport terminal. As soon as she stepped inside, she got into a long security line. Carefully, she observed people tossing small carry-on bags and other personal items into plastic bins that traveled along a conveyor belt. Even the heightened security didn't diminish her spirits. She trembled as her mind categorized a host of memories.

The trip marked her third this year. Each drew Lydia closer to her roots. Like the times before, she came back uncertain of what the future held for her family. In and out of crisis, her aunt's conviction, her iron grip held them together. Surviving the challenges in life without her aunt seemed unimaginable. Lydia shook her head in hopes of dislodging the terrible thoughts scurrying about like mice in search of food.

When Danielle's question popped into Lydia's head, it forced her to face an inevitable. The next generation wasn't a bunch of little old ladies sitting around in their rocking chairs lost in senility. Another thought frightened her. Who would she turn to for advice? Her aunt tackled difficult tasks without flinching. She welcomed change. Lydia's mind kept searching for reassurance in places littered with self-doubt and worry. Subconsciously, she heard the dinging and watched the *Fasten your seat belt sign* flash its warning. Like most frequent flyers, she ignored the mundane sights and sounds around her, except for the screeching of the landing gear as it safely broadcast her arrival.

Lydia pulled out her cell phone and made a quick call. "Danielle, I'm here, I'll grab my bag." Then she placed her phone back in her purse. She walked out as Danielle pulled up. Lydia threw her bag into the back seat then leaned over, and gave her sister a quick peck on the cheek. *No hello, big sister, or how are you?* Lydia thought. Danielle looked a mess. Her nappy edges cried out for a relaxer. Those blood shot eyes made her look like a wayward drunk in need of, but not searching for, an AA meeting.

"How's Aunt Regina?" Lydia asked.

"She's weak and not responding to the medication."

They made small talk. Of course, they stayed away from the topic of their aunt's failing health. God forbid if her dying crossed their minds. Lydia felt like a soldier heading into combat. Her warrior spirit was her weapon of choice. The enemy had many names, but its aim remained the same. Believing that God undoubtedly had a plan, she held steadfast to her faith.

She remembered her first test. It came early in her childhood. They've kept right on coming. Lydia and her sister Danielle shared a lifetime of memoires. Today, cloaked in deafening silence, they felt like total strangers. As soon as they reached the hospital, she jumped out of the car and headed straight to Dr. Charles's office. His nurse said she would find him on the second floor. Lydia took the stairs. She found him standing in front of the nurse's station.

"Good afternoon, Dr. Charles. I'm Dr. Giddens. We spoke earlier today."

"Oh, hello, Dr. Giddens, it's nice to finally meet you." Then he stretched forth his hand.

"Thank you."

His immaculate crew cut made him appear even younger than she'd imagined. "My sister's enrolled at St. Mary's specializing in pediatrics," he said. "It's a great teaching facility."

"I know. What a small world," she said.

They took the stairs. Together, they walked into an office decorated in shades of brown and black, set against a backdrop of glaring white walls. A vase of freshly cut flowers sat next to a black and white portrait that captured the essence of his family: a wife, three children, one girl, and two boys.

Medical journals stacked in a neat, orderly pile rested on the opposite side of the desk. His many degrees lined one wall. A collage of patient snapshots lined the other in a well-illustrated professional panel. Everything fit perfectly together.

"Please, sit down."

The slight hint of concern in his voice alarmed her. Her hands felt moist, as if she'd held them up to the sky and intercepted the morning dew. Then she remembered her aunt saying that fear was only fear when you succumbed to it.

Mentally, Lydia counted to ten, took a deep breath, and waited.

"Dr. Giddens," he began, "the surgery's necessary. Several clogged arteries leading to her heart need cleaning out. Right now, she's feverous and weak. Her elevated fever is the result of a virus attaching her body. Dr.

Matthews, her cardiologist, will perform the surgery once her fever breaks."

"Open heart surgery?"

"Yes. The standard procedure creates a greater, uglier risk. It takes longer. A robotic arm will help Dr. Matthews navigate the less invasive surgery."

The only time Lydia not so courageously watched a colleague crack open a patient's chest like a walnut, blood rushed to her cheeks, fear stole her voice, and she left her lunch on the observation room floor. Thank goodness Dr. Matthews opted for the less invasive method.

Finally, Lydia asked, "What about the scar?" If for no other reason than vanity, a tiny scar would certainly improve her aunt's attitude.

"This procedure leaves minimum scaring," Dr. Charles said.

"May I see her now?"

"Of course, I'll show you the way."

They walked out into the outer office.

Danielle stood up. "I believe you know my sister," Lydia said.

"Yes, it's good to see you again, Mrs. Camden."

Danielle's bewildered eyes stretched wide, but she left her questions for the person she trusted with everything. They left his office and took the elevator to ICU. When the door opened, Pauline ran into Lydia's arms.

Her aunt stirred then looked up. "Lydia, what're you doing here? You've got important work back home. Dr. Charles and Dr. Matthews can handle this minor glitch."

Lydia kissed her gently. Then she reassured her aunt that things back home would progress just fine without her. Of course, Lydia didn't dare say her condition presented a greater risk than any minor inconvenience. She knew Aunt Regina could die.

Dr. Charles checked Regina's vitals. Lydia kept their visit brief. Regina needed her rest. Pauline, Danielle, and the sergeant followed Lydia into the waiting room. They listened as she explained in layman terms the type of surgery and the associated risk. Lydia told them their aunt needed open heart surgery then prepared them for a long wait. The confidence in her voice gave them comfort. Lydia had done her job. Her earlier search showed both doctors had impeccable credentials, especially Dr. Matthews, the trail blazer. His record showed him instrumental in robotic cutting edge technology. Perhaps, if he needed a consultation, she knew that he was also a close personal friend of Dr. Martin.

Her sisters and the sergeant had spent every waking minute at the hospital. "Guys, I'm here now. Go home, and I'll call if anything changes," Lydia said.

Weariness won them over. They reluctantly agreed. Alone in the room, she sat quietly watching her aunt take one difficult breath and then another. The doctors had done everything humanly possible. The fever just wouldn't abate.

Lydia knew what she had to do. "God," she said, "I can't lead this family without her. Not yet. Please restore her strength. Amen."

Throughout the night Lydia dozed as nurses popped in and out of the room monitoring and administering medication. Somewhere in between her interrupted sleep, Lydia heard a faint voice calling out. Quickly, she moved to her aunt's bedside.

"Lydia," Regina whispered, "I'm very tired."

Fear gripped Lydia's heart. The muscles in her body grew tense. Patsy had made the same declaration before saying her final goodbye.

Immediately, her aunt saw the muscles in Lydia's face tighten. "Don't worry, child. I'm not going anywhere yet. I believe He has a few more things left down here for me to do."

Lydia crawled into bed next to her. There she stayed until her aunt fell asleep. The fever continued all night and throughout the next day. Shortly before midnight, the fever left her body. Lydia called her family right away with the good news. She knew they were waiting.

Oh no, Keisha, she thought. Her sisters didn't possess the stamina required for handling their hot-tempered sister. No problem. That job now belonged to her. Lydia rationalized that the new baby probably had her sleep walking. Anyway, she figured the news could wait a little longer. When morning came, Keisha took forever and then came a very alert, "Hello."

"Hello, Keisha."

"What's up big sister? I'm so glad you called. Frank and I talked. We want you and Jake as Stormy's Godparents."

"I'm honored. I'm sure Jake will be also." Keisha's request came as a surprise. Lydia paused.

"Is anything wrong?" Keisha's discernment kicked in.

Each of her sisters had some measure of it. Without any further delay, Lydia jumped right in. "Aunt Regina needs open-heart surgery. It's scheduled for some time later today."

Keisha screamed. Her hostility surged like a bolt of lightning through the phone line. Then she spewed language so fiery Lydia felt she might need special clearance if ever called upon to repeat those words.

"Why didn't you call me right away?" Keisha yelled. Explaining that she'd just given birth had no impact on her. "Lydia, don't ever play your silly games with me again. Not ever. I'm on my way."

All at once, Lydia heard absolutely nothing, except

for the sound of her own breathing. Sarcastically she said out loud, "That went well," and then placed her cell phone back in her pocket. Honestly, she knew her timing sucked.

Her family came prepared for a long wait. Danielle rested her head on Mark's shoulder while Rick and the sergeant went to the cafeteria to get coffee for everyone. By now, most of them probably needed a strong shot of caffeine. Nervously, Pauline paced back and forth like a caged animal.

Shortly before noon, Jake arrived. He wrapped his arms around her. "Are you okay, babe?" he asked.

"I'm fine. Thanks for coming."

He disregarded her impersonal comment, greeted everyone, and sat down.

The fever flared up again delaying her surgery. Finally, after two hours, Regina's fever broke.

Keisha arrived several hours after they wheeled Regina into the operating room. Leaving her newborn with a sitter terrified Keisha. On the other hand, leaving her in Frank's care had her rethinking that decision, too. He held her as if she would break and jumped straight up in bed if she sneezed. He hardly slept through the night anymore. Watching her tiny chest move up and down assured him that she was still breathing. In the end, Keisha decided on Frank. Hopefully, she'd made the right choice. Both of them had their own struggles to overcome as new parents. Keisha greeted Pauline and Danielle with open arms. Then she grabbed Lydia. Their bodies locked. "You can't do this alone, you know. I understand your role," she whispered softly.

Lydia always wondered if any of her sisters other than Patsy knew she had an obligation to take care of her family.

Dr. Matthews walked out of the operating room six

hours later. His sweat soaked scrubs clung to his torso, revealing all muscle. Everyone jumped to their feet. "The surgery went extremely well. Let's give it an hour and then we'll see how she's feeling."

"Thank you," they said. Their unified voices clamored like glaciers breaking apart in a space so cold, Lydia swore the windows shook. An hour passed. No word. Everyone started getting nervous again. Lydia found the doctor. The fever had come back. After an hour of close monitoring, the doctor brought them the good news. Finally, the fever was gone.

"You can see her now. Please keep the visits short. She's still very weak."

Lydia looked over at the sergeant and then at her sisters. Then looking back at him, she exercised her authority publicly for the first time. "Go ahead. I believe she's waiting to see you."

He nodded then followed Dr. Charles. When the sergeant entered the room, Regina looked up and smiled. The probability of any man loving this charismatic and stunningly beautiful woman from a distance certainly seemed impossible. He leaned down and kissed her gently on the lips. "Glad you decided to stick around, gorgeous."

"Me, too."

"Marry me, Regina?"

"Yes."

Strangely, her answer came without hesitation. Then her eyes closed. Sleep returned. He could only hope the medication hadn't inspired her answer. His heart fluttered. When he re-entered the waiting room, he had a noticeable bounce in his step. Lydia didn't need a tarot card reading to state the obvious. After his visit, Lydia carefully monitored each visit. Danielle and her family went in first. Pauline and Rick followed. Lydia sighed every time a relief-plastered face emerged from her room. Finally, Keisha went in.

"I'm a grandmother again," Regina said with pride filling her eyes.

"Yes, Aunt Regina. Stormy Regina is doing just fine."

"Thank God. Stormy Regina, that's such a lovely name. Thank you, sweetheart."

"You're welcome." They talked about family, life back in California and Frank. Keisha planted a kiss on her cheek, then whispered "I love you," before walking out.

While they sat around waiting, Keisha joyfully showed off pictures of her tiny bundle of joy. The light in Keisha's eyes shimmered.

"Jake, please go ahead, Aunt Regina's waiting."

"Come with me, Lydia."

"No, she's getting tired. I'm here all night. She needs to see all of her family."

He stayed just a few minutes. After he walked out, Lydia peeked in.

Her aunt raised her feeble hand and beckoned her inside. "Hey there, my girl."

"Hey, Aunt Regina." Then Lydia leaned down and kissed her forehead. "How're you feeling?"

"Much better. We still need to talk." Her eyelids drooped. Her soft babbling sounded more like a whisper. Lydia leaned closer. "Barton asked me to marry him. I said yes."

Then she drifted off again, unable to see the shock on Lydia's face. From a conversation on a distance shore, Lydia learned marriage scared Regina. Now, it looked like dying scared her more. Lydia stepped back into the waiting room. Their eyes locked. He held her gaze. Fearing the answer he'd sought for such a long time was a bit premature, the sergeant looked worried. As Lydia approached, his heart beat faster and faster, producing a sound so loud his ears popped. She moved in slow motion. *That's Lydia*, he thought, *methodical and in control.*

He allowed his mind to tease him with doubt. Maybe, he only heard what he wanted to hear. Timidly, he asked, "Lydia, did I hear her correctly?"

"You did." Instantly, his grin stretched from ear to ear. "Perhaps you should make an announcement," she continued. "The family could use some more good news right about now."

"Are you sure it's okay?"

"Positive."

The room grew very quiet. All eyes fell upon them. Gradually, her aunt had begun to step aside. To Lydia's surprise, some of them had paid attention. Even the sergeant realized he needed her blessing.

"What's going on guys?" Danielle asked.

Then her other sisters chimed in. He stepped into the center of the room. Lydia's private permission, coupled with her public approval, gave him confidence. He no longer feared the medication coerced Regina's answer. If he had, he didn't know Regina Mayers at all.

"Everybody!" His loud, overly dramatic voice rose to a shout. Everyone faced him. "Regina agreed to marry me."

Cheers rang out.

"Hoorah! It's time to plan a wedding," Pauline said.

Danielle shot her an annoying stare. "I'd like to wait until Aunt Regina's out of the hospital before planning a wedding, Pauline."

Embarrassed, Pauline lowered her eyes.

Lydia sent everyone home. She took the first shift. Jake came prepared, but she insisted he get some rest, too. He and his team had spent the last week working some very unforgiving long hours, triple checking DNA samples on a very gruesome double murder and suicide. A mother allegedly shot and killed her adult daughters before she took her own life. The police found some inconsistencies in the story of the mother's live-in boyfriend. The authorities needed the lab results before they could file charges.

Lydia folded her body into an uncomfortable chair that failed miserably at converting into a bed. Finally, after hours of tossing and turning, she found a semi-comfortable position.

The next morning, her sisters arrived not a moment too soon. Lydia woke with aches and pains in every part of her body. On the drive to her aunt's house, she thought about her future. Jake met her at the door and swept her into his arms. That long overdue shower could wait. He'd prepared breakfast. She ate, showered, and plopped down on the sofa tucked securely in his arms. Sleep came fast. Sometime later, she woke and followed the smell of freshly brewed coffee.

"Thanks again for coming."

"I need you to need me, Lydia."

Where had that come from? she thought. Of course, she needed him. She just couldn't say those words anymore. Not yet, anyway.

He grabbed his bag and walked out to the waiting cab.

"I'll miss you, babe."

"Me too," she said then waved goodbye.

CHAPTER 17

Lydia and her sisters rotated in and out of their aunt's hospital room every night for a week. When Regina came home, Nurse Rosa Lee Mooney came, too. They couldn't ignore Regina's loud protest. So, after much discussion on whether she could care for herself, they reached a compromise. Nurse Mooney took the day shift. The sergeant gladly agreed to monitor her nights. No surprise there.

Keisha stuck her head in the door. "Come on in sweetheart," Aunt Regina said.

"Hey Aunt Regina, How do you feel?"

"Pretty good."

Keisha sat down on the edge of her bed. "I've got to get back. Stormy needs me, but mostly Frank," Keisha joked. "I'll always be grateful for the all love and support you and Uncle Roy gave us throughout the years."

"Sweetheart, for our children, Roy and I always did what we had to do. Together, we did the necessary." As she shut the door to their open discussion, Regina whispered softly, "I love you, Keisha."

"I love you too, Aunt Regina." Keisha walked back into the family room where Lydia sat waiting.

They stayed up past midnight talking. "How's life in California?" Lydia asked.

"Good."

"What about you and Frank?"

"Better than I ever imagined. I know he loves me, Lydia. I see it in his eyes more now than ever before."

"Has he ever given you a reason to question his love?"

"No, but deep down I worried he still loved you."

"That's not possible, honey. You're the one who captured his heart. He loves you. I love you." Then Lydia gave her a big teddy bear hug.

"Thanks, Lydia, I love you, too."

They talked a while longer then said goodnight. The Mayers' household had order once again. Her aunt had Nurse Mooney and the sergeant. They policed her every move. Nobody knew how long either of them would last. They could only hope for the best. Very early, Pauline and Danielle dropped Keisha at the airport. When they returned, Lydia was sitting at the kitchen table with the newspaper in one hand and a cup of tea in the other.

"Where's Aunt Regina?" Danielle asked.

"Taking a nap."

Lydia smiled up at Danielle, her adorable sister. For better or worse, Lydia now owned everybody's secrets. Regina had kept an eye on everything happening in her family, especially Mark's gambling. He had no idea he walked a tightrope.

Their aunt lacked tolerance. Since Danielle couldn't shut her husband down, Lydia knew, for Mark's sake, she had to step in. After Lydia had that little talk with Mark, he began consulting Danielle on just about everything. His gambling quickly lost its appeal.

Honestly, Lydia hadn't realized he frightened so easily.

"How's the patient?" Pauline asked just as Lydia took another sip of tea.

"An attitude adjustment wouldn't hurt. Nurse Mooney has her hands full dealing with her."

Danielle turned, startled to see their aunt standing behind her. Their laughter sounded so inviting Regina had decided she would join them. Once again, those lively brown eyes sparkled. The earlier tension that threatened their hope no longer held any power over them. Lydia remained seated. She watched their affectionate display like a spectator enjoying a live Broadway show. Although, Lydia didn't applaud or bow, she acknowledged a great performance by simply blowing her sisters a kiss.

Lydia stood up and pulled back a chair. "Come sit here, Aunt Regina."

Her sisters always vied for their aunt's affection. Like any good parent, Regina always gave them a word of wisdom. Before she spoke, Lydia imagined her aunt's thoughts twirling gently like windmills perched high upon a Texas hillside.

"Girls, I've missed the spirit of laughter and joy you brought into this house the day you came. I miss everything about those times."

"Oh, Aunt Regina, I'm sure you don't miss my exploits," Pauline said, casting her eyes downward.

Who could've forgotten the hell Pauline stirred up? Lydia thought.

"My sweet, sweet girls, I miss everything. That journey brought all of us where we stand today. I wouldn't trade any of those blemished memories for a bushel of wholesome ones. Every unexpected turn helped define and shape this family. I'm grateful for the journey."

Pauline gave her aunt a big hug. Danielle poured everyone another cup of tea. These school girls who were now all grown up, once again sat around drinking tea and reminiscing. Everybody shared a tale from days gone by. Danielle bragged about her role as the son her uncle never had. Lydia reminded them of the time a boy with a crush on her asked her uncle's permission to take her out on a date. His massive presence, not to mention his thunderous voice, scared that boy nearly to death. Lydia swore he wet his pants. They went out once. He never asked her again. It had nothing to do with her uncle. He wasn't the one.

Every time Lydia told that story, they laughed hysterically. The things Lydia knew, but didn't say, would've shocked almost everyone around the table, except, of course, her aunt.

"Girls, the wedding's in three months," their aunt announced.

"That's wonderful!"

Her sisters appeared overjoyed. Lydia didn't feel the same excitement. She hated the idea that someone unaware of her struggles could possibly displace the memory of a man who taught her courage in the face of adversity. Early in her childhood, Lydia's dreams seemed more real than her reality. One night a bad dream chased her out of bed and into the kitchen where her uncle sat deep in thought. "Child, what are you doing up so late?"

"I can't sleep. I miss my mama and daddy," she whimpered.

Bravely, she tried to control her tears, but they came anyway. They warmed his heart.

Her Uncle Roy reached out then pulled her into his powerful arms. His booming voice softened. "It's okay to cry, Lydia. Dying is easy. It's living that's hard. Always remember, Regina and I love you girls."

Every time fear crept near, her uncle's comforting words barricaded the door.

Lydia remained visibly quiet, deep in thought. Somewhere in the distance, she heard her aunt say don't plan anything fancy. Of course, her sisters heard nothing after the wedding date.

Suddenly, Nurse Mooney entered the room. Her presence interrupted Lydia's private thoughts.

"It's time for your medication, Mrs. Mayers."

Their sophisticated aunt looked at her nurse and rolled her eyes. They couldn't believe it. Nurse Mooney ignored the attitude, administered her medicine, and then walked her back to her room. They fell to the floor laughing. Danielle held her stomach as she doubled over in pain. Tears rolled down Pauline's cheeks. Lydia tiptoed to the door, looked down the hallway, and then burst out laughing along with her sisters. The day kept getting better and better.

"We'll talk later, Lydia," they said after regaining their composure.

"Take care of her after I'm gone. You know she thinks she's a big girl," Lydia said.

"Absolutely!" And with one last laugh, her sisters closed the door behind them.

Lydia was still sitting at the kitchen table reading. "See you tomorrow, Dr. Giddens."

Lydia looked up from her paper. "You too and enjoy your evening, Mrs. Mooney."

Tonight, Lydia had the sergeant's post covered. Her aunt walked in and sat down across from her. "I'm glad you came back." Lydia got up, cleared the dinner plates, and then started putting them in the dishwasher.

"Leave them. Come! Sit back down."

Lydia obeyed. She sensed her aunt had something important on her mind.

"You're remarkably strong, Lydia. Never doubt your ability to do the right thing for the greater good."

Lydia strained to hear the faint words falling from her lips. Then her voice slowly rose above a whisper. Her message became very clear. "Lydia, our shipwrecked family survived over the years on broken pieces. Those difficulties made us strong. Out of them, a little black book with a family's encrypted secrets evolved. Who would ever believe searching for one insignificant book opened another more powerful one?"

One evening while searching her husband's study for a book borrowed, Regina's eyes fell upon a single newspaper clipping about a man found shot execution style in an alley. She froze when she saw the scribbled footnote of a $10,000 payment wired to Manny and the words, JOB WELL DONE in big bold red letters. No more pretending she hadn't suspected his involvement in their lives before that night. Now, in her hands, she held the difference between suspecting and knowing her husband's involvement in many things.

In the summers, he spent most of his time at the racetrack. Roy loved the horses and her, but not in that order. Certainly, he had a weakness for both. Shortly after they married, he and a friend formed a partnership in an import-export business. The venture kept him traveling between California and a few other east coast cities. The job had a downside. His constant travel and those spur of the moment trips drove her mad. They had argued before he left. When he returned, he found her still agitated. He pulled her into his arms and kissed her passionately on the lips. "Regina darling, I've missed you."

"Cut it out, Roy!" she shouted. Her anger apparent, she pushed him away. "Why don't you get cleaned up? Dinner's ready. The girls are out for the evening."

Regina sat down. He sensed something troubling her as he took his seat. His stomach growled. Dinner no longer looked appetizing. Her hands shook so violently her fork made a clanging sound as it hit her plate. She got up and placed the clipping down in front of him. He stared at it. When he looked up, he reaffirmed a very disturbing truth about the death of Ray Madsen, Pauline's ex-boyfriend. That discovery introduced Regina to a world she would later dominate.

Late at night while the girls slept, Roy and Regina discussed family business. Those nights while pretending she was asleep, Lydia overheard many things, some disturbing, others wonderful and worth marveling over. With the stroke of a pen, unfit parents eagerly forfeited their parental rights. Across the city, homeless shelters and centers for battered women received quarterly monetary gifts. These men, Roy, Edmond, and Jackson, made sacrifices for their families and for people they would never meet. The conviction in Regina's voice clearly showed that she supported those decisions.

All of them had highly visible imperfections. Roy's quiet reserve and fierce loyalty outweighed his faults. Sometimes, late at night, Lydia heard them arguing. Mostly, she heard the irritation in her aunt's voice. Her uncle never raised his voice. Usually, he said his piece and walked away. One time, her aunt got steaming mad and locked him out of their bedroom.

Today, her aunt couldn't stop talking. At times, Lydia followed her without effort. Then the conversation took a sharp turn. Had Lydia focused strictly on the agony in Regina's trembling voice, she might've missed an important message.

"Sweetheart, Roy's promise kept his affair from ending up with the rest of their secrets." Lydia's mouth flew open. "Sure, I knew before he told me what I dreaded hearing out loud. Suspicion's one thing, it's the knowledge that destroys all hope. I tried pretending this heartbreak wasn't real, but the pain came as a sharp reminder. His confession felt like an exploding boulder with a million pieces of rock flying toward me at full force. I accepted his moment of weakness. Unfortunately, I never forgave him."

Who was this man? Lydia thought. Surely, her aunt wasn't talking about her Uncle Roy. Lydia saw in her pain-soaked expression how much strength it took to reveal a disturbing fault in the man she loved. "I'm so sorry, Aunt Regina."

"Oh, it's okay, child. It hurt, but I loved him too much. I couldn't let him go. Pride's a beast, Lydia. The woman competing for his affection had a husband and two daughters, one born early in her marriage and a second born later. My husband and his mistress had a love child."

Her shocking piece of news discharged a torrential downpour of questionable feelings that left Lydia struggling with Jake's unfaithfulness. Regina grabbed Lydia's hands and squeezed tightly. "True love continues to love, despite the sins of the flesh. You made the right call even though forgetting and forgiving are light years apart. You'll figure out what needs to be done when the time comes."

Forgiveness, yes that was the word Lydia searched for among all the clutter in her head. Had she forgiven Jake's affair? How had her aunt found out? She quickly dismissed her dilemma and focused on her aunt's confession.

"Honey, that chapter of my life's over, and I settled the score. I promised I'd love him 'till death do us part.' I kept my promise."

"Why did you keep his secret?" Lydia asked.

"It belonged to him. It wasn't mine to share. After all, he was head of the family. Regardless, he knew that one day he would pay."

Lydia fidgeted. Her impatience showed. Slowly, her aunt spelled out the remainder of the story. "Roy kept a promise that protected the mother of his child. Despite his best efforts, he couldn't salvage my trust. As his life partner, I respected his decision. Of course, I didn't agree with him. We may suffer the consequences of our decisions, but we honor our promises. His daughter belongs in this family with all of his girls. I owe him that much at least."

Frustrated, Lydia blurred out the next question. "Where does his daughter live?"

"Jessie lives in Philadelphia."

Lydia gasped. "No way, not Jessie—Jessie Cooper?"

"Yes my darling, Jessie Cooper."

"Does she know?"

"Yes. Sadly, she missed a lifetime of his love. You and your sisters knew all too well what that felt like. Jessie's mother told her about him much too late. Of course, Jessie knew before she came to my birthday party. That weekend, I gave her my blessing. I needed to do this one final thing for him."

Lydia looked back, and, when she did, things looked a lot clearer, starting with Jessie's confession at dinner after too many glasses of wine. Later, at their graduation, Lydia got the distinct impression her aunt and Jessie knew each other. It didn't seem possible, even though Lydia felt sure that, somehow, she missed the connection. Then at her aunt's birthday party, Lydia noticed that her aunt tried to carefully pluck bits and pieces of Jessie's life from her.

"How're your parents, Jessie?" Aunt Regina had asked.

"They're wonderful."

"Where do they live?"

"Martha's Vineyard," Jessie said.

"Does your father enjoy island living?"

"He loves it."

"What about your mother?"

Lydia noticed her tone suddenly reeked of jealousy. Something seemed wacky.

"Mother loves the island, too." Jessie's eyes burned brightly, knowing that she and Lydia's aunt shared a secret. In time, her cue would come directly from Mrs. Mayers.

Back up. Settled the score? Lydia thought. What had her aunt meant?

Gradually, Regina started entrusting Lydia with their secrets. With each uncovered deed, she understood the importance of her role. Confessing his sin and giving up his daughter was more difficult than anything her uncle had ever done. Lydia had the easy part. She simply tossed pages filled with questionable conduct into the flames of an open fireplace. Then she watched the embers flicker, jump, and spit as specks of ashes floated upon hot air before falling back down into the rubble. The fire burned away only those things not worth remembering. Over many years, Lydia had stored all those tiny nuggets away.

Then it happened. Regina opened a door only she could shut. "Please forgive me this one last thing, Lydia."

Oh, no, what else? Lydia thought. Her aunt's eyes filled with the age-old suffering of time as she prepared to disclose a secret too painful to speak out loud. She pulled a small tape recorder from her robe pocket, set it on the table, hit play, then left the room. Lydia heard a familiar voice along with that of an unidentified man.

"Mr. James sent me. Your husband's the mark, right?" the unidentified voice asked in a cold, emotionless voice.

"Yes."

"Are you sure about this, Mrs. Mayers?" he asked again in the same frosty less animated voice.

"Yes, I'm sure."

The vengefulness in those words moved Lydia to tears. She heard the clicking of high heels against the pavement as the woman hurried away. With a loud pop, the recorder shut off. Shocked and gasping for air, Lydia shook her head from side to side. She felt her body falling deeper and deeper into a damp, dark place like the confines of an old abandoned well. The more she clawed and struggled the farther she sank.

Finally, Lydia knew what Regina had meant. "Oh God," Lydia cried out.

Those monstrous words kept ringing in her ears over and over again. As her throat tightened, she stumbled over to the sink, coughing and choking on the madness of her aunt's deed.

At that moment, Regina reappeared. She poured a glass of water and handed it to Lydia. "Drink this," she demanded.

"This isn't possible," Lydia said.

"Possible and true, I'm afraid," her aunt replied. "Sins are forgivable. It's the consequences that leave the scars. No injustice goes unpunished. It demands full restitution. Always remember that when dispensing justice. No one is exempt, not even me."

"Why did you do this? I thought you loved him?"

"With all my heart, but I loved the power more. You're the new gatekeeper, Lydia. Your decisions will affect this family going forward. Strong leaders make tough decisions sometimes. Just remember, power can be intoxicating and, if you don't control it, eventually, it will control you."

Even with all the noise going on in her head, Lydia heard and understood every heartbreaking word. Still, she had more questions. "Who's this Mr. James? How did you meet him?"

"He's the only daddy Jessie ever knew. Our paths crossed for the first time via an anonymous correspondence."

"Aunt Regina, surely you're not serious."

"Very."

Lydia's face registered the same shock heard in her voice. Life came at her so fast, her body swayed, as if the ground beneath her shook. They had known each other a long time. She never thought to ask Jessie her maiden name. It never seemed important.

"Aunt Regina, why on earth would he agree to help you?"

"Revenge, plain and simple, Roy betrayed him, too. They were business partners and friends."

"OMG! The affair. Aunt Regina, where did you get the tape?"

"From a cowardly little creature working for Max that he mistakenly trusted."

"Blackmail?"

"A failed attempt, but a lesson nonetheless. Max allowed a traitor into his camp. Eventually, he took care of the problem. He had no choice. Never leave secrets lying around. The enemy will use them to destroy you."

It wasn't just about the enemy anymore. How could Lydia accept what her aunt had done, even if she understood her reason?

Deep down, she feared her aunt's decision reflected her moral standards, too. Their unspoken code of flawed ethics got in the way sometimes.

"I'm tired, Lydia, I'm going to lie down for a few minutes."

"Wait, Aunt Regina, your medicine." Lydia's emotions kept bouncing all over the place, until the wind chimes whistling in the soft breeze outside the window corralled them. Her aunt looked feeble once again as she forced the pills down one at a time. The strain of disclosing such a horrendous truth had clearly zapped her strength.

"Thank you. Goodnight, Lydia." Then she walked down the hall to her bedroom. The door closed quietly behind her. Three powerful men and one extremely supportive and equally powerful woman kept them safe all these years. With a heavy heart, Lydia wondered who would stand with her. Clearly, Jake wasn't the one.

CHAPTER 18

Lydia had her own life back in Philly. This visit took longer than she expected.

When she heard the phone ring, she ran back inside.

"Hey, Rick."

"Are you heading out, Lydia?"

"Yep."

"Be safe, here's Paulee," he said. He'd given Pauline that nickname early on in their courtship.

"Oh, hey, girl, I hate to see you go. I'll miss you."

"I'll see you in a few months for the wedding."

"I can't wait," Pauline said.

"That's the doorbell. I've gotta go. I'll see you soon," Lydia said.

The sergeant arrived on time. When their aunt made a decision, no one argued with her.

"Hello, Sergeant."

"Lydia, it's good to see you again. Ready?"

"Sure."

The sergeant smiled at his soon-to-be bride and blew her a kiss. "Good to see you, gorgeous."

"And you too, sir." Then she gave him her familiar

wink. He picked up Lydia's bags and took them to the car.

Proudly, Lydia spoke those powerful long-awaited words. "Aunt Regina, I'm honored. For the duration of my life, I'll execute my duties to the best of my ability. I know you'll watch from the shadows, but please don't go too far."

Regina held Lydia's face in her hands as she looked directly into her eyes. "My darling girl, step up with my blessing. Remember, I'm always near. Besides, my view from the shadows is less restrictive." She kissed Lydia on one cheek then the other.

"Thanks, Aunt Regina." They hugged again then Lydia walked out of the door.

The first couple of miles, they talked about the weather and current events. Finally, he said, "Lydia, I love your aunt, but she's a very complicated woman."

Lydia looked over at him and smiled knowingly.

"Regina's exciting. In many ways she's so mysterious, it's scary." Then he laughed out loud. "She shouldn't scare me, I'm a cop."

Oh, yes, she should, Lydia thought. She fought hard to keep her inner thoughts quiet, but they kept getting in the way.

"You know, Lydia, I feel like I'm sharing her with another world."

Right again, Lydia thought. This time a fake smile decorated her face. Her aunt's ploy was working. The ride officially introduced the sergeant to the major player. As he merged onto the interstate, she stared ahead, memorizing the license plates of the cars in front of them in the same manner she'd done as a child.

Then she turned her head slightly. "Sergeant, it's true, my aunt's a very complicated woman. A long time ago, she built an empire with the first man she ever loved.

Her willingness to accept your marriage proposal suggests you've captured her heart. Therefore, you have my blessing."

He smiled not really sure what to say. This smart, successful detective of the Philadelphia Police Department, to his credit, had solved an untold number of crimes. Even if blindly in love with her aunt, Lydia hoped he understood the message if not the madness embedded in her brief summation. For goodness sake! Had loving her aunt made him a total idiot? Surely, he'd heard the rumors. Lydia worried their different lifestyle choices would one day present a challenge. Then the thought occurred to her that perhaps, he secretly planned a coup. Wow! Imagine the headlines. *Highly Decorated Detective heads up Suspected Crime Family. Not on her watch,* she thought. The minutes dwindled as they made their way through slightly congested traffic. When they reached their destination, he got out and helped her with her bags.

"Look forward to seeing you soon, Lydia."

"Hope the talk helped, Sergeant." She'd given him a lot to digest.

"You bet, thanks, Lydia." Then he waved goodbye.

Lydia sat down and pulled out a partially read book from her oversized handbag. After thumbing through a few pages, she put it away. Should she tell Jake what she and her aunt talked about? she wondered.

သသသ

The flight arrived on time. A half hour later, the cab pulled up outside her house. Dragging her bags behind her, she walked clumsily up the sidewalk. Jake opened the door, picked them up, and set them aside.

Then he pulled her into his arms and held her tenderly. "I missed you, babe. You okay?"

"Much better now that I'm home."

He sat very quietly and listened. Lydia skillfully circumvented an issue causing her tremendous anxiety. She shared only the need to know changes happening in their family.

"Babe, I'm glad you're home. I'm going into the office for a couple of hours. I'll meet you at the restaurant." Then he walked out.

Lydia unpacked then threw some dirty clothes in the washing machine. She had time for a quick shower.

When she arrived at the restaurant, the parking lot looked like a shopping mall on Black Friday. Better call Margie, she thought.

"Hey, Margie, how're you doing?"

"No complaints."

"Parking's pretty tight this evening. I've got you blocked in. Yell if you need to get out."

"Not a problem. I'm in for the night. Oh, by the way, how's Regina?"

"Doing great, let's talk later." Lydia entered the restaurant through the back and still had to plow her way through a crowd. Jake rushed in behind her.

Jennifer walked over. "I've missed you guys. Margie told me your aunt had open heart surgery. I'm so sorry. How's she doing?"

"Much better thank you. You wouldn't know by looking at her that she had major surgery."

"Wow, that's great. Enjoy your evening," Jennifer said as she walked away.

ひひひ

It was the beginning of summer. The restaurant was

busier than ever. Obviously, Jennifer needed more part-time help, but she felt conflicted about taking time away from her duties. Within a week a dozen applications landed on her desk, but the glowing references of a young woman named Julianne Davis stood out. "I think Julianne will mesh well with the rest of the crew," Jennifer said.

"Julianne," Lydia spoke her name out loud. Was it eerie coincidence or fate? No longer blindsided, Lydia had evidence that in a city miles away from Philly a woman named Julianne vied for Jake's affection. Naturally, Lydia didn't believe in coincidences. All of a sudden, she got this crazy idea. "Jennifer, would you mind if I conducted the interview for you?"

"Of course not, I could use the help. Thanks, Lydia."

When it came to her reason, Lydia kept Jennifer in the dark. The thought of toying with Jake made the whole idea worthwhile. When she got home, she told him Jennifer needed more help at the restaurant, about the interview, and Jennifer's high hopes for this potential employee. "The interview's Wednesday at six o'clock. Will that work for you, Jake?"

"Sure, sounds good." He figured that afterward, they would stay for their usual dinner and drinks.

The day of the interview, they arrived promptly and headed straight to Jennifer's office. An attractive young woman with calves like a marathon runner stood up when they entered the room.

"Hello, I'm Lydia Giddens, this is my husband, Jake. I'm helping Jennifer out this evening," Lydia said. *Let the games begin*, she thought as she eyed Jake.

"Hello," Julianne said. Her voice shook slightly. "Ms. Jennifer told me one of the owners would conduct the interview."

"Yes, we're the owners. Please sit down. You're Julianne, right?"

"Oh, I'm so s—sorry. Y—Yes, I'm Julianne, Julianne D—Davis," she stammered.

"My, that's a beautiful name." Lydia turned and smiled sweetly at Jake. "I imagine it would sound even more beautiful with a Spanish accent. Wouldn't you agree, Jake?"

Julianne looked puzzled but managed a smile. The muscles in Jake's body stiffened. Absolute terror registered in his eyes. Basically, as a formality, Lydia moved swiftly through the interview. Jennifer liked her. Enough said. Julianne's last employer, a well-known restaurant chain from her home town of Chicago gave her an exemplary reference.

"You look more like a fun-in-the-sun California girl." Again, Lydia glanced over at Jake. This time she had an amusing smirk on her face.

Julianne smiled. "No, I've never been to California."

The chair squeaked as he unconsciously twisted his body. He looked ready to jump up and run right out of there as if escaping a burning building. Of course, he didn't, and, while choking on his own fear, he coughed repeatedly.

"Jake, would you like a glass of water?"

"No, I'm good, thank you."

"Do you have any questions for Julianne?"

"No, no, I b—believe you've covered e—everything." His pathetic stammering made her smile.

"Yep, I bet," Lydia murmured underneath her breath.

Jake, you poor darling, why couldn't you see that I played to win? After all, her predecessors taught her well, especially her Aunt Regina. Perhaps, Jake's slightly upgraded ethics made him believe he had a higher moral code or just maybe, infidelity counted as a little white lie in his book. The interview was brief. Jennifer hired Julianne that same evening. Lydia knew that this Julianne wasn't her husband's mistress. Her sources had given her everything she needed to know about the woman her husband had enjoyed spending time with away from home.

The Wednesday evening crowd had already started pouring in as she and Jake took their seats. All through dinner, Jake struggled. No matter how hard he tried, he couldn't keep his composure. He looked like a prisoner awaiting his final meal. He had two dirty martinis. After chasing those down with a couple of beers, he still couldn't relax. Poor thing, except for that brief jolt of empathy, Lydia no longer felt sorry for him. Not in the least.

The affair was over. Lydia had seen to that. She hadn't planned on torturing him forever. A few more months wouldn't hurt. They sat quietly, each in deep thought until the waitress broke the silence. "May I bring either of you another drink?"

"I'm good what about you Jake?" He simply shook his head.

"Well, I guess we'll order now," Lydia said.

Watching Jake attempt meaningful relaxation was both stimulating and slightly boring.

Very shortly, another waitress appeared. "Good evening, Dr. and Mr. Giddens, may I take your orders?"

"Hello, Julianne, how nice to see you again," Lydia said.

"Thank you, it's nice to see you, too."

Jake nodded and then pulled the menu up over his eyes. His very noticeable discomfort showed. Forgiveness didn't happen overnight. Lydia planned on keeping Julianne around for a while to remind Jake of his dirty little secret. Eventually, she would release her. Not yet.

⚜

After a less than eventful dinner, they went home. Saturday morning, Jake fabricated his usual excuse. Lydia went to the country.

"Hey, Lydia, it's good to see you!"

"You too, Maria."

Alan came out of his office, "Hey, girl you look fantastic."

"Thanks, Alan."

"Where's Jake?"

"You know your friend. He's a workaholic, like you."

Alan smiled. He couldn't reveal his friend's secret without breaking a confidence. He loved his family. Naturally, the thought of handling a messy divorce pained him.

He didn't know it yet, but that would never happen. Marrying into the Mayers family literally meant "until death do us part." The first chance Lydia got, she would ease his mind.

"Alan, how's the patient?" Lydia asked.

"No change," Alan replied somberly.

Lydia took her customary walk. Her uncle sat facing east in the same room he once shared with his beloved B J. Lydia pulled up a chair, grabbed his boney hand, and held it gently. They no longer spent quality time together. Without any preparation, the words broke free. They gushed out like water escaping a broken water main. "It's a beautiful day, Uncle Edmond. There's not a cloud in the sky. The election's rapidly approaching. I'm not sure how I'll vote. Four years ago, I voted for the incumbent. It's a sad indictment. However, this time around his supporters can't swing the necessary votes for a victory. His opponent's impressive political record speaks volumes. Aunt Regina's getting married and Keisha just had a baby girl." Finally, she stopped, "I love you, Uncle Edmond."

His grip tightened. He had heard her. Her heart ached, realizing somewhere in that haze, her uncle could no longer find his voice. She stood up, kissed his cheek gently, and walked out.

"Maria prepared lunch, you're staying right?" Elaine asked.

"Of course." Then, joking, Lydia said, "I need some alone time with my attorney. Where can I find him?"

Elaine laughed. "He's in his office, and he's all yours."

Lydia stood outside her uncle's old office and watched Alan for a few minutes. The tiny streaks of gray around his temples made him look as powerful as his father had at the peak of his career.

He looked up. "Come in, Lydia, sit down."

She sat down across from him. Everything looked the same. Alan sat in his father's old worn leather chair. A portrait of their Aunt B J still hung on the wall behind his desk with a safe tucked securely behind it. Yep, she knew many things.

"How's Aunt Regina?"

"She's recovering nicely."

"Jake said you didn't want him to go home with you."

"My aunt needed me."

Alan never dropped his gaze.

Almost immediately, the moment felt right to her. Lydia leaned forward resting her elbows on his desk then fixed her eyes upon him. "Jake's a very lucky man or just maybe the advice Julianne received helped her see the error of her ways. Or maybe, she had second thoughts all on her own. Regardless, if you're not careful life can get pretty messy sometimes. I'm happy to say *this time* it looks like talking things out worked. Don't you agree, Alan?"

A wicked smile wiggled up from her core like the slithering spineless thing she'd given a voice. Her usual sweetness had vanished, and, in its place, coldness alerted him to the sharp emphasis placed on the words *this time*.

Alan didn't respond. She really didn't expect him to.

Jake, my brother, you've no idea who you're dealing with, he thought. Nothing about Lydia would ever surprise Alan again. Like always, she changed the subject so abruptly, he didn't get a chance to assess the dangerous and covert persona that reared its ugly head.

"Alan, I believe Uncle Edmond heard me today."

"I know. Every morning when I discuss my plans for the day with him, I'm convinced he hears me. My father's in there somewhere."

Lydia smiled and stood up. "I believe Maria prepared lunch."

He jumped up. "I forgot. Thanks for the reminder."

"Not a problem. I do know how to remind."

He held her gaze for a few seconds until Elaine's voice broke through. "Hey, guys, lunch is ready."

Lydia walked out of his office.

"I'll be along shortly." Alan sat for a moment wrestling with a distance memory. Long before his dad gave up his practice, Alan witnessed something he never forgot. At the time, he didn't understand. For over a year, he and his dad worked together on an important case. Finally, they settled a huge lawsuit. When the verdict came in that afternoon, his father opened a bottle of champagne to celebrate a defining moment. Its cork made a loud popping sound and then flew up into the air. The bubbling liquid fizzed then dripped down the side of the bottle. His father filled their glasses and then proposed a toast. "To the hard work that went into pulling off a sweet deal, and to the gatekeeper, may she dispense fairly her own brand of justice."

Alan remembered asking him, "Who's the gatekeeper?"

A mischievous glint appeared in his father's eyes as he took another sip from his glass. He ignored his son's question.

Hum, client confidentiality, Alan thought.

Today, he finally got the answer to his unanswered question.

Elaine, Lydia, and Maria waited for him out on the patio. Watching Maria move about, Lydia remembered their first meeting. Maria stood in the doorway, unprepared to meet the young guest. Her expression said as much. Noticing Maria's shock, her uncle quickly made the introductions.

"Maria, I'd like you to meet my niece. Lydia this is Maria, my long-time friend and housekeeper."

"It's nice to meet you, Lydia."

"Thank you. It's nice to meet you, too."

Her eyes and her mouth opened wide. Obviously, their uncanny resemblance caught Maria by surprise. The first time Lydia and her sisters met their Uncle Edmond, Keisha pointed out what Lydia tried to ignore. Today, at Alan's request, Maria joined them for lunch. Father Time had caught up with the spry young woman Lydia met long ago. Maria enjoyed talking. She had plenty to say. Who better to recall their lives than the person who spent most of her own caring for them?

Maria took a seat across from him. "Alan, it might surprise you to know that between Mrs. Stein, me, and Lydia, you didn't stand a chance. We chose Elaine."

Elaine laughed.

He winked at her. "You guys outnumbered me. I'm happy you did."

Everyone laughed.

Lydia rose. "Thanks for lunch and great conversa-

tion. I've got to get back to the city. It's getting late. I'll
see you guys soon. Take care of my uncle. Oh, before I
forget, Aunt Regina's getting married." Except for the
man she felt compelled to tell, her aunt's wedding date
momentarily loss it's' significance.

"That's a milestone," Alan said.

"You bet."

On the drive back into the city, Lydia had time to re-
visit that incredible one-sided conversation. Her uncle
had heard her. Politics, the catalyst that once fueled his
life's work like life-saving blood, continued to spark the
same desire.

CHAPTER 19

Her problem didn't just pop up overnight. Why had Lydia waited so long? She'd known about Julianne, Jake's mistress, for a very long time. In fact, long before that summer when Jennifer hired the lovely Julianne Davis from Chicago, she knew. Like most wives, Lydia knew the look and smell of trouble. Then, one day, she accidentally stumbled upon it when a jewelry store receipt for a rather expensive necklace found its way into the inside pocket of Jake's jacket. Apparently, his business trip included some pleasure. Her misplaced trust made her feel like a complete fool. Suddenly, she needed a sympathetic ear that wouldn't judge her.

"Everyone's entitled to one little mistake," her aunt said when she told her about Jake's infidelity.

"Little mistake!" Lydia shouted, surprised at her aunt's comment.

"I'm sorry, Lydia. I'm not trying to minimize an affair." What she said next didn't surprise Lydia. "Dispose of the situation, Lydia. This woman's a threat to our family's future. You've got too many years invested in Jake. We don't run away. We handle our problems. Do it now." Anguish coupled with the authority in her voice clearly showed she meant every word. "Call Max, he'll know what to do."

Lydia trusted her aunt. When she rattled off his number without pausing, Lydia jotted it down without stopping to think.

"Max's Investigation Agency," the soft very feminine voice announced.

"Max, please."

"Certainly, one moment please."

"This is Max, I'm listening," he said rudely.

The words stuck to the roof of her open mouth. Then nervously, she forced out, "Max, I'm Lydia—"

His abrasive tone interrupted her. "I know who you are. Tell me where you want to meet."

The next day in a park across town, Lydia met a short, pudgy man with greasy black hair so thin when raked across his head it barely covered his baldness. He took note of her choppy, yet brief directives.

"I'll be in touch," he said.

Then he walked away. Several months later, they met again at the same location where she paid him handsomely for the contents of a plain manila envelope. As soon as he rounded the corner, she eagerly tore open the envelope. The rush of blood felt so hot her fingers tingled as they brushed across her cheeks. If mad accurately described how she felt then something got lost in the translation. Mad didn't even come close. Wanting to rip their hearts out and trample them into the dirt beneath her feet painted a disturbingly more accurate picture of how Lydia felt about Jake and his mistress.

She'd learned a few things from observing her uncle. This was her chance to test that knowledge. First, she needed to make a call.

"Keisha needs me for a couple of days," she said as soon as Jake answered.

"Keisha okay?"

"Sure. She's learning that new mom equates to sleepless nights. Frank's away on business. She needs company until he gets back."

"If I leave now, I can take you to the airport."

"No, I'm good. I've already called a cab."

"I'll miss you, babe."

"I'll miss you more." When she spoke those words, they felt devoid of any real passion. That scared her. Then she hung up and called Keisha.

"Hey, girl, I need your help. I told Jake I'm spending a couple of days with you. Cover for me, little sister."

"Anytime, you know that. Is everything okay, Lydia?"

"Sure, everything's fine," Lydia said quite convincingly. "I'm looking into buying a time share as a surprise for him."

"Oh, that's great." Keisha didn't ask any more questions nor did she volunteer any more information.

One lie always led to another. Lydia had done enough of that for one day. On her way to the airport, she made another call.

"Hey, Aunt Regina."

"Hey, sweetheart everything okay?"

"Everything's good. I decided the matter needed a personal touch."

Regina paused. "There's another way you know."

"I know. I'm at the airport. I've got to go, Aunt Regina."

"Be safe, sweetheart."

"Always."

Before hanging up, her aunt reminded Lydia that she had everything she needed at her command.

Lydia disregarded the concern in her aunt's voice. "I'll be fine."

She regretted not handling the problem sooner. Lydia had let it get out of hand. Along with the title bestowed upon her, they had left her the necessary roadmap to handle any family crisis. Her predecessors never doubted her ability.

"Your first call will set everything in motion," her uncle had told her.

Her hands shook as she dialed the number.

"I expected your call sooner, Dr. Giddens. You need only to ask."

Her voice shook. How did he know her name? she wondered. That call officially realigned the hierarchy with Lydia fully cemented in the role as their new leader.

The flight took longer than Lydia imagined. Maybe, it had a little to do with her mission. At the hotel, she took a moment to freshen up. Minutes later, she gave the bellman an address. He hailed a cab. The driver pulled up in front of a very exclusive gated community and called out the address.

"Take the first left," the guard instructed him. "It's the ground floor condo."

"Please wait for me." Lydia stepped out of the cab and rang the doorbell. A very runway-thin woman with a silky brown complexion and high cheek bones appeared in the doorway.

"Good evening." She had a surprisingly strong Spanish dialect.

Lydia wondered where she owed her true allegiance.

"I've been expecting you, Dr. Giddens, please come in." The woman gestured boldly with her hand. "Would you like a drink?" she asked.

"No, thank you."

Julianne's lavishly furnished apartment suggested an affluent worldly lifestyle. It looked like the successful men she systematically chose contributed handsomely to her champagne taste. How much of her extravagant life-style had Jake supported? Lydia wondered.

"You've come a long way, Dr. Giddens." Then Julianne raised the glass to her lips, feeling an unrealistic sense of accomplishment. "What do you want from me?"

Confidently, Lydia stepped forward. "Julianne, the valuable merchandise temporarily in your possession belongs to me. I'm not here to relinquish my claim, not now or ever. As a matter of fact, I won't barter for something that already belongs to me. Besides, I hate bartering. Instead, I'll offer leniency." She reached into her pocket and pulled out her cell phone. As she dialed, her eyes held Julianne's stunned gaze. "Ms. Price, I believe this call will help you make the right decision."

When Lydia spoke her name, a less memorable vision popped into Julianne's head. She no longer heard the sweet whispers of Jake's promises.

Lydia's allies kept her abreast of everything. She knew more than just the name of her husband's mistress. Jake headed the long list of prey that had fallen into the snare of a predator who made her living dazzling undisciplined married men. Julianne stood motionless clutching the phone as tiny red blotches like hives quickly formed on her cheeks. It appeared that one of Lydia's foot soldiers had Julianne's undivided attention. It took just one phone call to summon a devoted member under her command to disarm an imminent threat. Julianne's hand gripped the phone so tightly her knuckles turned white. Her eyes swelled to the size of a half dollar. Lydia pried the phone from her grip then returned it to her pocket. Julianne now understood that Lydia's power could alter her circumstances. Lydia moved in even closer. Julianne felt her hot breath on her face. She shrank backward in fear. "If he's ever in your neighborhood again, I advise you to tell him that he's no longer welcome. It's up to you how you handle him, Julianne. Just make sure you get it done quickly. I'm not a very patient woman."

Julianne swung around, holding a half empty glass of vodka in her shaky hand. She moved unsteadily toward the bar, tilted her head back, and gulped down the last drop. The glass slipped from her hand. With a loud band, it hit the floor. Angrily, she picked up the bottle then hurled it forcefully across the room. The liquor trickled down the wall.

Lydia felt vindicated, seeing the last ounce of Julianne's dignity slip away. Gently, Lydia closed the door, put California behind her, and got into the waiting cab. That encounter felt almost as good as knowing the bread crumbs she planned to leave in Jake's path would give her an even greater satisfaction. On the ride back to the hotel, her mind kept going over that meeting. Had she handled her first personal attack as prudently as possible? She thought so but spent a restless night rethinking every detail.

The minute her plane landed, she turned her cell phone back on and, of course, it rang. "Hello, sweetheart."

"Oh, hello, Aunt Regina."

"I gather you had a successful trip."

"Yes. Everything turned out better than expected."

"Are you ready to start scattering the bread crumbs?"

"You bet."

Jake's affair threatened their family and propelled Lydia deeper into her role. She no longer second guessed her authority. Expeditiously, she began handling fallouts that jeopardized their lives. Protecting the family came first. Jake messed up. He hadn't realized yet that his stupidity placed him in a very precarious position. Until she got tired of the game, he could end up stumbling around

in the dark for a long time. Just like his masculine coun-
terparts, Jake wandered into a pasture he thought greener
than his own. Sadly, he discovered no difference. *Everything's relative,* Lydia thought.

After Lydia and her aunt finished talking, Lydia
called Jake. She heard something amiss in his voice when
he asked, "How was your trip?"

"All's well. Are we on for dinner this evening?" she
asked.

"Yep. I missed you, babe."

"I'll see you later." That's all she could say right
then and mean it.

Lydia stopped in at work for a few hours then went
straight to the restaurant. Jake sat waiting. On the way to
their booth, she stumbled backward then forward. Her
body felt like it was free falling off a cliff. Jake jumped
up and grabbed her. Jennifer dialed Nine-One-One.

As the ambulance sped away, Lydia heard the
squealing cry of the sirens dividing the night air.

"Dr. Giddens, can you hear me? We're almost
there." Before the EMS attendant uttered those last
words, the engine shut off and the ambulance doors
swung open. Jake pulled in directly behind them.

"Dr. Cooper," the attendant shouted, "it's Dr. Giddens. Can you hear me, Dr. Giddens?"

Suddenly, Jessie appeared. "Lydia, stay with me."

She and Jessie knew this disease thrived in a weakened body with stress a major trigger. Jessie stayed most
of the night. She left a couple of times when paged. Jake
never left her bedside. The next morning, Lydia sent him
to the cafeteria. Sworn to secrecy, he couldn't contact her
family. Jessie's oath tied her hands.

"Jake, I'm in good hands. I don't want my family
worrying about me."

He didn't agree but wouldn't fight her as long as she

had Jessie. When he left the room, she called her aunt. "How're you doing, Aunt Regina?"

"I'm a little tired today."

"Oh, is something wrong?"

"No, it's just those birthdays finally catching up with me."

Lydia laughed. Her aunt's admission shocked her. Where had her vanity gone? Admitting she felt old seemed out of character even for this timeless woman. Lydia sensed she omitted a few facts when asked about her health. Didn't any of them admit their human frailties?

From her very own hospital bed, Lydia offered her aunt encouragement. Before hanging up, the conversation moved on to the usual topics. Lydia walked over to the window. She looked out across the lot as cars pulled in and out of parking spaces like people moving briskly through a revolving door.

Jessie watched her from the doorway. Lydia sensed her presence and turned around. "I've signed your release. You can leave whenever you're ready. Please take your meds every day. No skipping. You know how this works. Soldiers guard their post with vigilance." Jessie's reprimand stopped short when her pager buzzed. "I'll call you later."

Had Jake been a minute earlier they might've collided. "You just missed Jessie. I can go home."

"Everything okay?" Jake asked.

"Yes, and I can take full credit for this little episode."

"Hum?"

Lydia didn't bother to explain.

"I'll get the car."

Again, Lydia no longer felt alone. She turned around quickly. "Dr. Barnes, what a pleasant surprise."

"Good morning, Dr. Giddens. Forgive my intrusion. You gave Jessie quite a scare last night."

"I'm sorry, I didn't mean too."

"Jessie's glad she took the call. I believe she said something about a promise to your aunt."

Lydia stared blankly at him. "Jessie had a terrific time at dinner the other night," she said.

"That makes two of us."

Lydia took his surprise visit as a sign. Dr. Barnes sat on the board of the clinic. She suspected that his recommendation alone secured her position. Since she had his undivided attention, Lydia decided she would tread carefully. "Jessie's a good friend. I don't want her to get hurt."

His eyes twinkled. *Gosh! What a good-looking guy*, she thought.

"Dr. Giddens." His authoritative tone demanded her full attention. "I'm not interested in a one night stand. Jessie's every man's dream." When he said every man's dream, the corners of his mouth turned up into a lustful smile. "I respect your concern for your friend. However, I believe Jessie's a big girl." He smiled again. This time his smile seemed very different from before, although his tone politely said butt out.

Slightly annoyed at her lack of diplomacy, Lydia offered an apology. "Forgive me if I overstepped my boundaries. Thanks for listening, Dr. Barnes."

"Anytime. Take care of yourself, Dr. Giddens."

As Jake turned the corner, he glimpsed Dr. Barnes coming out of her room. "Was that Dr. Barnes?" he asked.

"Uh huh."

"Is everything okay, Lydia?"

"Everything's great."

After that unexpected setback put her in the hospital

again, Jake threatened to call their aunt if she didn't follow Jessie's instructions. They reached a compromise.
During a two week trial period, Jennifer delivered all
meals, Jake came home at a decent hour every day, and
Lydia focused strictly on her health. Every day usually
started out exactly the same. Before Jake left for work, he
read the business and sports sections of the newspaper.
He folded it in half then left it on the kitchen table. Lydia
read the business, entertainment, and obituary sections.
Routinely, after her second cup of coffee, she'd put her
cup in the dishwasher. Today, a smile moved quickly
across her face when she recalled her mother's dislike of
dishwashers. For that reason, they never owned one.
Many times, her father offered to purchase one over her
mother's adamant refusal. No mystery there. Why bother? Her mother had five of them.

Lydia enjoyed those quiet mornings and late evenings with Jake, but she wanted to get back to the work
she loved. The phone rang in the distance and interrupted
her mundane morning.

"Good morning, Lydia."

"Hey, Jessie."

"How's my patient today?"

"I'm great."

"Would you like some company?" Jessie asked.

"I'd love some."

Until she heard Jessie's voice, she'd forgotten about
Dr. Barnes's comment. What promise? Had her aunt
asked Jessie to spy on her? Jessie wouldn't do that. Shortly past noon, Jessie arrived. "Hey, girl, you're looking
well. It looks like Jake knows what he's doing."

"I'm feeling great. He's doing a bang up job."

Jessie laughed. "Bang up? You sound bored."

Lydia didn't use words like that and, even if she
tried, she couldn't dismiss her aunt's deeply rooted eti-

quette training. Jessie and Lydia had that in common, too.

"With my permission, you can get out of this house and back to work next week," Jessie said.

Lydia laughed. *Mission accomplished*, she thought although, she knew she hadn't fooled Jessie.

Then Jessie changed the subject. "How's Mrs. Mayers?"

"Understandably not as agile, of course, I wouldn't let her hear me say that."

"And your sisters?"

"Everyone's good." Jessie had that happy and in love glow on her face. Her new beau had waited patiently for her to realize she deserved better.

"We'll talk later Lydia. I've got a late-afternoon appointment."

Jessie expected that Lydia wouldn't always work within the constraints of her illness. Everyone knew doctors made the worst patients. They usually ignored their own advice while expecting everyone else to blindly follow their lead.

As agreed, Jennifer brought dinner and then hurried back to the restaurant in time to greet the evening crowd. Lydia stood in the doorway, waved goodbye, then stepped back inside when she heard the phone rang. "Hello, Lydia."

"Hey, Margie, how are you?"

"I've had better days, but I'm not complaining. Lydia, this call isn't about me, it's about you. Please don't make the new medicine work harder than necessary. You must do your part, too. You don't want another hospital stay. People get sick in those places."

Lydia laughed. "I'll do my best."

Obviously, Margie had heard. *What a clever move, Jessie.* Without violating her doctor-patient privilege, Jessie probably called Tommy with an outline of the history of one of her patients then asked him for advice. He didn't need a compass. On his weekly call, he simply asked his mother about the wellness of a friend. Margie read between the lines. Then, as if an afterthought, he said something surprising. "Mom, the next time I come home, I'd like to bring someone special. I think you'll like her. Gotta go. I love you."

"I'd love that. Good-bye, Tommy. I love you too." That made Margie happy. Finally, someone made Tommy take notice of something other than genetic strands and blood disorders. He rarely dated after falling in love with his research. What woman could or would want to compete with that? Tommy's call gave her another confirmation. Margie already knew about Lydia's hospital stay. Lydia had a spy in her camp. The first day Jennifer brought Lydia lunch, she noticed the dark circles under her eyes. Lydia looked tired.

The paths Lydia and Margie chose had led them to a place neither of them expected. Penniless, alone in her darkest hour, Jacksons' light pointed Margie in the direction of a safe harbor. She loved him deeply. Sometimes, Lydia wondered if Jackson ever knew just how much Margie loved him.

"Are you okay, Lydia?" Jennifer asked.

"I'm running a slight fever. It feels like I've got a bad cold. So, I decided I'll take my own advice and stay at home. A contagious doctor running about the clinic would only compound existing problems."

Not believing a single word prompted Jennifer's call to Margie. "Lydia doesn't look well. She claims she took time off work because of a bad cold. Can you believe that?"

Margie didn't buy any of it. Jennifer's call then the way Tommy ingeniously handled his message told her Lydia needed a little reminder.

Margie worried that if she did nothing, she'd face the wrath of Mrs. Mayers. After Lydia's uncle died, a rumor surfaced that a less tolerant new commander smashed threats to her family like tiny insects. Most rumors started with a fact or two. Margie once served up enough drinks at those frequent meetings that she could identify their powerful infrastructure. Perhaps, Lydia needed a brief reminder of something a friend once told both of them.

"Hello, Lydia. How're you feeling, today?" Margie asked.

"Pretty good, thanks for asking."

"Lydia," she asked, "do you remember Jackson's philosophy about family?"

"Yes, of course. He had said you don't need a family you can't depend on."

"Good. I'm glad you remembered. Take care of yourself. We'll talk later. Goodbye."

❦❦❦

Lydia loved her work. It felt good being back, but it wasn't a marathon. No one expected her to reach the finish line right away. That was Lydia's idea.

"Dr. G.," her receptionist announced. "Your husband's returning your call. He's on line one.

"Hey, babe."

"Hey, Jake, did you have a meeting? You left much earlier than usual this morning."

"Uh-huh, and I've got bad news. I'm doing a quick run out to California for an urgent business meeting. I'll be back late tomorrow night. I'm sorry it's so spur-of-the-moment. I'm heading home to pack."

"Oh, Jake, couldn't someone else go?"

"I'm afraid not. It's my project. I'll miss you."

"Call me."

Flecks of red flashed before her eyes as her anger exploded then rose above the crackling sound of the receiver as it slammed against the cradle.

"Calm down," she whispered under her breath. Her head began throbbing. "You've already handled the problem. Everybody pays for their sins. Jake is no exception."

Did he think of her as stupid and blind? Hadn't he learned anything from her interviewing skills? While still fuming, she grabbed her stethoscope and burst into the first exam room. Lydia felt confident Julianne got the message. She wasn't so sure about Jake.

ↄↄↄↄ

The flight was turbulent. Jake arrived at the hotel somewhat bothered that, after leaving her dozens of messages, he hadn't heard from Julianne. Not one word. Surprisingly, this time Julianne answered on the first ring.

"Hey, baby, I'm in town. Let's get together."

"I'm sorry, Jake, I can't."

"Come on Julianne," he pleaded. "I've missed you, baby."

He didn't beg for very long. Julianne had fallen in love with a man who would never belong completely to her. "Give me an hour."

Had she forgotten the ultimatum?

An hour later, she opened the door and stared into his eyes. Realizing her mistake, she shrank back. Sheer panic took control.

"What's wrong?"

Julianne staggered over to the counter reeking of day old liquor as she sloppily poured up another drink. Jake had lied many times to enjoy the company of this sexy, wildly entertaining woman.

He knew he loved Julianne the minute he saw her sitting at the bar, but reserved that in-love feeling for his wife.

"I've got to go away, Jake. It's best for me and perhaps for you, too."

"What's going on, Julianne?"

"It's over. I can't see you ever again."

That ugly green monster rose up. It taunted him. Jake shook her hard. She belonged to him. "Tell me why. Is it another guy?"

"No, no, Jake, there's no one else. People in love make foolish decisions." Why didn't she lie? He gave her an escape. Her hands shook. The liquor bounced from side to side and then spilled out over the top of her glass. She never noticed.

He grabbed her glass. "You've had enough."

"You've no right to tell me when I've had enough. She came here, you know?"

When she spoke, a hint of jealousy colored her normally seductive tone.

"Who?"

"The Prima Dona."

"You're drunk. Who's the Prima Dona?" Jake asked.

"I'm not too drunk to remember your wife paid me a visit."

Her painful announcement took him by surprise. Resembling a scared little boy caught in a lie, he felt his heart join his mind in a desperate race to the finish line— competing for what, he wasn't quite sure. His grip tightened on her arm, and he swung her around. "What did you say?"

Her pitiful cry caused him to relax his grip.

"The great doctor came here. We had a little chat." Her voice trembled. "I'm scared, Jake. It feels like I'm in a horror movie. Will they really kill me?"

"Will who kill you?"

"I don't know."

Julianne started wailing. Her body shook. Finally, he saw his mistake. He'd underestimated his wife. In Jennifer's office that day, he previewed her ability to contain a situation. Ignoring the ramifications, he pretended the mousey little caregiver image he'd invented in his head represented his reality. *You fool! What's wrong with you Jake?* he thought. *Wake up!*

His nightmare had only just begun. He knew it. Hurriedly, he helped his now slightly sober mistress pack her bags. "Julianne, get as far away as you can from here and from me."

"Then it's true. Oh, Jake, I'm so scared."

Jake's body trembled as he held her close. The horror in her eyes pierced his heart. He sucked in her sweet, fragrant scent for the last time. "Please, just do what you were told. I'll miss you, baby."

He never asked about her plans or where she might go. He simply walked out. In hindsight, he questioned his stupidity. How could he not have seen the restructuring of powers from such a close vantage point? While he gallivanted across the country, Lydia stepped into custommade shoes then began the heavy lifting. The next day, he returned home, preoccupied with the mess in front of him. Lydia suspected he and Julianne finally had a heart to heart. Jake finally got the message. Later, her sources reported that Julianne cut Jake loose so fast, he was probably wondering if he'd dreamed her or if she really existed.

CHAPTER 20

Lydia had center stage and a lifetime commitment. Once she stepped into her own, her aunt saw no need to second chair. *Stop worrying*, Lydia thought. Perhaps, hearing Jessie's voice would quiet her doubts.

The phone rang once and stopped. "Dr. Cooper's office."

"Is she in? It's Dr. Giddens."

"Hello, Dr. G. Yes, she's in. Just a moment please."

"Hey, Lydia." Jessie's cheerful voice penetrated the mind numbing elevator music.

"Jessie, how're things with the new man in your life?"

"Terrific. He's a great guy. After you hooked Jake, I thought all the good ones stopped swimming in those dicey streams. We aren't exactly safe bait."

They laughed.

"I kept hinting. You kept ignoring me and the hints," Lydia said.

"Well, I'm paying attention now."

"Jessie, I know it's short notice. You free this evening?"

"Sure, what's up?"

"I'd like to repay dinner. Can you meet me around seven?"

"Sure, see you then."

She hoped Jake hadn't made any plans for the evening. He answered right away. A good sign, she thought.

"Hey, Jake. How's your day going?"

"Oh, hey, babe. It's slow. I'm even caught on some paperwork. Do you need something?"

"No. I thought I'd treat Jessie to dinner tonight. Do you mind?"

"No. I'll watch the game and finish up that leftover chicken spaghetti Jennifer sent over."

"Okay then. I'm heading over to the restaurant straight from work. See you later tonight."

"Enjoy. Say hello for me."

"Will do."

Jennifer looked up as Lydia walked in. Lydia had a fondness for bold jewelry like her Aunt Regina. Her favorite gold hoop earrings adorned her ears. Gold bangles jingled softly as they hung from her tiny wrist rendering the same whimsical melody like the wind chimes outside her aunt's kitchen window.

"Join me, Jennifer?"

"Sure."

"Jennifer, your day-to-day influence on our business has made it a huge success. Thank you for all you do. Effective immediately, we're giving you a raise."

Jennifer beamed. "Thank you so much. Please tell Jake and Margie how much I appreciate their generosity, too."

"I will."

Quite frankly, Jennifer felt she was paid extremely well for a job she loved. When she and some of the other restaurant managers got together, they compared notes.

Tantamount to suicide, Jennifer never broached her salary in actual dollars with her competitive friends.

"Thank you again, Dr. Giddens." She turned her head toward the door just as Jessie was making her way unescorted toward them. Jennifer stood up. "Enjoy your evening, ladies."

Jessie smiled at her. Lydia nodded her head. Jennifer walked off.

"Hey, Lydia," Jessie said and took her seat.

"Hey there, how're things at St. Mary's?"

"Good."

"And how's Dr. Barnes?" Lydia asked.

"Delicious."

"Oooh."

"May I take your drink order, Dr. Giddens?" the waitress asked.

Lydia ordered her usual. Jessie echoed the same. "*Huh.* I see Jennifer's missing that pretty waitress," Jessie said.

"Yes. Julianne accepted full-time employment at another restaurant."

"Good for her."

The last time Lydia went home, her aunt gave her two very important pieces of advice. First, no sin ever goes unpunished. Secondly, under weak leadership, empires crumble. Her aunt recovered from the shame of her husband's betrayal, but it wasn't easy. Although he repented, she later made the toughest call of her life. Now, Lydia was about to face one of the many challenges that lay ahead for her. She saw no point in trying to move forward until she dispelled some of the half-truths about her family. The lies and whispered rumors woven into the very fabric of their family's history made separating the truth from lies difficult. Forging ahead meant taking a great risk on the road to building an equitable family structure, but understanding the risk, she had no choice. The time had come for another equally responsible party to acknowledge his role in the death of Jessie's father.

Jessie's nerves tingled. She bit her lower lip. Lydia didn't know any easy way around the topic. So, too late to turn back, she began. "Jessie, my aunt shared an embarrassing part of her past with me." Jessie's eyes widened. "We've shared an amazing friendship. Why didn't you say something?" Lydia asked.

"About what? What are you talking about?"

"About my uncle, the man I now know was your father."

Jessie felt the blood drain from her face. "I really didn't know what to say or how I felt about everything. The painful stigma of illegitimacy like a parasite sucked the joy out of my life. The questions never ceased. Did he love me? Why didn't he fight for me? The mystery surrounding my father's death left me with a very tainted picture of a man my heart hadn't fully accepted."

The bitterness in her voice sent Lydia into a defensive mode. "Jessie, the man you so callously denounced died before he could right a wrong. He tried. Those who conspired and later ordered his execution did so without fully weighing future consequences. 'A house divided against itself cannot stand.'"

Jessie couldn't believe Lydia's absurd implication. Did Lydia honestly believe her daddy murdered her uncle in a jealous rage? "How dare you, Lydia. My daddy would never do such a horrible thing," she yelled.

Several patrons turned around when they heard her loud, angry outburst.

"Calm down, Jessie." Lydia waved her hand in the air. Jennifer rushed over, having heard the commotion, too. "We'll need your office for a few minutes," Lydia said.

"Of course," Jennifer replied.

Jennifer's secluded office seemed the perfect spot for a confidential discussion. The office contained the usual: file cabinet, desk, chair, and two large loungers. Jessie and Lydia sat across from each other in comfortable loungers like stoic opponents in a game of chess. The air so thick and stale it suffocated the mere whisper of silence until a knock on the door broke the spell.

"Come in," Lydia said.

The waitress looked at Lydia. She set two glasses of wine down in front of them and then backed out of the room. They had reached an impasse. Lydia figured that her next crucial move would set the tone. She lowered her voice. In a soft empathic tone, she began her explanation of their family's three-fold business model. "Jessie, as the newest member of our family, it's important that you understand us, as well as how you fit into this family. When Patsy shared her pain, you witnessed our unconditional love for one another. That's only one part of who we are as a family. We also provide financial security and guarantee protection from any outside interference." Ironically, the mayhem she and Jessie now faced came from within Lydia's very own seemingly secure borders, these same borders, she so proudly defended. Clearly out of her league, Jessie didn't speak. Lydia shifted their focus. "Jessie, I'm sorry you missed out on so many wonderful years with your father. He was truly my hero."

As she listened to Lydia calmly expose a murderous plot that stole her father's life, her thoughts whirled high overhead like autumn leaves fluttering in a gentle breeze.

Jessie came expecting one thing. It saddened Lydia that she ended up with something entirely different.

They turned around quickly after another knock on the door. "Come in," Lydia said again.

The waitress immediately noticed the two untouched

drinks. "May I get you something else?"

"No thanks." Lydia glanced at a very dumbfounded Jessie and then turned to the waitress. "Tell Jennifer we'll skip dinner tonight."

Visibly trembling, poor scared Jessie looked like she wanted to jump up and run out of there. How strange that Jennifer's office had that same effect on Jake. Still, Lydia moved forward with the painful story. "Every day those persons who conceived and executed such a heinous scheme live with the irreparable consequences of that action. I'm sorry things turned out this way. Killing my uncle solved nothing," she said sharply.

Jessie shook her head. Had she dreamed all this? She stumbled out of the office. For what seemed like hours, she sat alone in her car swept away in the flood waters of her own tears. Jessie didn't remember driving back to her condo.

After regaining a tiny bit of self-control, she called her administrator. Two days off would work. She packed, and then made two more calls.

"Daddy, meet me at the Waterfront Hotel. Please don't tell anyone I'm in town."

In her request, he heard sadness. He agreed. Her trip's suddenness alarmed the person she called next. Instead of pushing her for more details, Dr. Barnes called the only person who knew her better than anyone.

"Hello, Dr. Giddens."

"Hello, Dr. Barnes."

"I just heard from Jessie. Something unexpected came up. I'm wondering if I can do anything. Is she okay?"

"Jessie's fine. You'd better get ready. She's definitely a daddy's girl."

That's all that needed saying. After all, a watered down version of the truth sounded better than involving

him in problems that didn't concern him. Not yet, anyway.

"Thank you, Dr. Giddens. I appreciate your candor."

"You're welcome, sir."

Later that same day, Jessie checked into the hotel only a few blocks away from her daddy's office. Briefly, the
ringing soothed her raging thoughts.

"Mr. James's office," she said.

"This is Jessie Cooper. May I speak with him
please?"

"Oh, yes ma'am, he's expecting your call."

"Hello, Jessie."

"Daddy, I'm in room twenty-one, twelve."

"Jessie, you sounded upset. What's wrong? Should I
bring your mother?"

"Please don't, Daddy. No one else, remember?"
When she said "Please don't, Daddy," her razor sharp
tone cut through the outer layer of each syllable like a
paring knife.

He grabbed his jacket and rushed out. All of a sudden he felt weary as he stood outside her hotel room.
Momentarily, he hesitated then tapped softly.

"Come in, Daddy, the door's open."

"It's good to see you, sweetheart." He pulled her into
his arms. Immediately, he felt her withdraw.

"May I get you something to drink?"

"No, honey. I'm fine. What's going on? You sounded strange."

"Please sit down, Daddy."

He moved slowly like a much older man on the brink
of decline. She came, but just this one time, she desperately hoped that Lydia was wrong. "Daddy, what do you
know about Roy Mayers?"

Instantly, the color drained from his face. His lips
quivered. He turned his face away. His posture stiffened.

When he turned back around, he looked annoyed. Had he reacted this way because she knew his secret? Had he feared this confrontation?

"What is it you think you know, young lady?" His arrogance stunned her.

"Not enough. That's why I'm here, Daddy. I need the truth. Please, I want the whole story." Her pleading touched a deep-seeded longing. He'd carried that load long enough. Almost at once, his pride subsided, his tone softened. He delivered a chilling story.

Afraid of what his eyes revealed, she stared at the floor.

"Jessie, I'm sorry about so many things. You left home filled with so much anger. I should've stopped you. The affair hurt, but the most painful blow to my ego came knowing my daughter belonged to another man. Rage and hate consumed me. That impulsive decision made so long ago torments me even today. Never give in to hate, Jessie. Revenge cuts like a two-edge sword. The one you punish isn't the only one who pays." His voice, although shaky, still demanded respect.

Jessie's heart raced. In total shock, she listened. Her daddy unfolded a plot that took the life of his wife's lover and the father of her child. He accepted total responsibility for the crime. He never divulged the name of his co-conspirator. Had fear kept him from speaking the name of such a powerful woman?

Jessie looked up into wet, tired eyes. He blinked. "I'm sorry, Jessie. Please forgive me. What I've said here today never leaves this room. Do you understand me, young lady? I made a terrible mistake. You deserved the chance to know your father." His voice sounded genuinely remorseful as he stretched forth his arms. Without any reservation, she fell into his open arms.

"I understand. Good-bye, Daddy."

"Good-bye, Jessie." Fearing her answer, he asked anyway, "Will you ever come home again?"

"Yes, Daddy, it's home. It's the place where my family lives." She heard a sigh of relief as he grabbed his coat. Then he walked out the door.

Rather than face the world tonight, she opted for room service. Jessie knew her daddy had a less than stellar reputation. Young didn't mean stupid. Who needed a bodyguard twenty-four/seven? Out of spite, a boy Ginny jilted from their closely-knit circle spilled some pretty shady stuff about their daddy's business. Despite what they learned, she and Ginny kept his secret.

The next morning, Jessie left the hotel anxious to get back to work. The minute, she stepped off of the plane, she called her friend.

"Hey, Lydia."

"You okay?"

"I'm great. I had a long talk with Daddy. Lydia, I'm sorry. I behaved badly." Jessie sounded happy or perhaps resigned to her past. She saw no good in sitting around thinking about all the crap heaped upon her.

"I'm glad you're back, Jessie."

Nothing else needed saying. Jessie had as much truth as she could handle in any given day. Perhaps, her daddy thought that he had the command role that day so very long ago. Ironically, after setting aside his ego, he realized that someone else played an even bigger part.

While Lydia's predecessors fought a few private wars, an equally powerful warrior rose up from within their same ranks. Sure, Jessie's daddy chose the gunman, but her aunt authorized the execution then gave a superb Academy Award performance as the grieving widow.

CHAPTER 21

The RSVP's rolled in. The biggest shock came from Kellee and Mia. Finally, the entire family of the men who shaped their lives would unite for an occasion other than a funeral. That never happened before.

Lydia's sisters worked tirelessly leaving nothing to chance, not the decorations, the minister, or food. They labored over the smallest detail while everyone else went about their daily routines. Tommy's big mystery date had Lydia completely in the dark. Finally, she couldn't stand it any longer. "Jessie, I'm dying to know who Tommy's bringing to the wedding. He refuses to tell me."

Jessie laughed.

"What's so funny?" Lydia asked.

"Nothing."

Jessie laughed again.

"Well, I guess I'll find out soon enough."

Jessie couldn't believe something actually escaped Lydia's watchful eye.

On Friday, the thirteenth, Lydia and Jake boarded a plane for Sweetwater, Mississippi. From across this great country and abroad relatives headed home. Lydia and Jake's plane arrived on schedule. Mark met them.

"Hello, Lydia, great to see you looking well."

"Thanks, Mark. I'm told you're doing well too."

"Hum." Jake stared at them curiously.

Mark didn't need to tell her what she already knew.

"Hey, Jake, what's up, man?"

"Not much. Good to see you, Mark."

"Danielle's at the caterer's. As you can see, I'm officially her right and left hand."

They laughed.

Mark dropped them off at the house. "I've got another errand to run for my frantic wife. Can't stay, I'll see you guys at dinner tonight."

Before she reached the last step, the door opened wide. "Hello, Lydia, Jake." Then her aunt gave each of then a big hug.

Jake looked around. "Where's the sergeant?"

"He'll be along shortly. The wedding's tomorrow. Besides, I'm not superstitious, Jake."

"I bet you're not." Jake didn't realize he'd spoken out loud until he heard Lydia gasp. Had he taken a dig at Aunt Regina? *You're either brave or stupid, watch out Jake*, he thought.

Aunt Regina wasn't at all amused at his comment. She shot him an intimidating look. Quickly, he snatched up the luggage then rushed off down the hallway. Lydia followed her aunt into the kitchen.

"Are you hungry?"

"No, I'm good, Aunt Regina. Maybe, I'll grab a snack in a little while. Dinner's still on for tonight right?"

"Yes, sweetheart, the girls made reservations at a little seafood restaurant south of town."

"Then, I certainly don't want to overeat. I'd like to fit comfortably into my dress tomorrow."

Jake headed to his favorite spot. At once, he returned, looking slightly disappointed. "Sorry, Jake, I forgot to mention Danielle confiscated the backyard for the ceremony."

"It looks great."

Lydia walked outside with her aunt. "Gee, it's beautiful. What a spectacular job," Lydia said.

Oversized potted greenery placed alongside colorful blooming fall flowers added dimension to an already stunning yard. The purposeful arrangement of color along with size gave the yard a cozy, elegant feeling. Not a single weed popped up anywhere in sight.

Perfect for a small gathering, a white party tent set in the middle of the yard with chairs arranged in a semicircle.

Like her aunts, her sisters had paid particular attention to everything and everyone they loved.

"Yes, my girls have done a great job. I'm so proud of all of you."

The old swing squeaked under their weight. Lydia smiled. The sound was a reminder of those restless nights when she sneaked out of bed just in time to catch a glimpse of her aunt and uncle making out like teenagers under the stars. Other times, she watched them dance securely tucked in each other's arms as a tune played softly in the distant.

"Lydia, how're things with you and Jake these days?"

"Improving."

"Has the problem gone away?" her aunt asked.

"Yes, far, far away."

"Does he know?"

"Absolutely. I wanted him to what I knew. Most importantly, he needed to know that I took care of the problem."

"Good girl. What about Jessie?"

"I gave her an unedited, yet painful truth. Then as I

suspected, she went searching for her own validation," Lydia said.

"Her father's version, I suppose?"

"Yes."

"And how did that go?" her aunt asked.

Lydia smiled. "A wise woman once told me that the truth's harder to see with blinders on." She patted her aunt's hand before they headed back inside. Jake sat at the counter, eating a sandwich. He glanced up at them.

"This sandwich's delicious."

"I bet," Lydia said.

When the doorbell rang, he ran to the door. "Hello, Jake. Good to see you."

"You too, sergeant."

"Hello, Lydia. How're you feeling?" the sergeant asked.

"No complaints."

Then in a shockingly public display, the sergeant kissed her aunt passionately on the lips. At that moment, her aunt's new attitude reflected the sentiments of Lydia's favorite Sam Cooke song, "A Change Gonna Come."

Apparently, it had. She and Jake left them alone. An hour later, they were sitting in the same spot. The sergeant looked up at them, then down at his watch. "I've got to go. I'll see everyone tonight. Will six-thirty work, love?"

She smiled. "Yes, definitely."

He kissed her cheek. She waved goodbye.

"A continuous flow of calls started the minute you guys left the room. They're all here. Everyone's staying over at the B and B on River Drive. Keisha said with a small baby in tow, she needed more privacy. I agreed. Oh, Lydia, why don't you try the new fragrant bubble bath that I just bought?"

"Good idea, Aunt Regina. See you in a few, Jake."

Her aunt's obvious hint flew right over Jake's head.

As soon as Lydia left the room, she turned her attention to Jake. "Come sit, Jake." He recognized the sternness in her tone and readily obeyed her command.

"How've you been?" she asked.

"I'm doing really well. Thanks for asking."

"And work?"

"Work's good too."

"Any busier than a year ago?" she asked.

"Somewhat." Jake had no idea where this conversation was heading, but he could tell she knew exactly where it would end up. Her direct approach never changed.

"I bet those business meetings keep you on the west coast a lot. California offers a lot of forbidden fruit, I've heard. Is there any truth to that, Jake?" Not expecting a response to her rhetorical question, she grabbed his shaky hands. Like her husband, she kept close tabs on her family. "Jake, when we make a vow, we honor it. We overlook little mistakes, but an on-going affair—well, that's another story."

Regina gave him that familiar wink then walked away. He needed some alone time to think about what she'd said. Her intimidating choice of words made his flesh literally crawl. A chill ran down his spine. Then, it hit him. He now shared a bed with the woman who had inherited all that power. Slowly, Jake stood up and walked toward the bathroom. Feeling light-headed, he grabbed the door knob. The door opened. His nostrils sucked in the delicate smell of lavender.

"Is that you, Jake?"

"Yep, it's me, babe."

She looked relaxed, slumped down into a warm scented bubble bath.

His flamed nerves felt like they were on fire. A hard

stream of warm water splashed all over his body. Soap and water couldn't rid him of the guilt he felt. Not possible. Jake stepped out. Nervously, he paced the floor. Lydia had let time slip away from her until he called out her name. They hurriedly dressed. Ten minutes later, they walked out the door.

The sergeant and Regina had gone ahead. An army of family waited. Lydia and Jake arrived at the height of the meet and greet. It felt like a college reunion. Each of them discovered that apart from their birthplaces many of them had interesting careers or once lived fascinating lives. Tommy's guest had a work emergency that forced them to take a much later flight. The drinks and thoroughly entertaining conversation flowed like running water. Lydia watched the sergeant carefully. She wondered if he knew what he'd signed up for. *Probably not,* she thought. Her aunt kept secrets better than anyone. He would only know what she deemed necessary. Lydia smiled. She couldn't help wondering when they started referring to the man in her aunt's life as the sergeant.

Lydia made a mental note of everyone's behavior. She watched her aunt do the same. Everyone looked happy. The younger technologically savvy generation clung protectively to their gadgets. Mostly, they communicated electronically. From time to time, they made eye contact. Margie looked well. She bent the ears of Jessie and Dr. Barnes seated next to her. Margie once lived a very interesting life though not like the cautionary tale of Lydia's predecessors.

The suspense was killing Jessie. "Lydia, where's Tommy?"

"He called Danielle. His guest had an emergency. They won't make dinner."

"Oh." Jessie sounded disappointed.

After dinner, the out-of-town guest went back to the

B and B. The sergeant kissed his future bride on the cheek then said goodnight. "Tomorrow's the big day."

"Yes, it is. Goodnight, Barton." The excitement in her aunt's voice filled the air like the smell of an unforgettably fragrant perfume. When they got back to the house, she didn't tarry. "I'm tired. I think I'll turn in. Goodnight, all."

"Goodnight, Aunt Regina."

Jake echoed the same sentiment too as he headed off to bed. After tomorrow, new memories would infiltrate their old ones. Lydia wanted the old ones to last forever but knew that wasn't possible. As she wandered about an eerie quietness crept inside. It filled her with sadness. She headed to the bathroom. With her teeth brushed, her makeup removed, she crawled into bed and waited for sleep.

ɛ∕ɔɛ∕ɔ

"Wake up, sleepy head." Jake yelled and tossed a pillow across the room. It remained airborne for what seemed like minutes before landing on her face. "What time did you come to bed last night?"

"Not long after you."

"If you're interested, Aunt Regina made breakfast and coffee."

"Nope, just coffee for me."

"You sure you want to disappoint Aunt Regina on her wedding day?" he joked.

"Why not, it's just breakfast? She'll get over it. Me, the fat will attach itself to my thighs and hang around for the rest of my life."

He laughed. "Get up."

"Nope." Then Lydia turned over and covered her head with the sheet. He threw another pillow at her then left her alone. When she thought it safe, she dragged her weary body out of bed. A hint of lavender still lingered in the air. Jake poked his head back in the door. "Mark's here, we're going back to his house. It's a nice morning for a swim. Want to come?" he yelled.

"No thanks, it's hair and makeup, remember? Anyway, I'm not leaving Aunt Regina on her big day. Go ahead. I'll see you later." A few minutes later, she made her grand entrance. "Good morning, Aunt Regina."

"Good morning, Lydia. I know you prefer coffee."

"Yes, please."

"What can I get you to eat? I've got oatmeal ready."

"Please sit down, Aunt Regina, I'll fix it."

She took a seat.

She opened the cabinet and grabbed a small bowl. "Yum." Cinnamon filled the air. "This takes me back. I forgot how much I loved your cinnamon oatmeal with honey and blueberries. Thanks for making coffee especially for me." Lydia ate just enough then poured up a cup of coffee.

Lydia wondered what they talked about last night. Knowing her aunt, she probably gave Jake some sound advice from her vast chest of wisdom. In the distance, they heard a click. The door opened. Booming laughter followed.

Pauline, Danielle, and Keisha shouted, "Good morning, everybody," then they walked over and planted a kiss on their aunt's cheek."

"Girls, we've got some work to do," Pauline said then ran her fingers through her Lydia's hair. Girl, your hair's a mess." Before Lydia could respond, the doorbell rang. Pauline rushed pass her.

"Hey, Jessie, you're up early," Pauline said.

"Yes, I am. Good morning."

Pauline looked surprised. "Good morning, come on

in," she said waving her hand, "the gang's all here."

Jessie followed her into the kitchen. "Good morning, everybody." She looked over at Lydia. "I thought I'd take you up on your offer. I could use a manicure and facial."

"Great, I'm glad you decided to come."

"Come join us, Jessie. Would you like any breakfast?"

"No thank you, Mrs. Mayers. Barry and I had an early breakfast."

"Anyone else want breakfast?"

A big "No," rang out loud and clear before another soft chime of the doorbell announced the arrival of the hair stylist and her crew. Danielle showed them to the guest house. "Girls, I hope you didn't spend a lot of money on this weekend."

"You're worth every penny, Aunt Regina," Pauline said.

Everyone chimed in. "Absolutely!"

The Mayers women spent the entire morning in the care of a group of professionals who pampered them for a price. In the end, they stood in front of the mirror stunned at their transformations. Each chose a French manicure. Over already perfectly flawless complexions, they experienced the airbrushed look of supermodels. Their hairstyles varied. Pauline's sophisticated upsweep spun off tiny ringlets that trailed down her back. Suited to those early morning and late evening swims, Danielle sported a new chic boyish cut with closely shaved sides. Lydia and Keisha wore their freshly permed hair swept up into loosely tied pony tails. Jessie's big, bold curly afro framed her face perfectly. She reminded them of an African Queen. The stylist twisted their aunt's dark brown hair into miniature curls then fastened them with a crown of blue and white rosettes. Everybody looked red-carpet ready.

While their aunt sneaked through a side entrance into the main house, Lydia and Danielle entered through the front door. The guys sat waiting dressed in black tuxedos. They stopped, inspected bow ties, cummerbunds and shirt collars. Blue and white boutonnieres stuck conspicuously out of their lapels. They stood back looking on in amazement at the finished unmarred product on the way to their aunt's room.

Danielle opened the door then stepped back with her mouth ajar. "You're beautiful, Aunt Regina."

"Thank you, sweetheart."

The beautiful illuminating signs of maturity showed whenever her aunt smiled. Soft definitive lines formed at the corners of her big brown eyes with a gentle wrinkling at the contour of her mouth. Her aunt remained an ageless beauty. Proudly, they stood next to the woman they emulated. Unlike her sisters, Lydia confronted their physical likeness every time she looked into a mirror. Their sameness kept bouncing back like the waters in a reflecting pond. Time had chiseled away the crude edges of her wild youth while smoothing out a more disciplined replica of her aunt.

Lydia walked over and kissed her gently on her cheek. "You're a show stopper, all right. I can hardly wait to see the sergeant's face."

"Thanks, Lydia."

Lydia left her in the capable hands of her sisters. When she stepped out into the backyard, a melting pot of familiar faces greeted her as soft music played in the background. She turned around as Tommy walked out with an attractive woman on his arm. Jessie watched from across the lawn.

"Hello, Tommy."

"Hey, Lydia, I'd like you to meet Ginny."

"Well, hello again, Ginny." Tommy looked at her in

wide eyed surprise. Even after he confessed his love for
Ginny, Lydia never bothered to mention they'd met before.

"Oh, hello, Dr. Giddens, how nice to see you again."

"Please call me Lydia. It's so nice to see you again,
too."

Jessie rushed over looking like she'd won the lottery.
She winked at Lydia, hugged her sister, then greeted
Tommy. While Jessie and her sister chatted, Tommy
pulled Lydia aside. "You never told me you knew Ginny."

"The last time we talked, I recall you saying a future
with Ginny wasn't in the stars since your travel schedule
and her work load kept getting in the way. After that
comment, I didn't see any reason to say anything. So
what happened to not in the stars?" From where she
stood, Tommy looked star struck.

"After we accidently bumped into each other last
month in DC, we spent an entire week together. Everything felt exactly the same."

"Good for you. Of course, if you must know, I met
Ginny when she visited Jessie a few years back."

On a perfect day, the fidgeting sergeant stood front
and center. Whatever happened to the relaxed Southern
gentleman? His posture appeared unsteady as he shifted
his weight from one foot to the other. The Mayers women
took their positions to the right, and to the left, of their
aunt then walked her down the aisle to her waiting
groom. Like Pauline on her wedding day, she carried a
single white rose. "Who gives this woman to this man?"

"I do," Pauline said.

"I do," Keisha said.

"I do," Danielle said.

Finally, Lydia stepped forward. "I do."

Then they took their seats. His mingled gray hair

made him look outlandishly distinguished. They exchanged beautiful vows then later danced to a classic ballad. Lydia vaguely remembered what time they left the ceremony. Literally, she *crawled* into bed. But when she turned over, Jake had gone.

See you in an hour the note read. *I'm joining Mark for an early morning swim.*

Lydia searched the kitchen high and low. No coffee anywhere, instead she brewed a cup of tea. Just as she took her first sip, the phone rang. "Good morning, Lydia."

"Hello, Aunt Regina. You're up early."

"Yes, sweetheart, we're on our way to Myrtle Beach. Lock up when you leave. Enjoy a safe trip home. Give my love to Jake."

"I will. Enjoy your honeymoon, Aunt Regina. Call me when you return home."

❧❧❧

Two weeks seemed like an eternity. Lydia missed their long, sometimes short chats. Then from across the room, she heard a vibrating sound. She picked up her phone and quickly switched it over from vibrate. "Good morning, sweetheart. Barton and I just got back. How's the world treating you?"

"Wonderful. What about you, Aunt Regina?"

"Never better, sweetheart."

They talked about everything, including the time Joey sneaked out of the house to attend a house party. Yes, they slipped. Occasionally, they still called him Joey. "Joe's a good kid, Lydia. We've had a long talk. Don't worry. I've kept an eye on him." As always, Regina had some sound advice. Just before hanging up, she issued a stern warning. "My sweet girl, take care. Be careful not to bend too far right or left. Stay as close to the middle as possible. You'll find the ground solid there."

As usual, she hung up before Lydia could ask what she meant. Regina believed an answer would less likely go unheeded if sought with fervor. After several hospital stays within the same year, Lydia no longer needed a reminder about the importance of staying healthy. Because of Tommy, she actually hadn't felt this good in years.

This time her phone actually rang. She had remembered to switch it from vibrate.

"Hey, girl, Barry and I had a wonderful time. He said your aunt's as charming as ever." "Oh." Then Lydia laughed out loud. Surely, he couldn't possibly know any more than she knew about this master manipulator. It took her years to get an accurate read on her aunt. Occasionally, she missed the target.

"What's funny, Lydia?"

"Considering Tommy's surprise guest, I'd say nothing much. You knew didn't you, Jessie? I can't believe Tommy's dating your sister."

"I knew, and I'm happy Tommy chose her. He made a very wise decision."

Jessie never told Lydia that when Tommy came for a conference in her home town, he fell in love with her sister in front of God and her parents. Jessie wasn't the only one with secrets. Lydia and Regina had some they could never tell another living soul. Lydia hoped that when they took their last breath, their secrets would vanish like steam evaporating into the air.

Lydia lounged undisturbed. Her housekeeper had the day off. She and Jake had dinner plans for later. Suddenly she got an urge to hear Keisha's voice. Her sister stopped working after the baby. She loved her new role of stay-at-home mom.

Keisha had come a long way. Finally, motherhood

agreed with her like it had their mother and their aunts.

"Hey, Keisha, what's up?"

Keisha laughed. "As always, diapers and formulas."

"And how's Stormy?"

"Cute and adorable. We're super excited you and Jake agreed to become Stormy's Godparents. Everyone's coming out for the christening next month."

"We're honored. How's Frank?"

"Really good. He took a new assignment so he can spend more time with us."

"That's wonderful." She wondered if Keisha realized the irony in her choice of names. For her sake, Lydia hoped gifting her child with their aunt's name wasn't a bad omen. However, the perfect footnote would read a *forceful personality*.

"Lydia, has Aunt Regina called?" Keisha asked.

"Yes, just this morning. They had a great time. Honeymoons tend to do that."

Keisha laughed. "I'm glad she found a loving companion."

Lydia agreed. Other than greed, Lydia often wondered why some children denied their surviving parent their blessing. Sure, alone as well as lonely existed, but on separate planes. Lonely scared even Lydia. "I've got to run Keisha. I'm meeting Jake for dinner."

"Enjoy. Give Jake my best."

Life turned out radically different for all of them. Their uncles treated them like defenseless young women. Initially, their aunt bought into the same fallacy until she saw the defect in their premise.

Then, out of new chartered waters, she raised strong, independent daughters.

Jennifer waved as Lydia entered. "Hello, Dr. Giddens, are you dining alone this evening?"

"No, Jake's coming straight from work."

"Well, talk about timing. Hello, Mr. Giddens, how was your day?"

"Not bad, Jennifer, thanks for asking."

Then Lydia stood up. "Well, hello, handsome."

He kissed her. "Hey, babe, I'm starved. I skipped lunch."

"Thanks to a stricter regimen, I'm eating well-balanced meals these days."

"Good for you. Okay, guys, what's your poison this evening?" Jennifer asked.

"Give us a minute," Lydia said.

"No problem, I'll be back shortly."

He looked perplexed.

"You okay, Jake?" she asked.

"Yeah, I'm good." His pensiveness started long before tonight. Lately, there were so many restless nights, she stopped counting. They sat quietly looking out at the crowds. Finally, he couldn't stand it any longer. "Lydia, what happened to Julianne?"

At first, Lydia ignored his question and continued gazing at the couple seated across from them. They looked like they'd found the secret to true happiness. After a long pause, she turned then looked directly into his eyes.

He flinched under her intensely penetrating stare.

"Does it matter, Jake? Does it really matter?" Her tone sounded creepy calm like the stillness before a turbulent storm.

"Yes." His voice quaked. His hands shook. He quickly dropped them to his side.

"Why does it matter, Jake? Why?"

"I messed up. I'm sorry. Whatever happened between us is my fault. I never meant to hurt you. I love you, Lydia. I've always loved you. I fell in love with you the very first moment I saw you. After you visited

Julianne, I panicked. I thought you would never forgive me or worse." He paused, as if he had trouble catching his breath, and looked absolutely petrified.

"Jake, I'm sure you never meant to hurt me. Perhaps, you never meant for me to find out. But, sadly I did. The people we love always end up breaking our hearts. You brought Julianne into a place reserved only for me. I forgave you. As for Julianne, I flicked her away like an unimportant speck of dust."

Her arctic words made him tremble. He wondered what price Julianne paid for loving him. He sensed ice water rushing angrily through her veins and knew eventually, he would pay, too. Then with precision abruptness, Lydia changed the subject.

"Jennifer's a jewel, how did we get so lucky?"

It took every ounce of his willpower. Sill, Jake couldn't hide his fear. Beneath the table, he wiped his sweaty palms on his pants leg. For an uncomfortable few minutes, they sat quietly. Together they watched the crowds dart in and out of the restaurant like lighting bugs flickering in the night. Only let them see what you want them to see. Julianne played that game very well.

Although Lydia's predecessors considered themselves somewhat religious, they never sought true spiritual guidance to solve their problems. Her Aunt Regina sought God when convenient. She used him as her own personal Ouija board. No more! Lydia thought. Their scandalous story needed rewriting.

The waitress stood staring down at Jake. "May I get you a drink?"

Startled, Jake looked up. He ordered a dirty martini. Lydia smiled inwardly. No doubt tonight, he would need more than two or three. Nobody made that sinful libation like Jennifer. Her secret to a great martini started with the exact proportions of vermouth, olives, gin, and olive juice shaken sharply a half dozen times then poured into a chilled glass. As she predicted, he had several martinis. Much later in the evening, they went home after a quiet, but rather somber dinner. She planned to tell him some-day that she gave Julianne a new lease on life. Not today. Her source had told her Julianne fled to Argentina. As suspected, she quickly returned to her old tricks.

Foolish, foolish Jake! Did he honestly think he picked Julianne up that night in the bar? Men—gotta love 'em.

Lydia had been taught that no sin goes unpunished. Even with her at the helm, real change would take time, discipline, and prayerful consideration. She wasn't power hungry like her aunt or an empire builder like her uncles. She had found that middle ground.

About the Author

Bertha Connally Abraham is a retired ATT manager. She attended Southern University and, although the South is in her blood, she lived on the East Coast for a while. The love of traveling fuels her desire to write. She and her husband often hit the road for business and pleasure. Her hobbies include reading and gardening. She is a Master Gardener and public speaker. Wildly diverse and unforgettable characters fill the pages of her books. As founder of The Writer's Workshop for Children, she helps children realize their love of reading and writing. Currently, she is a member of (OTC) Off the Chart book club and The Red Hat Society. She lives in the countryside of Wharton, Texas. Her works include *Woven*, *If Only for a Season*, and *In the Pew*.

CPSIA information can be obtained
at www.ICGtesting.com
Printed in the USA
BVOW06s2130261217
503650BV00026BA/1379/P